ABOUT THE AUT
Genghis Chase is a
Chichester and lives
Hampshire.

Katabasis

Genghis Chase

insta@genghischase

Small Tree Books

For Anna

Acknowledgements

Anna Pope

Chase Winters

Jeanie Simpson

Alison Macleod

David Swan

Genghis Chase

Copyright © 2021 Genghis Chase

All Rights Reserved.
This is a work of fiction. Names, characters, places and incidents are either a product of the author imagination or are used fictitiously.

No part of this publication may be reproduce, stored in a retrieval system, or transmitted, in any form or by any means, electronic, mechanical, photocopying, recording or otherwise, without prior permission of the copyright owner.

Reunion
Just like old times
Jacob's Ladder
Celebration
Morning After
The Guest
Party
Roof Top Rendezvous
Morning After the Night Before
Somnambulist
Pain and the Pleasure
Eateries of the Gods
The Box
Wildman
A Trip
Ray the Tramp
Ray the Poet
Speed Date
The Vale
Redemption
The Deal
Imogen Discovered
Crisis
Tension with Tea
The Father of Nyx
Grave Intent
Fandango
Panic
The score
The Punch
The second Punch
Epilogue

Reunion

The chirpy voice of Margaret Knight the counsellor chimed.
"Welcome everybody, if you would like to take a seat, we will start in a minute." She moved to the trestle table at the back of the church hall and poured a coffee. The effect was like sheep being corralled at sheep dog trials. The crowd, younger than before, broke cover, moving towards the chairs arranged with mathematical precision into a circle. Micah wondered how he was here again, jostling for a good seat near the exit, at a meeting of the "self-harm/self-help" group.
Micah considered sloping out for one last nicotine hit but the Portsmouth Tricorn centre, a dilapidated concrete monolith, offered a drab shelter from the rain. The Chichester meeting he had attended over the summer was across the road from his house, whereas Portsmouth was anonymous, big enough to swallow him whole.
"Ah, nice to see you again, how are you?" Margaret Knight had seen him, worse; still remembered him from months before. She shook his hand with the force of a woman who had forged a career in male-dominated medicine.
"Fine, thank you."
He felt her trying to read his face, sifting and evaluating. Her eyes were slightly downturned, disarming and passive like a heavy dope smoker. Once, in a private session, he had commented on "Cheech and

Chong", attempting to excavate her youth with one cultural shibboleth.

"How are your scars?"

She could probe; it wasn't the scars he was worried about. As long as she didn't push, as long as he could sound convincing, she could tick her list, and write him off as rehabilitated. Then she would never find out the about his new angry red scars.

"Shall we?" She said ushering him over to the chairs, the heart of the strip lit linoleum confession box. She positioned herself at the far side of the circle with a clear view of latecomers. She gathered her long auburn hair into a ponytail and pulled a pad and paper from her Gucci bag that matched her skirt suit perfectly.

Micah glanced round the mostly new faces as he sat. Children he thought. A support network to be dumped, once he was given the all clear by Dr. Knight.

This time it was different. This time there was no Jacob.

He had known Jacob since they were kids and they had been inseparable throughout school. Then that long balmy summer after exams pushed them in different directions.

Micah spent the summer trudging across the muddy fields of Greenland. He had expected barren white wastelands; he found mud, stone and midges that bit with the ferocity of piranhas. The one item on his wish list had been to see the majestic polar bear. The guide woke him one night to midnight sun and a scraggy bear rummaging through the bins. To

Micah's horror the guide then shot the bear as a safety precaution.

Micah returned home to discover Jacob had transformed into a black clothes-wearing, snakebite-drinking Goth who listened to 'Sisters of Mercy'.
He had not seen Jacob for eleven years. Then one summer evening, six months ago in a church hall with fire exits thrown open, he saw him. Jacob was standing rummaging through a biscuit barrel at an identical meeting, still draped in black.
"Jesus fucking Christ, I can't believe it."
Jacob shook Micah's hand like a Richter scale needle measuring an earthquake. Handshake exhausted, Jacob slapped Micah's back, laughing.
"How have you been?" He asked dropping his voice and turning to the coffee
urn.
"Good I suppose apart from…" Micah glanced around.
"Yeah, slashers of the world unite."
He tried not to smile, tried to fend off Jacob's irreverent tone.
"Man, seriously, this lot are a bunch of losers," said Jacob, straightening his tie.
"That's a bit harsh."
Jacob shrugged and rifled the biscuit barrel for the chocolate Bourbons. "Look at this one."
Micah followed Jacob's gaze to a girl at the end of the table talking to Margaret Knight. A summer dress cascaded off her shoulders, falling uninhibited by curves. She was smiling whimsically, her face full of her features, like Princess Mononoke

under a magnifying glass. Big eyes, long lashes and thin lips that seemed constantly in motion, even when she wasn't talking. She wore her long brown hair scooped up, pinned at the back in an attempt to balance her petite head.

"Pretty, yeah?" Chided Jacob.

"I suppose," Micah agreed, without enthusiasm.

"Fucking nut job."

"Why's she wearing a long sleeve top and leggings under that dress? It's like thirty degrees in here."

"Hiding the scars. I swear, there is not an inch of that girl that is free from scars, and I mean not a single inch." Jacob winked, lent conspiratorially closer, and whispered. "If you know what I mean." He smiled to himself and glanced around to confirm he had kept volume in check. "And that guy there." There was only one other guy in the room, a carbon copy of how Jacob was after that long summer they had drifted. The kid looked like a roadie for Metallica. "Absolute idiot got caught because he didn't use sterile objects. Collapsed in a pub with blood poisoning."

"Surely that's good, getting caught?"

Jacob stepped back. He had finished the Bourbons so he popped a custard cream into his mouth as he looked Micah up and down. "Yeah, okay, then."

"Come on, Jacob. I know it's been a long time, but you're not getting away with that."

"Alright then." Jacob lent close again. "Thing is… cutting is a coping mechanism right?" He paused and Micah realised quickly that it was not a rhetorical question.

"Right – I suppose."

"Exactly right. It's our way of coping with whatever shit we have to live with. Keeps us on an even keel. Except we are all here trying to deprogram ourselves, so Ms Knight can tick a list and write a report, and we can go home and drink, or do drugs, or get into fights." Micah tried to move away as Jacob's voice began to rise. "But that is just me" His eyes darted around, as he drank his coffee, trying to judge who had heard.

They synchronised sipping from their polystyrene cups. Micah could tell the coffee was cheap; six sugars barely hid the bitter after taste.

"Oh, for Arabica." Micah muttered to himself.

"What?"

"Nothing."

"Go on?" Pressed Jacob.

"Nothing, it's just this coffee is nasty. It reminds me of my dad."

It hadn't until then. His eyes prickled, hot from holding back tears.

"Reminds you of your dad? You make it sound like he's dead."

"He is."

Micah looked at the ceiling, traced the foam tiles as they moved toward the point of infinity, tried to think about perspective in the drawings of Escher – anything. Just not his dad.

"Cigarette?" Suggested Jacob. "I mean, I assume you smoke, and if not, well now is as good a time as any to start." He winked again.

'They're about to start."

"Don't worry, it's very informal; you can come and go. As long as you stay for most of it she still marks you down as present." Micah relented, following Jacob and the possibility of a cigarette.

Outside the heat haze blurred the ends of the road. It was eight o'clock but the sun still hung ferociously over the baking city. Jacob passed a pre-lit cigarette from his mouth.

"Sorry man, I had no idea," said Jacob

"It's alright; we haven't seen each other for years."

"I know, but your old man… I liked him."
It was true they had got on well. In their youth Jacob had been a latchkey kid. He'd spent a disproportionate amount of time at Micah's house being fed by Micah's dad.

"He always made wicked scrambled eggs," Remembered Jacob.

"With cream," Added Micah.

"Yeah." They chimed simultaneously, remembering shovelling food as fast as they could, while Dad warned of indigestion. They withdrew into their own thoughts.

Micah was trying to think shopping lists, move his mind on, but Jacob fidgeted at his side. He lit another cigarette, then thumbed the Zippo, forcing it open by applying pressure between two fingers and a thumb. It popped, and he immediately closed the lighter and repeated. Micah went to speak but thought better of it.

"Do you mind?" He said instead, pointing to the cigarette packet.

"Knock yourself out."
He cupped his hands to shield the flame as Jacob held his Zippo steady.
Then, flick – pop – click, as he fiddled again with the lighter. Micah inhaled, head spinning a little; this was the first time he had smoked in four months. Death makes people re-evaluate.
   Flick - pop - click
Some people re-evaluate, and decide that they need to drown themselves in whisky, rum or gin. People have vices to indulge in times of emotional crisis. Micah wondered if his was smoking.
   Flick - pop - click
He certainly remembered playing a lot of Sonic the Hedgehog, and drinking quite a bit, but drinking felt acceptable as long as it didn't jeopardise his job. He had a vivid image sorting through Dad's belongings and finding the single malt and drinking nothing else but that brand for the next three months. It helped him sleep.
   Flick- pop - click
   Flick-pop-click
   Flickpopclick.
   "Jacob please stop it" Micah placed his hand on Jacob's, disrupting the action.
   "Sorry," He said.
   Jacob's idle hand moved up to his neck, and he began to fiddle with his necklace. Micah was about to take issue a second time when he noticed the Star of David pendant hanging from the dark leather cord.
   "I didn't know you were Jewish?"

"What? I'm not." He followed Micah's gaze and pulled the pendant forward for a clearer view. "It's a pentangle."

"Oh." Micah shrugged.

"As in pentagon, five-sided, or should I say five-pointed."

" Is that not Jewish then?"

Jacob smiled, standing, instantly animated. "The star of David is six-pointed, two equilateral interlocking triangles. This is a pentangle, or a pentagram."

Jacob had always been better at Maths than Micah. Jacob was pacing now, explaining that the pentangle was an ancient symbol, a talisman. Micah smirked, thinking of teenage boys playing Dungeons and Dragons wearing talismans clasped in sweaty hands. Jacob stopped mid-flow.

"Alright, sod ya then." He sat down, looking away. The lighter came out again – flick - pop - click – then he realised. "Sorry." He pocketed the Zippo. Then Jacob tapped his finger on his chin as if an idea was forming. "If there was a way that you could speak to your dad again would you be interested?" Jacob's fingers were twitching for something to play with.

Micah just shrugged his shoulders; fantasy never helped.

"The thing is" Jacob hesitated locking his gaze. "I dabble in the occult and I have a pretty good success rate with contacting the dead. Ask around."

"I wouldn't know who to ask."

"I'm just saying. It doesn't matter, anyway. It was just an offer." He flicked his cigarette, hitting the lamppost and sending a cascade of embers to the pavement.

"No, no I'm interested Jacob. It's just been a few years, and 'hello, I speak to the dead' caught me a little off-guard."

"Cutting comment."

"Self-harming humour, I like it." Micah smiled. "Jacob, I have to ask why the suit?"

Jacob tapped the side of his head with his index finger. "Playing the game. Look good feel good, she-who-decides-our-psychological-state ticks the box and I'm outta here."

"Makes sense," agreed Micah.

Jacob nodded now tapping the side of his nose with his finger. "Fancy a drink after this?"

Micah was forced from his memories of over six months ago by the one connecting sound. Dr Knight was repeating her mantra of self-help.

"My body is a vehicle in life, I choose to treat it with kindness" She paused waiting for the group to repeat back to her. So much had changed since before. So much was back to the same.

""My body is a vehicle in life, I choose to treat it with kindness." Micah chanted.

It seemed strange that he was back here again in a sterile lit circle in the depths of winter, listening to the sycophantic chatter of a bunch of people desperate to gain some self-esteem from a word or glance from the all-powerful Dr Knight.

Just Like Old Times

Jacob's weakness was that he had a gravitational pull towards trouble. Under different circumstances he would have served prison time. Micah listened as his friend outlined the simple plan of destruction, as he stood on the bonnet of the car brick in hand.

"Leave it Jacob it's not worth it." Micah laughed nervously half turning, watching to make sure that he was climbing down.

"Mate they can't get away with that." He was still rigid, brick raised. Micah touched his face in recognition of the beating. He could feel the blood pulsating, the skin pulling tight as the bruise on his cheek bone began to swell. His nose had stopped bleeding. He was pretty sure it wasn't broken.

"If I wanted them to pay I could ring the police but I haven't." Said Micah, his pride hurt more than head.

"Besides you can't be sure it's their car." Jacob had that look in his eyes the one he used to get. The one Micah remembered from their childhood, the one that always led to trouble. He was beginning to regret agreeing to go for a drink after the self-help group. He was starting to remember why they had stopped hanging out; his destructive habits and Alice Magreaves. His stomach tightened but he ignored the feeling and focused on his brick wielding friend.

"You don't know it isn't?"

"You can't put a windscreen out because I don't know it isn't their car. That's stupid." Micah tried to reason with the brick-wielding mad man.

Jacob dropped his raised arm. "It's a blue Subaru with custom rims and spoiler. Of course it's their car." Micah thought of the brilliant white trainers jabbing as he went down. Status symbols, trumpeting the self-proclaimed title of *kings of street corner*. They fitted with the car.

"Yeah now you're getting it." Said Jacob raising his hand again.

"Wait if we are going to do it then we have to be sure."

"How?" He lowered his arm again.

"Hide out and see if they come back to car. It's only twenty minutes till closing." Micah checked his watch it was forty-five minutes till closing and he knew how this could go.

When they were younger they had visited the superstore on the outskirts of town and had attempted to break the enormous windows at the front. Micah had watched Jacob hurl stone after stone. Glistening with sweat, Jacob sighed as each missile bounced off. The glass flexed taunting the ineffectual teenager. He would inspect the impact point, just traces of powdered flint that brushed off. Micah threw one or two half-hearted. Eventually an old man whose house backed on to the car park threatened to call the police. Jacob and Micah screamed abuse at him then scrambled down a footpath and went home via the football pitch, cemetery, and allotments to avoid detection. Jacob admitted three days later that he had returned and torched the skip at the back of the store. The same wide wild-eyed glare looked back at Micah now. Destruction used to be a favourite hobby. He had to admit there had been satisfaction in breaking things. From fourteen they had burnt and smashed their way through barns sheds gravestones, and various parts of cars. It was release, a perverse freedom. The only true freedom they had back then. There were no adults telling them not to, and the very fact they knew their parents would disapprove made it all the more emancipating. Except now they were in there twenties and could do what they wanted.

"I'm over this. I'm going down the Nuts for a pint." The 'Nuts' was the Horse chestnut and although a good ten minutes' walk further than the nearest pub it was cosier. Micah's tone was final and this time he turned and walked away. Deprived of an audience Jacob tossed the brick into a hedge and followed.

"Since when did you get so serious?" Called Jacob as he ran after his friend.

"*Since I grew up you prick.*" Micah thought but instead pointed out that there were no doubt security cameras were near enough for the police to incriminate them.

"Good point, always the thinker." He wrestled an arm around Micah's neck and rubbed the crown of his head with his fist. The squeeze smarted as the bruising on his collarbone began to bloom.

Jacob considered the attack as unprovoked, a targeted beating, and sport for these smart burberry wearing animals, whose idea of a night out was not complete unless they had jumped somebody. Micah's crime had been wearing a Rolling Stones Tee shirt. But Micah knew the truth and the truth hurt more than the exquisite pain of a storm of punches. Micah remembered marvelling at his main attacker. The guy had been wearing a chequered shirt that was more expensive than Micah's whole wardrobe. He marvelled as the apparent disregard the guy had as he smashed him five times in the face while his three mates held him. On the third punch blood exploded from his nostrils and the fourth punch splattered blood across the front of the designer shirt. The guy didn't stop until they dropped him to the floor so they could bloody their trainers.

    It probably was sport, a way for friends to bond against a common enemy, a way to show the world, that in some archaic Darwinian pecking order that they were top predators. It had been almost two hours ago in a different pub, not Micah's usual. He had been waiting for Jacob to return from a phone box. Soon after the two friends had arrived a pager had gone off in Jacob's pocket. He had read the number made his excuses and left to find a phone box, promising to return in a few minutes. A few minutes was all it would take.

    He had spied them at the pool table marking their territory. One of them had passed him to go to the toilet and had made some remark. It had been mumbled, the details lost. Micah's eyes kept flitting to the door for Jacob. As soon as he returned then Micah would feel better. One of the other men drew up to him at the bar to order another round of drinks. He ordered four pints with whiskey chasers and downed his as the barman stood hand on tap.

"What you looking at." He growled shifting his weight onto his front foot and pushing away from the bar. Micah, who had been looking at the bar, glanced up to check the guy was talking to him. The man had squared up staring.

"Nothing mate." Micah replied quietly.

"Mate? Mate? I'm not your mate you faggot." The guy scowled drawing his hands in front of his body to brandish his clenched fist.

Micah felt rooted to the spot. This guy was bristling with adrenalin and testosterone. Micah slid away from the bar slowly, with careful movements so not to face the man fully.

"Sorry I don't know how I upset you but certainly didn't mean to." He said raising his hands up placating.

"Hey I recognise you."

"I don't think we've met mate." Micah said genuinely puzzled.

"Told you I'm not your mate." The guy swung dramatically wide giving Micah time to dodge. The other fist fired like a piston tight and straight from the shoulder. Knuckles dug into his cheekbone and he reeled. The guy went to punch again and this time seeing it coming Micah threw himself at the fist head-butting it. Why had he done that he thought? Pain seared through his brain and he fought to stay focused on the bewildered face in front of him cradling his hand. Why had he done that he thought.

Suddenly the other three were there holding him as a barrage of fists pummelled his face and shoulders. They finally let go and he crumpled to the floor in a flurry of blood glass and booze caught in a storm of feet. Then they parted and the guy handed over a ten-pound note for the drinks. The barman refused

"I think you'd better leave." He said, removing the two beers he had already poured.

Then Micah spoke. He should have stayed quiet. The sport was had and the lads would leave most likely, after all it was late afternoon and the pub was half full of respectable older clientele who might phone the police.

"Fucking dicks" escaped before he could catch the words. They fell into dead space and the guy turned, his hand still stretched out with the denied note. This could go bad. He knew he needed something to happen. The entire pub held their breath.

"I sit here minding my own business and you decide to take a disliking to me for an imagined filthy look that I never gave you. And suddenly what?" Micah was now on his feet with a fevered pitch to his voice.

"What? I've given you permission to use me as a punch bag, work out some of the week's stress. There is no reasoning, no chance of dialogue for me to put straight your misconceptions." His word lengthened as he saw the guys' confusion and hesitance. He wasn't hitting, which was a good thing. Micah needed to keep talking. It wasn't a barrage of fists he threw but the effect was still a stunned silence.

"I make no judgements of you and your friends, although you clearly have judged me. I don't look for trouble I don't want trouble but every fucking weekend some bloke thinks it is fine to punch someone for entertainment. Go to the cinema or something. Just stop punching people who are minding their own business. Because one day, yes, one day they might fight back." He was in full rant; globules of spittle had pooled at the corners of his mouth and now he was spouting about fighting back. Where was he going? But the four blokes were ridged as if paralysis had set in. Micah locked eye contact with the largest guy, the guy who had hit first, still rubbing his hand.

"And the thing is when someone who doesn't like fighting or who doesn't want to fight suddenly does, it's because they have crossed the Rubicon." The bloke who had been riveted word for word now screwed his face up.

"The what?"

"The Rubicon. The point of no return. I'm saying that when someone who does not like fighting is forced into a corner and has to fight, they have nothing to lose. That is a dangerous man." He chose his words carefully impersonalising the confrontation but leaving the seed to burrow deep. All four blokes stood staring. Micah slowed his breathing and the speed of his talking and sat down on the bar stool behind him, hands on the bar deliberately not looking at them.

" Now" he cleared his throat, "May I buy you all a drink by way of apology?"
The bloke stood staring unsure. He looked at the bar. He looked at his mates standing to one side. "Fuck off you twat" He said and punched Micah hard catching him on the neck. It wasn't so much the

force as the speed and the surprise that caused him to fall back off his stool, and as he tumbled into the laps of two old boys who darted with unexpected agility to move their drinks, the blokes left in a cloud of threats and bravado.

By the time Jacob came back Micah was on his second complimentary free beer. The barman was paying off a debt of inaction. Micah would have done the same, yet while the publican was buying he was drinking. Unfortunately the freebies only managed to fortify plans of revenge that led to Jacob astride some ones car with a brick in his hand. Micah retold the story, small details changing as he repeated for the third time on the way to "The Nuts". By the time they were entrenched in the back bar, he had swung twice and landed one punch.

Jacob's Ladder

Later that evening the distant throb of the stereo echoed like a heartbeat through the empty upper rooms, moody and loud to ward off unwanted callers knocking on the door three storeys below. Tonight Jacob was closed for business. He stood at the foot of the narrow stairwell after climbing two flights in total darkness. Beyond the landing and the reach of the street lamps, was the inky black pool of shadow leading up the stairs. He blinked hard trying to claw every last scrap of light, trying to see the twelve steps and the door above him.
"Do we have to do this without clothes?" Came a hushed voice at Jacob's shoulder.
"Think of it as a sacrifice."
Jacob was scared of the dark to the point of phobia but he was glad of it now standing there with Paul, both in their underpants. The tight elastic clung to Jacob tensed buttocks and he had that strange uncomfortable notion he often got next to strangers in public urinals. He was sure Paul wasn't gay.
Step one.
Jacob took a deep breath allowing himself to be wrapped in darkness. Thick dust scuffed the bottom of his feet like sand at the beach. His hand stretched out with his fingers searching the details of the wall, preparing to find the shelf at the top of the steps that held a black candle and a box of matches.
Step two.

Another step and he could sense a void above. It expanded and contracted resonating to the distant throb from the stereo. A wave of goose bumps broke at the nape of his neck sweeping down his shoulders. He felt terrified and sharp. He was a bat, sensing his surroundings. He looked up imagining he could penetrate the dark, see the shape of the ceiling and of course, the door ahead.
Step three.

The walls seemed to pulsate. The darkness swirled with movement and he blinked wrestling his feral imagination now bubbling with unseen menace.
Step Four

He faltered at the next step. What if the dark contained other things? Stuff you couldn't see with the lights on. He imagined a spectral figure guarding the stairwell; hollow eye sockets staring, inches away and an insidious grin pulling tight over protruding teeth, just visible through almost translucent skin. He shook the image out of his head, breathing deeply. What had his *games* released?

He forced himself to take another step then another and another, each feeling heavier than the one before. His gut tightened as he became aware of a presence very close behind at his shoulder. His skin tried to shrink away. Paul walked into his back. As Paul steadied himself against the wall, his naked chest brushed Jacob's back. The feeling of bare skin and a few hairs was uncomfortably intimate in the dark. He tried to remember if Paul had a girlfriend.

"Are we supposed to stop?"
He felt the heat of Paul's breath on his nakedness.

"We must embrace the dark, confront our fears." Not too trite he hoped.
Jacob rechecked the void ahead delicately with fingers spread wide. What if he had missed the shelf? What if his fingers had trailed too low? The next step could be cut abruptly short. There was nothing else to do, but step purposely up. Paul mumbled under his breath. The consonants tickled his eardrums with a hot moist air. The step beneath him creaked and instantly he knew he was eight steps up. The soft underside of his foot sought out the floorboard nail that popped its jagged head above the age-bleached pine.

"Are you praying? It's just, praying tends to fuck things up." Jacob asked.

"I'm not praying, I'm chanting."

"Chanting what?"

"It's a Krishna chant." For some reason Jake thought of dreadlocks and tie-dye.

"O.K. But remember, it's fear that generates the energy and the energy attracts them?"

"Got it. Do you want me to stop chanting?"

"Try chanting something more direct. This isn't a Hindu temple."
He took another step and the stair creaked again as he lifted his weight off.

Paul began to chant quietly. "Spirits come, spirits come."
Jake ran the palm of his hand along the wall feeling the chalky gypsum residue coming off on his hand, separated by the constant damp of a house without central heating. Thankfully summer was here.

"Spirits come, spirits come."

He could feel Paul's breath on the base of his spine and with every step and every word muttered Jacob felt hairs stand erect.

"Actually, chant in your head."

Another step closer, he was counting in his head now, searching for the shelf.

"The thing is" came Paul's voice at his shoulder again. "I'm not scared of the dark."

He looked down into the black space where he thought Paul must be standing, imagined him close. Too close.

"Well, what are you afraid of?"

"Spiders."

Jacob smiled to himself. "We must all face our fears at some point Paul."

Two more steps and his finger found the shelf. He quickly picked up the matches.

"Remember fear is the energy that's a beacon to those beyond the grave.

Are you ready?"

"Yes."

The match flared.

Celebration

Micah tried the back gate. It was locked, as he knew it would be, so he jumped the fence marking his hands with creosote and agitating his bruised body. Home was a caravan situated a third of the way down the garden, still a fair distance from the house.

Thanks to the original council house status of the property, all the houses in this road still had their long wide back gardens. In a wave of private ownership people had begun to add their own individual touches. A porch here a garden pond there; it made the 1960's brick blocks of conformity individually stand out. His parents had added a garage. It was originally supposed to have a pitched roof with a studio flat for him to live in once the twins were born, but it would have exceeded a certain height and needed planning permission. Instead his mum and dad bought a twenty-foot caravan and parked it behind the garage. Of course, all this was before the illness.

Beyond the back lawn with its neatly trimmed and edged grass, was the rest of the garden divided by the swing set and a trellis adored by Zephrine Drouhin a thorn-less pink climbing rose. The back two thirds of the garden had been his dad's domain. Now brambles crowded the vegetable beds, grabbing at people's ankles as they walked past. Micah stopped at the second smaller shed. Undoing the aluminium bolt more at home on a bathroom door, he waded to the back of the shed past slowly rusting tools and tins of paint, a roll of chicken wire, chicken feed and an old car seat. Tentatively fingering the edge of a stack of terracotta pots, he felt for the chipped rim of the one with the key in it, a crude form of Morse code for moonless nights or half-light with a hangover.

    Key in hand Micah walked towards his caravan past the chicken coup. The other side of the green house was arranged as if some half crazed gardener was trying to hint at a Darwinian evolution of sheds. Proto-shed was an apex chicken coup on two wheels home to Harriet and Chicken Licken. Next on the evolutionary ladder was a green house, stuffed with selection of rarely used bikes, then the "potting shed" where the key was hidden, and last in the line, the big shed like a Neanderthal in pine cladding with the lawn mower, hedge trimmer and tools that mum used to regularly press dad into using. The right side of the garden was like a distant cousin, The Homo Erectus of sheds,"Brentmere Kadet 28 foot" as the brass plaque proclaimed. This was his home with its habitable, rust proof, shiny tin, single glazed and built in fixtures and fittings. Finally, the pinnacle of garden building evolution was the brick built garage with lead flashing, a damp proof course and drainpipes that channelled the water to soakaways.

    So perfect, so redundant.

    As he opened door, the heat of day leaked from the caravan like sebum from an open wound. He drew back the curtains, threw open all the windows and popped the skylight. An empty cereal bowl and cup still sat on the low table in front of the television. The milk residue had baked to a rancid lumpy mess filling the open plan living area with a sickly sweet smell. Peeling off his top, he made directly for the comfy chair. This luxury was a single seat jumbo corduroy chair. It had belonged to his Grandparents before they moved into the nursing home. This piece of luxury with its high back and jutting wings all padded and puffed up was perfect for relaxing on. A plastic wood effect handle on the left side, shaped like a sheep's clavicle would catapult his feet up and throw his head back with a sharp snap.

It was gone six and the sun still had not abated. He could already feel the heat begin to creep over his skin in the confinement of the caravan. He flicked on the television, trying to distract himself from the beads of sweat disentangling themselves from the hairs at the nape of his neck. He punched the channels, found the news amongst the early evening dross; it was the local feature so he watched to see if he recognised anybody or place.

"Aah it's too fucking hot!" He jumped up tugging at the back of his hair. He picked up a sheet of paper and started to fan himself, trying to force the warm air over his face to bring relief. He walked outside again. The hot concrete of the path on his now bare feet drove him down towards the house and respite in the manicured lawn. There in the middle of the lawn, like a vision, was a toddler's paddling pool still with a good foot of water at the bottom.

"Yes." He stepped in feet in-between the plastic toys and the bits of floating grass. His swollen, tired feet soothed by the tepid balm. As the sensation of his blood cooling began to spread, he regretted picking up a piece of paper rather than a cold beer. He looked down at the paper and saw that it was the flyer Jacob had handed to him last night. He'd dumped it on the side with his keys, last night forgotten about it. He scanned the picture of a woman dressed in a bikini cavorting in a pseudo-sexual pose in front of a psychedelic landscape worthy of Hendrix or Santana.

Jacob had thrust it in his hand with a wink saying, "The future of entertainment is within us". Micah couldn't even work out what the flyer was for. There was no time or venue just a date, a list of phone numbers and the title saying "Spiral village". It looked as if it had been done on an old typewriter and the psychedelic background was definitely hand draw. *'The future of entertainment was shoddy.'*

He pushed the flyer into his pocket and went to get some beers. Ten minutes later, having peeled off the last of his clothes except his nuthuggers, he was now laying in the paddling pool with his legs sticking out over the side. A half deflated Donald Duck serving as a pillow, allowed him to comfortably drink his second beer while listening to his Mum struggle with the twins. The battle of bath time was in full swing. He picked up a brightly coloured frog that would swim if you wound it up. He considered taking it upstairs as a weapon to tip the balance in Mums favour but he knew better than to get involved in bed times, he was, after all, the son that was banished to the garden. Mum always extended a dutiful invite but the lines had been firmly drawn and every night, after dinner together, those patio doors were locked. He threw the frog to the undergrowth and reached for a third beer from the depths of the pool, breaking it free from the plastic. He was entrenched until the call for food.

Mum had never been a great cook, though she had endeavoured, with the aid of cookbooks, to conjure up exciting meals. Since Dad, her enthusiasm had waned. Nowadays, it was microwave meals and a lot of beans on toast. Not that he complained. His mother was still cooking and cleaning up after him.

Tonight it was no different, he was happy with the microwaved meal and peas emptied on to a plate. She sat opposite seasoning with extra salt.

"Guess who I bumped into the other day?" Said Micah as he skilfully shovelled in a fork of peas.

"I don't know darling. Someone I know?" She piled her frizzy hair upon the top of her head fastening it with a band from her wrist.

"Jacob"

"Oh?" She picked up her fork and started on her meal.

"You know my old friend from school."

"Ooh." Her fork stopped half way to her mouth.

"It turns out he's got some issues too" They never discussed the cutting and burning. There was a thesaurus full of euphemisms that allowed them to navigate conversations like this.

"Butter?" It was margarine but she always called it butter. She scooped two large dollops on to her peas before turning attention to the fish pie. He took the hint.

"Anyway he's doing great and I think we are going to catch up next week."

"Oh alright." She pushed the "butter" around the peas as it melted. Then took mouthfuls of pie, chewing and swallowing, chewing and swallowing. Masking the silence with functionality. He stopped talking and ate, staring intently at his food.

"Sorry darling, I'm just exhausted."

"I know Mum. I can always help out with the twins." She looked up at the ceiling as if suddenly frightened they might wake.

"I'm sure you've got other stuff to do. Girls to meet."

"I'm twenty-two Mum, not sixteen."

"Well you know what I mean. You need to be out having fun meeting girls and making friends"

"I'm just saying that I can help out a bit more if you want."

"Thank you." She reached her hand across to grab his and squeezed it. "I'll let you know."

He knew she wouldn't. This was her role; a martyr being punished for still being here after her husband had gone.

She cleared her plate and put it on the draining board while he continued. She lent forward, hands resting on the side back facing him. "Are you sure about spending time with Jacob again."

He shrugged. "Yeah why not?"

"I thought you two had fallen out over some nonsense."

"That was ages ago Mum."

"Yes, but you were upset for months."
He shrugged again smiling at his Mum's hunched shoulders. The questions and concerns were nice.

"As you said Mum, I need to be out there making friends. It's just some of the friends are old friends rather than new ones."

"Well you aren't a teenager any more are you?" She stared out the window arms folded, eye contact avoided.

"Can you wash up for me before you go out. I'd like to have a bath." She asked in an almost whisper then remembered what day it was.

"You are out tonight?" She added.

"No."

"Well you should be. Do you want to celebrate this weekend?" Micah shrugged.

"Happy birthday darling." She ran her hand over his head, smoothing his hair then left him eating and trudged upstairs.

He could hear the hiss of the hot water tank refilling after being emptied for the bath as he had washed and dried everything and put it away, before getting the breakfast cereal and bowls out for the morning. Then he slipped out the backdoor.

After the sun had finally set, Micah sat down with everything laid out neatly in front of him; a small cup cake with a lone candle, a packet of John Player Specials and the kitchen knife. He lifted the bottle of vodka, draining the last of it. The low murmur of Led Zeppelin's "You Shook Me Baby" mournfully vibrated the speakers. The drink burnt his gums as he held it in his mouth before swallowing. It always seemed right, getting drunk alone on neat spirits. He slouched forward, the skin from his naked torso peeling away from the leather sofa, dropping the spent bottle to the floor. It was amazing, a whole year had passed already. The record finished and he got up sparking a cigarette as he moved to put the LP on for the eighth time.

He stood gazing at himself in the mirror, seeing the tear-streaked face staring back.

"He loved this song." He whispered to himself. The reflection stood glaring back silently.

He swayed, lifting his arms like a matador subduing a rampaging bull. He skipped and twirled, catching the empty vodka bottle with his foot sending it spinning off across the hard flooring. It struck the wall exploding like a firework. He used his foot to roughly sweep the glass into a pile in the corner to deal with later.

He drew another cigarette from the pack, lighting it directly from the glowing cherry of the last.

"Happy birthday to me, happy birthday to me." He sung to his reflection.

He took the lighter and lit the candle, watching it as the blue wax dripped onto the white frosting. Drawing heavily on the cigarette dangling from the corner of his mouth, he extinguished the flame in a plume of smoke.

His hand ran across his chest and found the scar. Like a third nipple, centre left, just below the dip in the sternum.

A perfectly round, scar.

A white beacon on his tanned torso.

A stuttered braille sentence cut short, a sentence he was going to add to.

He had never known the full story. He knew it had something to do with his childhood but as far as he remembered it had always been there. He still remembered the moment of revelation in the film 'Breakfast Club' when the character John Bender brandished the scar on his arm identical to Micah's.

"Do I stutter?" Bender had grimaced. He had once asked his mother if his father had smoked cigars. The conversation abruptly changed. He did not remember his dad as a violent man. Sure he would shout some times when he was angry. Micah remembered his dad's red face close as he screamed obscenities. But then Micah had left the greenhouse door open in February and killed next year's seedlings.

He inhaled hard three times on the cigarette then rolled the end on the edge of the ash tray, blowing the end till it was a glowing lipstick.

"Happy birthday to me, Dad" He spoke to the ceiling while holding the cigarette end close to his chest just below the old scar. He could feel a little pool of warmth; acrid smoke caught the back of his nostrils as fine dark hair singed.

"One" he uttered, his eyes tracing across the coffee table he had made in design tech. The large, round indent of a clamp a reminder of his inability to pay attention during class.

"Two" his eyes rested on the lounge door and the coat-stand beyond in the hallway. Shadows cast from the solitary lamp made the jumble of coats resemble the silhouette of his old man.

"Three." He pressed the end into skin. Holding his hand firm as the butt burned through the subcutaneous layer of fat sinking deeper. Sebum finally flooded the wound, extinguishing the end. Then the pain, searing, scratching heat, lights flickered in front of his eyes, cerebral fairy lights.

"Fuuuuuck." He exhaled the word with relish, and felt his mind begin to clear for the first time in a week. Even the effects of the vodka were clearing.

"Happy birthday to me."

Sunday morning

Jacob woke, head cradled in his own arm. His mouth tasted like it was full of ash-flavoured treacle. Peeling his tongue from the roof of his mouth, he looked around, and remembered where he was. Spread across the decoupage floorboards of the top room were hundreds of dry husks of insects laid out uniformly in display cabinets. Last night, by strained candlelight, Paul had nearly missed the detailed content of the ritualistically lined up glass fronted display cases, as the dust covered glass obscured the carcasses in the half-light. Long after the memory of the insects had waned the creeping primal fear of being watched would still stalk Paul. Jacob got up from the floor, the shiny surface peeling like Blutac from his skin. He must have been really stoned to have fallen asleep up here. He left Paul sleeping, in his underpants, mumbling about millions of eyes.

Down two flights of stairs, Jacob found the bathroom. He ran the hot tap, firing up the boiler which sprung into life with a series of clanking pipes as hot water wound its way to the sink. He urinated as he waited for the hot water, and noticed the deep Citrine colour of his stream.

"The trouble with highs is lows."

As the sink filled, he scooped handfuls of water over his arm to wash away the dried blackening blood. He was aware that music was still playing downstairs. Ambient soundscape 5 on continuous loop thanks to auto-reverse on the tape deck. Then, above the steadily rising electronic crescendo, he made out another noise, a high tincture like a little bell or a teaspoon being tapped on the side of a teacup. It was from downstairs, and Paul had not yet come down. The floorboards on the top three floors worked like the ping of an unforgiving radar. Jacob had two thoughts, firstly, where were his clothes from last night? Secondly, where was the baseball bat? He knew the answer for both was near the sofa. He crept to the top of the stairs; from there he could see a three metre squared section of the downstairs. Near the base of the stairs was the kitchen door. He could see the bottom corner, see that it was shut, he hadn't shut it last night. Something warned his groggy mind that this wasn't his imagination but a flesh and blood intruder. He took four steps down, the muscles in his legs tightening. He could see a large section of the red, white and blue rug hand woven car-boot purchase. Surely this was just a bad case of come down paranoia. His ears picked up a sound like the flare of a match. He strained to listen over the music, then he realised, the music was quiet. He tried to remember if he had descended last night to turn it down, change the music to be considerate to his one deaf neighbour. But there was more. The lounge was light, not from the various lamps and candles but from daylight. Jacob never opened his curtains in the lounge. He took another step revealing the near end of the sofa and by confirmation saw a large, black brogue shifting to the music.

"Fuck fuck fuck" he whispered under his breath and retreated to the bathroom. He searched the cabinets to arm himself but they were bare apart from two bars of soap and a spare tube of toothpaste. He checked the other two rooms on that floor but they were empty, not even a chair to wield. All the time his mind was racing. He leant against the wall feeling a little light headed. Who would be in the house? He was up to date with the brothers and they weren't exactly stealthy. Police would definitely not be this quiet and would have come much earlier in the morning. He sneaked back up another flight of stairs and checked the loose floorboard in the far corner of the back room, all secure. Downstairs the music changed to U2, then Clannad, finally Bob Marley.

"Who the fuck?" This guy was sitting on his couch rifling through his tape and record collection. He returned to the bathroom, and unscrewed the shower-head and gave it a few cursory swings. Step by step he moved down slowly, bringing the room back into view.

He saw the rug, his heart pumping.

He saw the lamp stand, his muscles tensed in his leg.

He saw the corner of the low pine table. His grip tightened around the showerhead.

He saw a cigarette rested in the green glass ashtray, a tendril of smoke rising from the end. A tailored, noted Jacob. His head was racing, he didn't know anyone who smoked tailored cigarettes. He shivered, half with fear and half with cold as a breeze from an open window raked across his near naked body. Then he remembered the Picts, fierce ancient blue Scottish warriors that fought naked because it terrified the enemy. Keeping his eyes fixed on the few metres squared downstairs, he hooked a thumb under his waistband and dropped his underwear to the floor. He felt sick with adrenalin.

Then… "AARRGG"

Jacobs's brother, Robert, jumped up from the couch so fast he knocked his cup of tea all over the his suit trousers.

"Jesus Jacob, what are doing?" Robert attempted to avert staining with futile brushing. Then he swung his attention to his baby brother.

Jacob could feel his eyes tying to take in the scene. Jacob dropped his arm and cupped his privates with one hand and tossed the showerhead behind a chair.

"I thought you were a burglar."

"That is not what I meant."

A 'tap, tap, tap' began to steadily beat a tattoo on to the floor.

One of Jacob's wounds had been deeper than he had realised. In the moment, he had forgotten to dress them, the sudden excess of action had re-opened it and now he was bleeding. He heard his brother begin to work himself up to a rant worthy of their father. The familiar mantras "do something with your life", and "what happened, what's going on?" all merged. He wasn't listening properly as he knew this script, he was watching the thin trail pulsate as it ran down his arm and thinking how he had never seen it gush so badly.

"Mum and Dad are coming home in four months. They have been trying to get hold of you to tell you for weeks." These words caught in the net of Jacob's fragmenting mind. He looked his brother squarely in the face, questions lining up, but the lights were spinning like a hornets' nest of aural disturbances. He opened his mouth forcing out words

"HEam. A chicken wing, five." Robert stopped berating him, and looked puzzled then jumped forward to catch his brother before he keeled over into the coffee table.

By three thirty, a half-moon hung low over the chip shop at the end of the terrace leading away from the back of Micah's house. Standing, surveying his handy work, he counted seven new, small cigarette-sized siblings to the old scar. Shiny, bulbous, white blisters winking at him in the reflection of the bathroom mirror. He felt calmer now and the vodka haze was retreating. He knew the headache would nag behind his eyes tomorrow morning. This wasn't a problem beyond painkillers. He could stack and pack books at the warehouse with his eyes closed, he just needed to keep clear of the boss. He rummaged through the bathroom cabinet and found Paracetamol, unsure whether Nurofen would be better for the now angry wasp sting sensations that spread across his chest. He made a mental note to go and change the flowers at his Dad's burial site. His mum had decided on cremation. Somehow the constant reminder of finality that came with a head stone scared her so she opted for a cheap hard wood veneer coffin. It all went in the furnace in the end anyway. After a quick fifteen minute service, they had been ushered out a side door as the chimney belched the last earthly remains and the next party of mourners lined up at the front; a conveyor belt of grief from nine til four thirty. The next day, his mum collected an urn and scattered them at Dad's favourite place. Unfortunately, his favourite place, an allotment, was now a supermarket car park.

"Half an hour of television, with hot chocolate then bed" he announced to his reflection. Too many times he had switched off the television and gone to bed as the milkman rattled past on his deliveries. He moved through the open plan living area to the kitchen, poured a glass of apple juice, and necked the painkillers, while he waited for the kettle to boil. He had a special mug for hot chocolate, with the words *hot chocolate* written fifteen times in different fonts and sizes. He liked it.

"Where's that gone then." He muttered opening various cupboard doors. He flicked the light on piercing through the fug of smoke, and spied the mug by the television left unwashed. Micah sought the simple life, sometimes to the point of distraction. He had considered joining a Buddhist monastery once not because of any deep held belief in the teachings of Buddha but rather for the idea of the middle way. Not too easy, not too hard, just keep it simple. He liked the idea of not having to worry about things like mugs. He could live shut away from the world and sit and chill or meditate as the more religious were fond of calling it. Eventually, it was the aversion to orange that put him off.

If he thought about it, he had considered lots of religions since his dad had died. He was not blind to the proximity of his curiosity. There was the old vicar in the cold, flint church with the kindly, soothing voice who *loved the sinner but hated the sin*. Unless of course they were gay; he couldn't quite love those kinds of sinners in case they got the wrong idea. Micah had chuckled to himself, the vicar was a very ugly man.

There was the Rastafarian that spoke eloquently of his body being a temple to worship, to be pure for Jah, with a perfect Jamaican accent then promptly switched to Scouse before cramming it with as much harmful chemicals as he could lay his hands on. Rastafarianism seemed fun but not as a spiritual path. He tried a raft of other pseudo -religions and self-help gurus but they were either hypocrites or dogmatic. He sat sipping his hot chocolate as the painkillers kicked in and the heavy cowl of sleep wrapped itself around him. He slept in the chair, half a cup going cold on the table in front of him. As with religion, he could never get comfy.

The Guest

They sat facing each other over the table littered with banal paraphernalia. Somehow Micah had expected more "Goth", skulls, black magic, and incarnations penned in red ink looking like blood. The best he got was three candles. "Stolen from a church", Jacob assured him. That and an odd-looking box roughly six inches deep, four inches wide. It was light brown wood, probably ash but the corners had splintered away to reveal a thin veneer covering a rich darker wood, with the initials J.A.S stamped in small, simple type font.

"Have you ever done anything like this before?" Asked Jacob.

"No." Micah hesitated. "Well, I had my palm read on Bognor pier once."

"O.K" Jacob seemed uninterested in the minor dabbling and continued to unpack more items. It looked as if he had put a lot of thought into this since they had loosely arranged it the first night they had rekindled their friendship. Indeed Micah had assumed the hasty, half made plan was just a polite suggestion. Jacob pulled something out of the box that glinted.

"The thing is, this kind of stuff, I mean the real stuff, not the television dance around the grave three times at midnight with the right spell shit, but the real stuff, is a bit different." He placed a knife on the table purposefully.

"It's more like poking them with a stick to get a reaction," iodine, a roll of bandages, and a wad of cotton wool. He lent closer.

"And we're the stick."

Micah had known Jacob for years, he was the kind of guy most people knew from around and made sure they stayed that way. Before all that, before it mattered who you knew or where you hung out, they had been friends. As they grew up and got proper jobs their lives had separated. That was the sanitised version.

"There is no method to crossing the divide, just blood."

"I thought you mentioned something about a guide?" Micah lifted his eyes from the growing pharmacy to meet Jacob's; two brown eyes ringed by thick black eyeliner.

"Yes, but I can't just pick up the phone and dial the underworld."

Having set everything up to his satisfaction, Jacob pulled out a pre-rolled cigarette, then a matt black Zippo lighter, which matched his monochrome outfit, though his black jeans were somewhat faded to an off grey. He lit the candles, superfluously flickering in the afternoon light streaming through cheap, Ikea curtains. Then lit his cigarette before offering one, Micah declined.

"So is there stuff I need to know about your dad? Was he involved in any way?" Micah looked blank.

"You know, witchcraft, demonology, any weird family stories, hauntings or murders, stuff like that?"

"Err no."

"Did you get on?"
"Yes. I think so."
"Did he have unfinished business?" Jacob continued to probe.
"What?"
"You know, affairs, historical arguments with family members, that sort of thing."
"Why don't you ask him in a minute."
"Look, if I summon up your dad and he was in to dark shit, that kind of history is going to attract attention. We don't want attention."
"I thought we wanted to poke it with a stick?"
"What?" He inhaled heavily on his cigarette, ignoring Micah's tone.

Micah had prepared it as he had requested, removing all furniture except three chairs and the table that they now occupied. All mirrors were taken down throughout the house and placed in the downstairs toilet, which was locked. This had been the first point he had checked when he had arrived, the first time Micah had seen him since the support group.

He had been expected at the funeral. The obituary had gone out in the local newspaper and a load of people Micah recognised from his childhood appeared. Even John Steiner, his old piano teacher who, by way of being a next door neighbour, ended up trying to teach Micah. Since Dad died, he had been visiting his grave on Sunday afternoons making the corner of the car park look like a shrine to a hit and run victim strewn with flowers. Sundays had been their father and son ritual, They would cook an average roast; chicken, potatoes, parsnips, peas and four cans of Carling. The old man would then insist on watching the EastEnders omnibus. They ate their food from trays in front of the television while he interjected with his philosophies on life. Mum took the twins to her parents for the afternoon.

Jacob lit another cigarette from the glowing ember of the last, offering Micah another.

"Thanks, I don't smoke" It wasn't quite true but he was trying to quit.

"Probably best in the long run." He seemed to veer away from the seat as if it was a magnet of the opposite polarisation, and found himself leaning against the wall over by the window.

"So how's your Mum?" He asked

"Away at my aunty's for a week with the twins."

"Wow, your mum had twins, how old are they?" He inhaled again and caught Micah's eye briefly. The red veins in the whites of his eyes made patterns like crazy paving.

"They're six."

"It's been a long time," he said.

"Seven years, I think."

"I used to really like your Mum." Why wouldn't he? She used to feed him regularly when he followed Micah home to supposedly help with homework. Micah's Mum took pity on him. Jacob's parents weren't bad, they just weren't around much.

"Right we better do this thing then, did you bring an item?"

"Yep," He pulled his dad's watch from his wrist and placed it on the table.

"Good" he sat back down, scratching his arm and glancing at the window then door. Micah could see his friends' latticework, angry red scars covering his pale arms.

"And all the mirrors are definitely locked away?" He nodded reassuringly.

"Right then, we can begin."

"No Ouija board." He nodded his head side to side, picking up the knife lightly. He waggled between his forefinger and thumbs staring at Micah, as if trying to perfect Alistair Crowley's transcendental stare. Micah smiled back, waiting patiently until he was not sure what he was supposed to be waiting for.

They sat in silence for two minutes. The muffled sound of the street drifted through the tightly closed windows. They could just make out the low mumbles of Mr. and Mrs Sollomovici. It was strange how walls distorted sound making their heavy Slavic language almost understandable. Suddenly Micah realised that he had no idea where they were from. He knew they always had one full fat milk and one skimmed milk from the milkman. He knew that Tuesday night was their special night in and that Mrs Sollomovici always did her white wash Wednesday morning including the bedclothes, but there was always the barrier of the wall. From his mobile home in the back garden he would occasionally see them in their garden lolling in the sun, speaking softly, sharing meats and pickles.

"Look Jacob, I'm sorry to hurry you along, but I can't be waiting for some witching hour. Are we going to do this then?"

"You do understand what's required?"

"I imagine a little bit of bloodletting." His shoulders dropped and the knife ceased its restless twitching. He held the point steady over his thumb and pushed, forcing the skin into a small divot and remained poised till a pinprick of blood oozed, held in a perfect orb by the surface tension. He passed the blade across to Micah who shrugged and wiped the point of the blade then inspected it, chasing away concerns of HIV. Somehow his friends' fingers seemed too chubby to be desperately grasping syringes in abandoned houses.

The inexperience of cutting to cause as little damage as possible showed as he exerted a little too much force and, instead of a pinprick, drew a nasty cut about half an inch along the pulpy flesh of his thumb and it stung.

"Is that alright Jacob?" But Jacob was white and his eyes were glazing. He opened his mouth to speak but seemed to stall, then slumped off his chair.

"You've got to be kidding me." He was out cold, head hitting the corner of the table as he went down. Micah pulled him out straight from the uncomfortable ball he had landed in and did his best to remember the recovery position. When he had him arranged in a rough semblance of it, he suddenly thought about tongues and choking but beyond dire warnings and the general whereabouts of the tongue he was lost.

"Bollocks to this." He rushed into the kitchen and picked up a saucepan he had used to cook noodles for lunch. He had been living in the house most of the week and there was a growing pile of dirty saucepans he could have chosen from. Filling it with water, he moved as quickly as he could back to the dining room, and threw the contents over his prostrate friend.

"Ahh!" He jumped up, "what happened Micah?"

"You passed out at the sight of blood." He blinked and rubbed his eyes then touched his scars, stroking them like they were a secret message in braille. There was a knock at the door.

"You alright for a second?" Jacob pushed himself up and rested on his elbow but did not reply.

Micah moved into the hallway, sunlight striated through the ribbed glass illuminating dust that hung pensively. He wasn't expecting anyone, and could only imagine it was the Jehovah Witnesses. He opened the door and stepped back surprised to see a gentleman standing close to the threshold.

"Afternoon, can I help?" The gentleman, tall and slender, had a face that seemed to be exaggerated around his skeletal features, as if all flesh had been sucked away leaving tissue paper thin skin over cheekbones. Even the rugged grey stubble failed to mask his gossamer complexion. He was wearing a double-breasted pinstripe suit and was holding an umbrella. Blood vessels were visible beneath the surface, flexing and changing direction as he smiled and extended a hand which Micah left hanging.

"A little over prepared there." He motioned to the umbrella.

"Expect the unexpected I always say." He tugged on his tie with meaning, attempting to realign what was already straight.

"And you are?"

He extended his hand again with more force. Micah noticed his hands matched his face, only the veins on his hands stuck out electric cabling violet-blue and tracking across his hand like a river delta.

"Mr. Able-Smythe."

"Not today thank you I'm a Watchtower subscriber" He began to close the door, but Mr. Able-Smythe pushed his umbrella across the threshold.

"I am sorry, I am a friend of Jacob's. He called."

"Pardon?"

"A friend of Jacob's."

"He didn't mention a friend."

"Less of a friend, more of an acquaintance." Micah had to strain to hear him clearly as he purred his words.

"And he said to meet him here?"

"I assume you are Micah."

With the recognition, he swung the door open and began to walk back to Jacob who he could hear stirring. The suited gentleman remained stationary on the doorstep.

"Well, come in then." Micah screwed his nose and pursed his lips half annoyed at Jacob making arrangements without consulting him and half annoyed at Mr. Able-Smythe's reserved behaviour.

"I thought you would never offer."

He closed the front door with a precise air and followed Micah through to the dining room.

"Jacob, friend of yours"

"What? Yeah my head." He groaned, focusing on the floor as Mr. Able-Smythe stepped into the room.

"What happened?"

"You passed out at the sight of blood."

"Did anything happen?"

"Apart from you passing out?"

"Anything supernatural?"

"What like apparitions? Spooky voices?" Jacob steadied himself against the table.

"Yes like apparitions and spooky voices." He was still rubbing his arm and Micah wondered if he passed out when he cut himself, if he had to mutilate with his eyes shut or if it was only other people's blood. He decided now was not the time to ask.

"I'll make a hot drink. Tea or coffee?" He moved closer and picked a stray noodle from Jacob's shoulder, an escapee from the saucepan.

"Tea please."

"Coffee." Added Mr. Able-Smythe.

"Keep an eye on him, he knocked his head" Micah motioned to Mr. Able-Smythe who stood grinning inanely in Jacob's direction having not sat down. Jacob was still looking at the floor with a glazed expression and his brow screwed tight.

In the kitchen, Micah attended to filling up the kettle and pulling mugs out from the overhead cupboard while straining to overhear their conversation but beyond Jacob's occasional moan there was silence. Maybe Jacob should be driven to the hospital to be checked out. The fake French café clock on the wall read four forty and by now homebound shoppers would be clogging up Spitalfield Lane.

"Sugar?" He called in.

"None for me thank you I have more than enough vices to be getting on with" said Mr. Able-Smyth appearing behind him.

"Shit!" He half dropped the cup he was holding, having not heard the old man come in.

"Is Jacob alright?"

"He'll live." Mr. Able-Smythe shrugged then chuckled sucking in air over his teeth. Teas were poured and milk decanted into a jug.

"So have you known Jacob long?" Mr. Able-Smythe asked.

"A while."

"Here" He passed the old man the tray with tea, but his hands stayed motionless by his side.

"Oh, I couldn't possibly; I'm a guest." He smoothed his hair down against his scalp and Micah caught flashes of black amongst the thin grey hair.

"Well after you then." Micah's smile was all teeth with lips drawn wide like a Cheshire cat forced to politeness under torture.

They filed into the room to Jacob resting his head on the table. He raised himself up and smiled. Suddenly black seemed such a slimming colour as he shrank back into the chair.

"I'm sorry Micah, I'm not really feeling up to it now."

Micah arranged the chopping board doubling as a tray, glad that Mr. Able-Smythe would be denied access to any of his family past.

"Tea?" He placed a cup in front of Jacob with the inscription "You don't have to be mad to work here but it helps" a smirk ran across his lips. His dad got it for him the summer he had worked at his shop.

"I think I'm going to be sick." Jacob's face was suddenly pallid white. There was a bucket under the sink.

"Watch him."

"Wha? Huutah," spluttered Jacob retched, but managed to hold it down as his mouth watered. He curled armadillo-like into himself.
Under the sink there was washing detergent, dishwasher tablets, polish, shoe polish, and a hoard of used Tesco carrier bags. What was missing was the bucket. Then he remembered washing the floor last weekend and emptying the grey water in the garden. He threw open the back door and placed his hand on the handle. Mr. Able-Smythe was standing there.

"Jesus! What are you, a gliding ninja?" Mr. Able-Smythe had snuck up on Micah a second time. Adjusting his tie, he announced his departure. Micah moved to the sink and he stepped sharply to one side staying out of the young man's way. The bucket smelt of earth and snails. He rinsed it.

"How is the patient?" The sound of retching answered the question.

"On reflection, I am never what people expect so I will no longer impose myself upon your company, as clearly there will be no séance. But please do me one favour, don't bother mentioning I was here as I really came to meet you."

"I think he probably saw you?"

"No." The aged lips paused puckering "No, I don't think he did."

Mr. Able Smythe stood, his thinning eye brows raised high in a manner that smoothed the skin on his forehead giving it a plastic quality.

"It's been great." Barely concealing his sarcasm Micah indicated the conversation was over. He held his hand out to usher out the guest. Re-entering the dining room, he forced the bucket between Jacob's legs just in time. He didn't hear Mr. Able Smythe leave.

"I think you might be concussed," Micah murmured to the back of Jacobs's head as he threw up into the bucket, rubbing Jacob's back as a mother would a child.

"Let's get you to hospital." Jacob didn't argue and in one movement Micah swiped Jacob's possessions into his blue duffle bag then lifted the box. It was unusually heavy. He remembered Mr. Able-Smythe's last request and ignored it.

"Who was your friend anyway?"

"Friend?"

"Sorry, acquaintance?"

"I don't know wh…" He reached for the bucket again and hacked dryly at his empty stomach.

"Hospital. Now." An arm slipped round Jacob's shoulder to steady him and another under his elbow to catch him if he went down again as they struggled out the front door to the car to battle through the rush hour traffic of Spitalfield Lane.

Party

Micah was surprised at Jacob's phone call after the last debacle. He would have at least preferred some time catching up properly, having one of those conversations that in twenty questions dissect your adult life and compartmentalise existence into cars, kids and career. Not that there was any of that. Part of him hated those conversations. He hated the self-analytical categorising. Judging how well he was doing in his life from the poverty in others. Jacob didn't want to disclose that kind of information. His neglect of these conventions only made Micah want to know more and he was mildly excited about seeing him at the next self-help group, but his friend had not been for two weeks.

    He turned off the television silencing the repetitive murmur and wandered to the fridge where he removed cold custard and spooned it straight from the bowl by the light of the open fridge. He should have gone to bed an hour ago but the 6am alarm still seemed so far away. He considered adding tinned fruit, but with reflection, retrieving the can opener, and rummaging through the top cupboard was too much effort. Instead, custard finished, he left the bowl on the draining board and stood by the back door smoking a rollie. He waved his hand in token gesture as a sickly breeze carried the smoke back into his mobile home.

    He flicked the lighter on holding the flame until the wind blew it out and wondered how Jacob was doing. Was he embarrassed at a relapse? Was he still seeing Doctor Knight for private sessions? The metal casement of the lighter was hot now from continual playing. How easy to press the hot metal into skin. Knowing that if Ms Knight asked he could square it away as a youthful prank as the burn would be shaped like a smiley face, and he knew at least three old school friends who had these marks. Was Jacob avoiding the Thursday group because he was embarrassed about the farcical séance? Micah just wanted to know he was all right.

    He spent another hour smoking, making cups of tea and cutting his toenails in the bathroom. He calculated how much sleep until the alarm. If Thatcher could run a country on four hours then he felt confident he could stack and pack books on five.

The phone rang a little before dawn. Outside soprano sparrows were fluttering around rehearsing for the main event. A weak dull light leaked over the horizon throwing a stale grey haze in through the edges of the ill-fitting curtains. He lifted up the phone and listened. He rarely gave out his number. A phone was one of the things he had insisted when his Mum had put the mobile home out in the garden, that and a television.

    Late night phone calls always stirred a sense of inevitable dread. They were only received for deaths, births, car crashes and the occasional wrong number from Saudi Arabia. Once he had received a string of phone calls from a man with a thick indistinguishable accent. Every time he asked, in broken English, whether the deposit had been received and when he would get confirmation of the booking. At first Micah would hang up but as the calls continued he tried to help the guy. He suggested phoning the police or Embassy. The phone call of his dad's death came in the early hours. The old man had got up to the toilet and had a heart attack mid ablution. The shrill bell jangled his nerves. Of course the ultimate late night phone call was a booty call; though it never had been to date. He picked up the receiver.

"Hello who is this?" Micah said. All immediate family were now dead or safely in the house up the other end of the garden. The only concern was that Jacob had cut himself too deeply.

"WAIT A MINUTE." Somebody shouted over loud music.

"Who is this?" Micah repeated, but the late night caller had abandoned the phone in search of a volume control. He hung up and rolled back over burying his head under the pillow more in frustration than to ward of the slowly brightening sky. Just as the eyelids began to drag the phone went again. This time he sprung up.

"Do you know what time it is?"

"4am at a guess." Music was quietly playing in the background.

"And who the fuck is this?"

"Jacob. It's Jacob."

"What do you want Jacob?" Micah tried to sound cross, as the aggravation bled from his voice."

"Just ringing to say hi."

"Well. Hi then."

The line went silent except for breathing. There was a female voice in the background and the music began to creep up again.

"Sorry Micah, wait a second." There were raised voices and the music suddenly stopped. He returned to the phone.

"Anyway how are you?"

"Tired and until recently fast asleep. You?"

Jacob missed the sarcasm and replied. "Good, really good. I was wondering what you are doing tomorrow night. I'm having a party thought you might like to come. Low key kind of thing."

"Can't this wait till tomorrow?"

"Parties tomorrow night. What do you say?"

"Ring me in the morning. I'm too tired to think." Said Micah stifling a yawn.

"It is morning. I'll put you down as a yes. Oh and I thought we might have another go at contacting your dad."

"Yeah whatever." Micah put the phone down and unplugged it from the wall.

He turned over and over in his bed digging a rut into the mattress. He was thankful for the invite, a chance to put things right. Micah had expected an awkward reticence, instead Jacob's easy manner left a slight powdery taste in his mouth, or maybe that was just custard hadn't dissolved properly.

It was hot and sweaty the way it always looked in those films about the Vietnam War where they were stuck in the jungle waiting for Charlie. Micah wished he had not worn his summer jacket. He wasn't sure what time the party was starting and planned to arrive around nine. By the time he turned down the right road any benefits of the shower were obsolete. He stopped off at the corner shop and bought beers. Jacob still lived in the family house. His absent parents lived somewhere abroad. When they were young his parents had worked in the city but were always off to America and increasingly the Far East as market opportunities opened up. Micah had met them occasionally in the six years they been at school together. They were always gone, the early commuter train to London. But occasionally in the evenings his mother would be home, dressed in a uniform grey pinstripe suit smelling of Yardley and authority. Once she invited Micah for tea, and after ringing his dad to check he sat watching television in silence with Jacob eating Chinese takeaway, the mother flitted from plate to telephone to a stack of spreadsheets she had brought home from the office. You could count the words she spoke on one hand.

    Micah knocked on the door. There was no sound, no music or voices from inside, and as he stood waiting he wondered if he had misunderstood the invite. He knocked again louder while picking green paint from the flaking wooden frame.
The door opened and a guy with a shock of peroxide blonde hair squinted at Micah with half open eyes.

    "Yeah?"
    "Hi I'm a friend of Jacob's."
    "Wait there." He slammed the door.

"How fucking rude." Micah mumbled as he looked up at the windows. Every curtain was pulled shut. The door opened again and this time it was Jacob.

"You made it. Great."

"Only just. I thought rude boy was going refuse me entry for a moment."

"Don't worry about Paul he thought you were somebody else."

"Some body he doesn't like I assume?" Jacob laughed and ushered his friend inside.

"Coat?" He held out his hand as if to receive stigmata. The relinquished jacket was tossed onto a large pile of coats on top of a leather Winchester.

"I remember that old sofa" commented Micah.

"Yeah, sold the rest of the set." He followed Jacob as he weaved through a crowd of faces towards the kitchen.

"Drink?" Jacob offered.

"Oh I bought these." Holding out the offering which Jacob took and placed on the kitchen roll top amongst an assortment of spirits and mixers. Jacob peeled off one of the Fosters and passed it back.

"Beers in fridge, spirits on table, ice in the freezer and party's in my pants. Oh yeah." He turned his attention towards two women leaning against the kitchen doorframe engrossed in conversation. The taller girl, glass in hand, ring in nose, lifted an eyebrow and disapprovingly pursed her lips.

"Lesbians" Jacob shrugged "Oh and toilet, well I'm sure you can remember where that is."

"Nice party." Micah commented following social convention. Jake shrugged
"I like what you've done with the place. Very minimal."
"You like it? You should see upstairs. I'll give you a tour."
They went back into the lounge. He had the Winchester and a miss matched chair, opposite an old tube ray television in the corner. Next to the television was the record player balanced on top of a milk bottle crate with two enormous speakers flanking like bouncers. Someone had decided that it was time for the party to properly start and had put some music on. The room filled with sound; eye shaking, vision distorting base pulsed.

Up the tight steep stairs it became apparent that minimal had been an overstatement. Sparse or barren was more apt. Jacob moved from room to room, waving and babbling. Micah wasn't listening. He was engrossed. It was as if the house had been emptied, as if it had thrown up until it hurt then continued heaving. The first thing he noticed was that all the carpets were gone. All was bare. He wondered if Jacob's parents had taken carpets and furniture with them when they had moved abroad or if he had them stashed in storage. Jacob waltzed around pointing enthusiastically to the lack of possessions. In two bedrooms everything was gone, carpets, lampshades, and furniture. There were faint faded outlines on walls, ghosts of the pictures that used to hang there. Micah remembered the family portrait that Jacob hated so much. Jacob's bedroom had a few items of furniture but nothing he recognised from the old days. Two wooden forklift pallets with a mattress served as a bed, while all clothes were stuffed in an over crammed chest of draws as tall as a man. Everywhere were books piled up a meter high, spines facing out. Nearer the bed the book stacks became smaller and served as a nest of bedside tables, with one stack sprawled across the floor. Each room was a glimpse. Jacob opened the door and closed doors at a frantic pace announcing the room with a single word or phrase until they reached the foot of the stairs leading to the third floor.

"Toilet as you know and the temple but we'll get to that later" he pointed up the stairs to the attic room.

They descended to replenish drinks. The cans were still nestled like dwarves between their elegant towering cousins. Jacob disappeared back into the throng of twenty or so people that crammed into his front room so Micah stepped outside onto the patio, bedecked by candles and a string of fairy lights missing every other light. Paul was sitting on the low wall that marked the boundary with next door. Looking across there were at least six manicured gardens with the exception of next door; a tangle of brambles and nettles. He sat down to next to Paul and introduced himself.

"We didn't get to meet properly at the door. Micah." He extended his hand.

"Paul" said Paul and he grabbed the hand firmly shaking it then slipped from one odd grip to another in a flurry of hand holds before punching a loose dishevelled fist and adding "Safe man, safe."

"So how do you know Jacob then?" Paul asked.

"We were school friends going back years."

"Oh right yeah, St James."

"No, St Richard's."

"Oh yeah, I remember now."

"How do you know Jacob then Paul?"

"We just kind of found each other. We're like kindred spirits. When we met we just clicked. I got him, you know, on a deeper level."

"So down the pub then?"

"What, yeah I think so. I mean probably. I mean we worked together at the local pub."
Micah smiled and said "He's a good guy, if a bit serious some times." Just to cover up the obvious mockery.

It was then Micah spotted her, flitting from group to group, social hopscotch. She seemed familiar; stick thin and angular with sad shiny eyes. The half empty, half full smile turned down at the corners made him want to hug her even if it meant cutting himself on a clavicle or a hipbone. She spotted Paul and walked over. Casually she slinked through the crowd sidling up to them and sat on Paul's lap much to his surprise.

"Hi Paul." She purred.

"Hello Imogen."

"What are you talking about?" She asked.

"How me and Jacob met." Smiled Paul

"Oh the pub. Such a shame. Jacob got fired for stealing seven hundred odd pounds." She addressed Micah. Then turned attention back to Paul.

"Got any weed?" He shrugged, but she wrapped an arm around him and whispered in his ear. He pulled out his tobacco pouch.

"Who's your friend?" There was a strange tone in her voice Micah could not place.

"Micah, Imogen, Imogen, Micah." She nodded as she began to construct a joint. Micah watched her thin nimble fingers crafting away aware that her short skirt had ridden up her thighs as she sat. From this angle he could see the lithe line of her thin legs rising up to her crotch and caught a flash of pink knickers. He pulled his eyes away.

"So, Micah, you enjoying the little gathering?"

"Yeah seems nice enough." He stayed non-committal, eyes straying again. He looked away again but this time when he looked back to her she was staring at him. He needed to say something and quickly. He added "I recognise you from somewhere."

"It's a small city. I guess you've seen me around."

"No, I'm sure we have met before?"

"Nice line but you'll have to work harder than that." She licked the edge of the paper holding the joint steady, tilted her head at an angle keeping her eyes locked on Micah's. There was something about the deliberate precision that reminded him of an old typewriter.

"'Do you come here often' or 'heaven's missing an angel' would have at least been slightly more obvious." She said

"But equally unsuccessful I am guessing?" He replied and she smiled.

"Paul, lighter." She held out her hand. As Paul tried to negotiate retrieval from his front pocket Imogen made no effort to move pinning his hand in an awkward position. Micah took the chance, reaching up with his and she cupped his hands in hers to shield the flame in the still night air. He took the opportunity while she concentrated on the flame dancing on the tip of the joint, to glance again at the strangely hypnotic glimpse of pink between her legs, though this time it was the ghost of white scars half hidden on her thighs that caught his attention.

Imogen took three long drags and then passed it to Micah. He obliged and quickly passed it to Paul as it was his dope in the first place. They sat silently, savouring the joint. As soon as it was finished Imogen stood up kissed Paul on the cheek then turned to plant one on Micah's cheek.

"Nice to meet you Micah. See you around." Then she was gone back into the house enveloped by the crowd.

"So that was Imogen then. She's a bit crazy, I'd keep your distance if I were you." It was then Micah remembered where he had seen her. It was the first night at the self-harm group. Jacob had said something similar about her. He could feel the warm glow of the kiss on his cheek noticeably close to his lips, at least too close for a first meeting. His mind over worked itself as the weed kicked in and he decided to go and get a cleansing beer. He offered to get one for Paul, but he declined leaving Micah free to wander off into the party and mingle.

The lounge had transformed into a dance floor, what little furniture there was had been pushed a side and bodies crammed close. The walls were beginning to run with sweat. Electronic beats, shrill perverse sounds, staccato and repetitive, drove the crowd into frenzy. The base clawing at people's insides.

"Acid House." He muttered rolling the words round his tongue, thinking that if this lot were on acid it would get very messy very quickly. He stepped into the kitchen swiped two cans and entrenched into the corner within easy reach of an ashtray as he began to chain smoke and listened to the music. For twenty minutes it seemed the same song played rising to crescendos only vaguely distinguishable from the breaks by the tone of the bleeps and the frequency of the bass drum.

He swiped another can and ascended the stairs to take a closer look at the house. The trouble with houses with very little in, there is very little to look at. Draining the can of beer, he went to the toilet in the least changed room. It was the same off-white bathroom suit and matching cabinet with back lit mirror and shaving point. The feminine touches, Jacob's mother used to add, were no longer visible.. Now there was no matching towel set or pot pouri. He pulled the door shut and realised there was no lock. Facing away from the door towards the bowl he began to urinate. The throb of bass from down stairs masked the sound of footsteps on the stairs and it wasn't until the door slid open that he realised someone else was planning on using the toilet.

"Busy in here" he called out to late.

"Sorry" said Imogen, shutting the door and waited outside.

"No lock" He said as he exited.

"I've told him before to fix it but he's not exactly what you would call a handy man." Said Imogen.

"Wait for me while I pee." She went into the bathroom and left the door ajar.

"So Paul said you've known Jacob since forever?"

"What?"

"You're an old friend of Jacob's right."

"Yeah that's right. Sorry do you want some privacy."

"We're all adults here." She went silent for a second.

"Could you do me a favour and talk? Any old rubbish will do."

"I could shut the door?" Offered Micah.

"And sneak another peek? Then I'd really wonder if you're a pervert." He was glad the half closed door was between them as his cheeks flushed.

"Well I've known Jacob since primary school but we lost touch after secondary school and I hadn't seen him since until about two weeks ago when we bumped into each other at self-harmers self- help group."

"Ah yes, Doctor Knight, what a joy. Have you had the pleasure of her one to one interviews or were you a volunteer?"

"No I had a consultation. She basically put it down to father issues and told me not to stop cutting and gave me a leaflet on how to harm safely." He heard the sound of a steady stream hitting water like a localised rainstorm.

"The only place for ice cubes is a Gin and Tonic." commented Imogen.

"My pet theory is that she has major father issues and projects them on to her patients."

Imogen appeared at the door. "So not a pervert then, just your average red blooded male. I'm sure Doctor Knight would say the way I dress invites that kind of attention." She stood very close.

"And do you?"

"Do I what?"

"Dress for attention."

"Doesn't everybody? When you came out tonight did you have a shower? Did you make sure you were clean just in case you got lucky? I assume you dressed like that because you thought it looks nice and you want to look nice for people's acceptance. From your male peers and to be attractive to the opposite sex?" Her eyes flicked up and down.

He looked at her straight into her eyes not sure if this was some sort of aggressive flirting whether Paul was right and she was crazy, a predator circling her prey. She had dark brown eyes almost black in the low-lit corridor. He searched her face for the slightest hint a lift of the lips at the corner of her mouth or an arching of one of her plucked eyebrows that as he studied, he noticed were a little crooked.

"How do you know Jacob?"

"He's my pusher"

"Oh!"

"Things changed since primary school?" He considered correcting her pointing out that I knew him through secondary school as well.

"I mean he is more than that. We have an odd arrangement. But drugs was our first love."

"And sex was your second." He remembered more of what Jacob had said that first night at the group.

"No, oh my god!" She recoiled in mock horror as far as she could in the space and pressed herself against the far wall lifting her knee so it touched Micah's outer thigh.

Predator?

"Well you know him, nice guy but I couldn't be doing with all his mumbo jumbo black magic bull shit."

"Ah yes, that"

"I see." She said lengthening the vowels at the end of the statement giving him a knowing look. He shrugged not wanting to talk about it.

"Have you seen the temple yet?" Her eyes flitted beyond Micah.

"Temple?"

"Yeah, apparently it's where the magic happens." The corners of her mouth turned slightly causing elongated dimples in her cheeks.

"Nope."

"Neither have I. Let's take a look." They simultaneously, conspiratorially glanced towards the stairs going down, looked at each other, then at the stairs going up. He shrugged, not committed, rather allowing her to take the lead.

Predator or potential partner?

She darted past him and flicked the light switch at the bottom of the stairwell. Nothing happened. Even the light from the bathroom could not pierce the impenetrable shadow.

"I'll go first." offered Micah.

"Brave hero leads the way into the unknown?" She pushed him aside and stepped up two or three times till the only sign of her was the pale white of her lithe legs.

"Come on then." Came her disembodied whisper. Micah followed. As he stepped up he noticed a sudden change in temperature.

"Wait up." called Micah and then accidentally walked into her. Face awkwardly pressing into her bottom.

"Sorry. Why did we stop?."

"If Jacob has removed the light bulb, what else has he done?" He could hear her shallow breath. The throb of music disorientated their senses. The dark fuelled their imaginations. Primal, unknown fears crept up their spines. Hairs on end, teeth gritted. Micah slapped himself on the cheek like a prize fighter psyching up.

"This is fucking stupid. Excuse me." He went to push past but her arm shot out blocking his way. They were close. So close the smell of her perfumed skin was intoxicating.

"No way hero boy. Follow me." She began to tentatively move up again. The lack of sight heightened Micah's other senses. A stair squeaked, a sonar ping in the dark. His nostrils filled to a musty smell. He tried to remember what was up here before. His foot reached the squeak and the sound seemed muffled as the surrounding space shrunk. They must be nearing the top.

"Imogen. You at the door?" Collusion was exciting. Then suddenly a voice from down stairs bellowed up the stairs.

"Micah. You up there?." It was Jacob. They froze, her arm reached down gripping his arm.

"It's…"

"Shh." She silenced him, stepped down and bent to whisper in his ear. "He's a bit touchy about his temple thing. He'll go mad if he catches us." He felt her hand begin to push him back down and he allowed it. They descended on tiptoe.

" Micah?" Jacob called again.

"Yeah." Called Micah popping his head over the banister looking down.

"What you doing?"

"Toilet."

"I'm thinking of going out for a bit. This parties getting a bit mad." Jacob glanced back into the lounge. "Besides I'm not a massive Acid House fan."

"But it's your party." Said Micah now walking down towards Jacob.

"Well the thing is." He stopped mid-sentence staring up beyond Micah at Imogen.

"Hello Jim." His eyebrow raised like a Lancet arch.

"Fuck off Jacob." She said pushing past them both.

"Roof hop. Back gate. Five minutes." Jacob shouted after her. He then turned back to Micah. The eyebrow now joining the other in a furrowed glare.

"Seriously don't go there. It is not worth it." Jacob warned again.

Back in the lounge the frenzy had increased. More people had packed into the room jumping and writhing waving hands sporadically as if they were having some kind of musically induced fit. This was dancing like he had never seen. This summer newspapers reported illegal raves in abandoned warehouses thrown up at a moment's notice. That was London, this was quaint little Chichester. It was youthful rebellion, except no one cared. Jacob's neighbours were old and deaf and just turned off their hearing aids.

"Micah. You up for a little roof hopping?"

"Definitely." Said Micah, with no idea what roof hopping was. Five minutes later he slipped out the back gate with Jacob and a few others. Acid House wasn't his thing either.

Roof Top Rendezvous

The claustrophobic alley opened out into New Park Road and beyond the park itself, a recreational ground and memorial park separated by a hedge. They regrouped in the memorial park at the enormous cross inscribed with the World War One dead. It was stepped at just the right height to afford seating. Micah looked around to see who had joined them. There was Jacob, Imogen, Paul and a couple who were glued to each other introduced briefly as Claire and Sean. They all wore black and dark grey making Micah navy blue shirt seen positively rainbow. No consensus could be reached as to where to go. Claire and Sean fancied McDonald's which had recently opened in town. It had taken over the site of the Old Corn Exchange with its Romanesque columns, which were now painted bright red. Certainly no other town had a McDonald's that looked like a Roman temple. Micah began to wonder if this would be as boring just without the Acid House.

"Roof hop, roof hop, roof hop." Chanted Jacob. He was dancing around on the spot like a five year old. "It'll be great." He looked at Imogen.

"Why not?" She said, and with that seal of approval, Paul, Claire and Sean nodded and the motion was carried.

Cutting across town via the back street was an education. Micah had lived here all his life and he knew this place well. But Jacob led them a tortured route that left Micah dizzy. They intersected the car park behind the swimming pool then under an arch way that tunnelled through the old Roman walls this brought them out into a maze of roads known as "Little London", so called because of a small community of tailors who came down from the capital hundreds of years ago. Here Jacob slipped through an inconspicuous gate in a wall that opened out into the courtyard of a hotel almost hidden from the road. They traversed the cobbled rectangle and entered the back of the lobby walking straight through and out the front door. The waist-coated gentleman sitting at reception registered little interest, assuming they were guests. Past the museum, another cut through between a taxi company and a private house and through two interconnected car parks and finally a crooked narrow pathway that forced them to walk single file, and out onto the main shopping street.

"Nearly there." Called Jacob.

"Where?" Micah was sure that if they had walked straight down east street they would have reached the same point in half the time.

At the Market Cross they headed north cutting across the cathedral green heading for the darkness behind the towering monolith away from the bright spot lights that illuminated the city's largest land mark. Micah brought up the rear trying to catch Imogen or Paul's eye. They finally came to a stop in the shadows of the cloisters: Gothic arched windows facing an inner courtyard which let moonlight spill in to the grey stone walk way. There was just enough light to see the doorway in the gloom on the far side.

"Alright, who's done this before?" Everyone raised their hands except Claire and Micah.

"For the virgins this is how it's going to go. Through the door at the end of the passageway second to last house is little shed climb on the roof from there up on to the flat roof then up the old drain pipe painted green. Move fast and head towards the Cathedral." He looked around for nods.

"Yes, we got it." They chorused. He grinned, and his teeth caught the moonlight like cats eyes. Imogen was busy fastening buttons on her cardigan and tucking everything in to her tights it looked comical but practical.

She glanced at Micah. "Ready?" He could see her teeth shining in the moonlight too.

"You bet." Replied Micah.

They moved like un-caged tigers. The moment they reached the shed, Jacob's hands grabbed the top and he launched himself. The next second he was gone, bounced off up the drainpipe and over the lip of the roof out of sight. Claire had to be pushed up by Sean. First hurdle completed, she gained confidence but Micah felt invisible eyes watching him as he crouched vulnerable on the flat roof waiting as she shimmied up the lead down pipe.

Imogen was less patient. "Get a move on Claire." Once she'd made the top, Sean quickly followed. Imogen turned to Micah.

"You next." She said.

"Ladies first."

"A true gentleman." Her face recoiled in mock shock. "Or do you want to sneak another peak?" Her eyebrow arched and before she could see him blush he vaulted the first few meters of pipe. At the top he turned to give Imogen a hand up to discover her right behind him.

"Out the way." She said pulling herself clear of the edge. They both lay flat against the gentle slope of the roof for a few seconds catching their breath. Laying up slope with their backs to the slate was quite comfortable.

"Nice bum, by the way" Imogen said as she followed Sean and Claire disappearing over the peak of the roof in search of Jacob.

They all regrouped in the lea of three roofs, lead flashing offered a small flat area where they could sit.

"Excellent, everyone's made it." It was clear from Jacob's tone he had not expected it. "Our destination for tonight's adventurer is the great cathedral spire." He looked to the beacon of limestone rising above them. It was ever present over the city yet never really seen. From here one street away and already three storeys up level with the guttering of the cloisters it seemed so much bigger. Once everybody had rested, Jacob stood.

"Quiet as we go. The local clergy live in the houses underneath." He pressed his finger to his lips.

These were old higgledy-piggledy house with miss-matched roofs creating a maze of pitches and troughs, until breaking left of a mansard roof. They reached the cloister roof; a moss cover steep pitch with tiny little terracotta tiles.

"Where's Sean and Claire?" Asked Micah when they stopped again.

"Stuck to each other like leeches." Answered Paul with an odd sneer.

"Their loss." said Jacob, standing staring up at the spire. Then he pointed.

"Look can you see the route. Along there to the point where that flying buttress comes down. You can't see from this angle, but you can climb up on to the green roof and follow it along to the base of the spire. I reckon from there we can shimmy up and get in through the windows half way up the spire."

"You reckon?" Said Micah. The gap from the peak of the green lead roof to the spire windows looked a good ten meters.

"Easiest route." replied Jacob.

Then from the passage below they heard urgent, busy voices and torchlight raked the guttering at the edge of the houses. Eyes widened and looks were shot between members of the group.

"I'll take a look." Said Jacob and lying on his belly he slid to the roof edge. Waiting till the torch beams moved away, he poked his head over the side briefly stealing a glance. Then slowly slid back to the rest; crouched on haunches, his legs beginning to cramp.

"It's the pigs." He snapped in hushed tones.
"What we going to do?" Paul asked.

"Just sit here and wait. They can't get us up here. After a while they will figure we've gone." Suggested Imogen.

It was a good plan, and in fairness it was the only plan they had. They sat down passing around cigarettes and lighters. Suddenly a window light flicked on illuminating an attic room inside the mansard roof. More worryingly was the policeman standing talking to an old gentleman in a suit. There was a set of keys being riffled through. Without warning, Jacob was up over the Cloisters roof, a clod of moss flying off as he scrambled. He vaulted the top and slid down the other side, his feet catching on the stone balustrade. Micah, Paul and Imogen stared at each other and then as one, they followed. There was still no sound of window opening by the time Micah reached the balustrade. Jacob was already gone. Thirty metres away, climbing back up, heading away from the cathedral towards South Street. Micah followed breathing hard. As he reached the point where Jacob had climbed upImogen was right behind him.

"Keep going slow coach." She chided. Micah couldn't reply; he had to keep sucking in air.

He cleared the top of the roof and spied three torches moving across the rooftops away to the right where they had come from. Voices carried on the breeze.

"Wait a moment" Said Imogen catching up. Her hand held his, as if its very position had the power to freeze him.

"Now" She said and they slid down the other side stepping on to another row of houses before dropping down on to a wall.

"You have to be kidding me. This is really narrow and more importantly seriously fucking high!" protested Micah.

"Chicken."

"I'm not chicken, I just have a heightened sense of self preservation." Micah looked at the sheer drop both sides. The wall was only narrow enough to place one foot in front of the other.

Imogen shrugged. "Suite yourself, wait here. If you're lucky the cops won't come over." She stepped out gingerly then stopped before giving a little laugh and walking off confidently.

"Shit." Micah stepped out. His heart thumped through his chest reverberating in his ear so loudly it felt as if he would over balance. But one step at a time he began to move along. He concentrated on one foot then the next foot, reminding himself that if this wall was a metrehigh he would manage without a problem. It was going well until he looked down. There was pitch-black one side and a well-lit fatal drop the other. His legs seized and he could feel a shaking beginning in his knees that he needed to control before it was too late.

"Come on Micah." He encouraged himself and forced another two steps, eyes straight ahead. His palms were sweating and he could feel his feet sweat saturating his socks.

"Oi! Down here!" Came a whisper. Somewhere below in the dark was Jacob calling but his eyes couldn't adjust.

Micah crouched precariously. "Where are you?" A hand reached out of the gloom.

"Here hold my hand, jump down."

"Thanks." He said landing on a gravelled flat roof, a spray of stones to the ground below. His eyes adjusted to the darkness and he could make out a precarious jumble of steps consisting of lower and lower roofs. Another wall offered another palm sweating balance across to an iron fire escape. Jacob was already sneaking down. He disappeared between the two buildings and Imogen ushered Micah to go first.

It seemed easier balancing on a lower wall. He strode across, bracing for the vault. "Shit. Shit. Shit." Whispered Jacob under his breath as torches flared up to the shadows at the top of the metal stairs.

"There." Jacob pointed to another route going back the other way that led up to the roofs. A dog barked from the bottom of the fire exit. They scrambled up keeping low, staying in the shadows. Micah glanced back. The torches were on the move, drawing closer. They crossed to the street of the roofs, running along a wide parapet. Below South Street bustled, unaware. They were forced up by a crow stepped gable facing them end on. Jacob leapt up two steps at a time. The others followed. Both Jacob and Imogen skipped over the ridge. Micah straddled the peak and shuffled over. His eyes constantly darting back to voices and torches moving back and forth along the back gardens. His foot slipped on a loose tile and it clattered down, catching in the gutter. The noise that echoed seemed to draw the light beams and chatter.

"Shit." He said as his shuffle transformed into a four crouch, hands and knees on the ridge tiles. They stopped again, all breathing heavily.

"Do you reckon Sean and Claire are alright?" Paul said.

"Fuck Sean and Claire. We've got to get down." Jacob's eyes were flitting all over. Without another word he was off again loosening clods of moss. Then suddenly he stopped.

"Bollocks."

"What?" Said Imogen keeping pace. He pointed to the chasm. There was a natural break in the shops. A beer garden and alleyway put ten meters between them and the way forward. Micah caught up again.

"The police are up on the roofs. They're getting closer." He spluttered dropping on his haunches.

"Great we're fucked." Jacob motioned to the void.

"For a bunch of people that voluntarily cut themselves, you seem very scared of pain." Said Imogen moving along the gutter to where a tree canopy reached up level with where they hid.

"We roll off into the tree. It slows our fall, we land, we walk off." She shrugged. "Easy."

"It's two storeys!" countered Jacob.

"Two big storeys. The size of three really." Added Micah. Imogen shrugged again and lay flat then rolled off. There was a rustle, a crack and the sound of someone landing hard. They peeked over to see her pick herself up.

"You alright love?" A man sitting in the beer garden enquired. He had been sitting back against the wall unseen.

"Right then." said Jacob looking at Micah.
"What?"
"After you."
"Why am I going first?" said Micah.
"Because the police know me, they don't know you. Unless you want to go first Paul?"

"I'm fine." Said Paul quickly. Micah lay flat and rolled, mimicking Imogen. He hit the floor still in the horizontal. Then curled his limbs like a spider crab, then moved slowly, checking nothing was broken.

"You alright mate?" The man from the beer garden had come over to check on Imogen and now offered Micah the same attention. He pulled Micah to his feet.

"How many of you hiding up there?" At that moment Paul came tumbling. He caught his side on a branch, his head just missing a table as he landed.

"Shit, it's raining people." The guy laughed and finished his beer. Then Jacob fell landing on his feet and rolling to cushion the impact.

"The names Gareth." Said Gareth, the pub's only customer. Everyone smiled not speaking, watching the roof tops.

"Way out?" Asked Jacob.

"Through there and then out into the front bar. Shouldn't be locked just yet." Gareth pointed.

Jacob nodded and they filed into the pub then out onto the high street.

"Evening" Came the low rumbling voice of authority from the window of a patrol car.

"Evening officer." Paul Chirped back.

"Any of you seen anyone climbing about on roofs?" Then he added. "Evening Jacob."

"Officer Crowley."

"You been climbing on the roofs have you?" This time Officer Crowley was directing his question to Jacob.

"Na, sounds stupid."

"Well if anyone was to be climbing they would probably want to stop because I will arrest them if I catch them. And no amount of wearing black will hide them." He locked glares with Jacob.

"Fair enough officer. Like I said, sounds stupid."

"I didn't say it wasn't. But I will arrest them." Jacob shrugged as Paul shifted looking more and more guiltily.

"We will be sure to tell them." Said Paul.

"Tell who young man?"

"The people who were climbing on the roof. I mean if we see them. I mean if there was someone on the roof." Paul smiled, all teeth. The officer slowly looked each of them in the face. He took note of Micah: dark brown hair undercut long on top, blue eyes, wide set chin. Paul: peroxide blond mop, thick, dark brown eye brows and Imogen: stick thin, dark, messy hair, big brown eyes. He committed the new faces to memory.

"Say hello to your parents Jacob." With that, the window wound back up and the patrol car pulled away slowly.

"Do you think he knew it was us?" Babbled Paul.

"I reckon he suspects." Said Imogen.

Jacob cut the speculation short. "Thank fuck he didn't search us." He proffered a hand full of pills.

"One each according to my calculations." He necked one before anybody else could reach in.

"They're all different." Noted Paul.

"Job lot." Shrugged Jacob.

"Job lot? So you have no idea what they are?" Micah spooned on the sarcasm hiding his genuine concern.

"Acid, speed, Ecstasy if you're lucky."

"It's like Revels with drugs." Said Imogen, reaching across and picking a small, white pill." She locked eyes with Micah. "You're not scared are you?"

"Just hope I don't get the coffee flavour." He replied picking a lozenge shaped pill.

They made for last orders at the Mute Swan. As they made their way up South Street and turned into East Street, Jacob marching off ahead like an urban Tonto with Paul following close, Imogen held back and passed Micah a piece of paper.

"Give me a ring some time. A drink, just you and me" She smiled before hurrying to catch up with the others. Micah looked at the scrap of paper it was a non-local phone number scrawled in eyeliner. He tucked it safely in his condom pocket and followed everyone towards the pub.

The morning after the night before

There were eight women; seven were naked covered in oil snaking their way towards Micah, undressing him, caressing him with their eyes, while he stood passive. The eigth woman stood separate. She was taller, her physical features somehow sharper, and a black-patent leather mask obscured her face. Her pitiless eyes seemed to bore into his head but the seven curvaceous virgins soon distracted him; all lips oil, and augmented breasts. In moments they stood next to him, pushing themselves against him, their oil running off them, soaking his checked pyjamas. He felt himself harden as he questioned their virginal credentials. He caught a last glimpse of the masked lady and she lifted her finger pressed it too her deep rouge lips and whispered.
"Ouch"
Micah heard it clearly although she was twenty meters away. The bed sheets tightened and he woke in a sweat.

Opening his eyes, he stared blank at the room. He waited for his addled dream soaked thoughts to reorganise, but still he couldn't place the bedroom. A lava lamp shot a plume of green gloop in slow motion, bathing the room in a science fiction tint. In the half-light he could make out a room tidy to the point of obsessive. Even the curtains matched the bed linen. Not his homemade creative mess, that was certain.

An alarm clock blinked 06:02 in an angry red light from the bedside cabinet, casting its eye over a small metal key placed in the exact centre of the bedside cabinet, giving the impression of care and precision. It was wasn't a front door key, too small, it looked more like the kind of key little girls had for secret diaries.

He needed to get up for work. He tried to lift his head, and searing pain forced him back down. His pulse thudded behind his eyeballs, and with every beat the world jumped. After a minute the sensation subsided. Why couldn't he remember what happened last night? He remembered getting ready to go out. The fuss of not being able to find his 'lucky shirt', then finding it discarded, and unwashed stuffed behind his bed. He remembered his Mum giving him an opinion on which T-shirt best defined his personality. He remembered the taxi drive into town, slightly fuzzy from a few vodka mixers, the meal with Ray, dropping acid and starting to come down. After the third pub the memory came adrift. There were lights, drinks, recreational drugs, faces he thought he knew. Lights blurred with images as if he watched the night through the window of a speeding train and now it was gone with all definite sequential moments.

Micah rolled over delicately. Shit! There was a girl in the bed with him. He was sure he would remember something like that. She was facing away from him, face half buried in the covers. Micah froze, all he knew was this girl was blonde from the shock of bed-ruffled hair. He listened but she seemed to make no sound. That was good. Sneak out write a little note; leave it on the kitchen table, assuming she had one, and out the door. He made a mental note not to mix chemicals and drink. What did he take last night? He slid from under the covers legs first, thankful for the soft carpet cushioning the knees. Again he waited and listened but not a sound. The blonde was not just quiet; there was a complete absence of sound. What if she is dead? The thought stalked him as he crawled hands and knees to the door and out to the hallway. Beyond the green glow it was pitch black. He weighed up options. Naked on the floor was not good, Micah needed to find clothes. Fumbling, he found a light switch then pulled the door too and switched it on. The sudden glare started the drumming behind the eyes and he sank back to the momentary safety of the floor. Nearby were his pants, close to the blondes' knickers, starting a breadcrumb trail of seduction which he followed, steadying himself against the wall. The trail led downstairs to the lounge and two half-finished glasses of wine sitting by a half finished bottle of Frascati, a more informed choice than your usual Pinot Grigio. He wondered if they had got on. He rubbed his head and scratched his stubble then went to the bathroom, after accidentally discovering the kitchen, the front door, and a broom cupboard in the process.

    Standing waiting to urinate he looked around. A small print of an old painting hung above the toilet depicting a naked woman chained to a rock pulling away from a serpent lapping at her feet. The small print read *Andromeda,* then he wondered if there were any photos of the blonde girl around. Suddenly urine shot off at an oblique angle. Well at least he had sex with this girl last night. Back at the bedroom he pushed the door a jar and peeked in. She had not moved. The white light of the hallway glinted off something at the top of the headboard, something that had gone undetected in the subdued green light. Now, from this distance, he noticed her arm behind her head under her pillow, then straight up attached to the bedpost by hand cuffs.

"I have killed her, I really have." Micah thought checking the bed spread. Crisp white, no blood.

"I didn't stab her; there would be blood if I stabbed her, buckets of it." Maybe that was it? Maybe Micah had blocked it out of his mind. That was why he could not remember a thing, a suppression of hideous amounts of blood.

"Now my DNA was sprayed all over the bathroom floor for the police to find. Shit." He quickly returned to the bathroom and started wiping the floor with toilet paper.

What was he thinking? There would be blood, he couldn't have killed her. *"Go back and check, pull yourself together."* He told himself. On all fours, slowly, using the bed as cover, he crept back into the room, shuffling round to her side to get close. He was quiet not wanting to wake her, just wanting to hear her breath. He drew near and held his breath so the only interference was his own heartbeat and a low level electrical buzz from that angry eyed alarm clock. He listened… nothing. Could people be this quiet without being dead? There was no blood for sure, but what if he had suffocated her, part of some weird sexual game? He didn't do that type of thing though, the closest to kinky he had ever been was swapping underwear with an ex girlfriend, more of a point to prove than a method of arousal. Fuck, what was that? Did she breathe or was that a car passing outside? He had not been listening. He looked into the face but couldn't see it really as hair was cascading down, just her nose sticking out and the shape of her lip barely glimpsed. She was perfectly still. Her nose glowed green from the lamp giving it the patina of a corpse from some fifties B movie and still he could not detect her breathing. Micah felt hot, sinking to the floor hot tears burning like sulphur on his cheeks, head spinning. What was he going to do? Why couldn't he remember? He must have done something awful.

    He left the room, the key, the cuffs, the girl, as they were and retreated to the brightness of the downstairs kitchen. Leave a note, act innocent, leave his number and when she rings, pick up, hear a very alive stranger on the end of the phone then hang up and never have to think about last night again. But what if she doesn't ring? Then make no attempt to cover his tracks. That would make him look guilty. If he left everything as it was then he could tell the truth. God, the truth, if only he knew the truth, but she'll ring, she must. He opted for the a quick note *"Thanks for last night, ring me"* he scribbled, with his number using a tiny blue pen like those from Argos or betting shops and gathered up the rest of his belongings. He opened the front door.

Feeling the heat of the day already beginning to bake the unfamiliar city outside, he wondered where he was. No immediate landmarks looked familiar. Then without hesitation he closed the door, and walked quickly away clutching his wallet; in search of taxi rank, bus stop or sign post.

Somnambulist

Micah waited, nursing a cup of coffee and fiddling with the menu. A petite waitress with dead straight blonde hair came over with her biro poised over a tatty little waiter's pad.

"Are you ready to order?" She raised an over plucked eyebrow.

"Not just yet but another coffee would be nice." She hustled the cup away for a refill as he feigned indecision, scanning the menu. He checked the clock on the wall. It was over an hour since he had rung Jacob. He had assumed no reply, an expectation formed in the few weeks of their re-acquaintance. He never knew Jacob to be out of bed before midday. He stared out of the window encrusted with the grime of passing traffic. He had realised where he was as soon as he had emerged from the rows of terraced houses. Southsea common stretched east, a long strip of green grass reminding the sea that this was lands true identity, rather than the sprawl of concrete, and brick that encroached on to the beach further round the shore line. There, arcade and promenade gave way to dock and diesel boats, listless after a hard week of pleasure cruising. The road, the last urban insult, ran the length of the park, and on hot summer's days like this, it crawled with cars spewing out their passengers, transforming the park, with a mass of weekend sun seekers. Above, white puffy clouds sailed regally, moving at a slower pace than the breeze.

The petite girl returned his mug, spilling it on the Formica grey tabletop as she placed it down.

"Sorry, I'll get a cloth." She blushed, and he noticed her white shirt and dark blue skirt were the colours of a local secondary school. Sweet sixteen on minimum wage marking time until she left to do bigger and better things.

"Don't worry." He called wiping the spillage with his jacket sleeve. Moments later she returned with a cloth to discover no mess. She hesitated then decided to wipe the table anyway, lifting his mug spilling more at the same time.

Micah noticed a man seated near the front of the café. He seemed from a different era. A semi=circular ring of wiry white hair cut just above the shoulders encompassed his bald head. A kink just below the nape of the neck belied the habit of wearing a hat. Of course men of a younger generation would simply shave their heads. But that hair cut would denote allegiance to far left politics and a tendency towards violence. His outfit caught Micah's eye as well. He wore smart suit trousers, shined, black brogues and, because today was his day off, a Dunlop polo shirt. Several small, empty, china cups littered the table and the ashtray was already overflowing. He would sip his coffee then throw his head back and look at the ceiling while he puffed on his cigar. He had the look of a man embedded for the long haul.

He must have been a regular as he and the proprietor were nattering like an old married couple.

In quieter lulls, the proprietor would even pull up a chair and join him. The pair would haunch forward in secretive collusion. The line between customer and restaurant owner seemed blurred. The old boy would get up and help other customers through the door and carry heavy bags to tables for frazzled mothers with children. Every time he went up to order another coffee he would clear a table and take it up with him.

Micah caught snippets of conversation, local gossip. Like some lazy spy network they traded information seen or heard over the last day about customers or local business owners. They even traded information on the rumoured love life of a road sweeper who called in for a takeaway tea. Micah wondered what they would make of him and proceeded to act out in an attempt to peak their interest. He had time to kill. He ordered a third cup of coffee with a cup of boiling water as a side then added eight sugars to both. He sat motionless, bolt upright with his eyes shut for long periods of time as if deep in thought and when he finally opened his eyes he would move to one of the other three seats around the table he was situated at and then repeated. He kept rotating for a good twenty minutes before he finally risked a glance in the direction of the two gentlemen to see what he imagined would be confused and intrigued faces. Both men faced away looking out through the floor to ceiling glass plate windows onto the Southsea strip; busy collecting their intel. Then Micah remembered he was in a big city. Here he was one of hundreds of crazy people who talked to themselves and shuffled along on their own little missions. The rule of thumb was to avoid eye contact.

The door opened and Micah glanced up. A tattooed man swaggered in, high-count polyester sweat pants and bright white Nike trainers trumpeting his street status. He pulled up a chair and beckoned the waitress. She shuffled over. The café slowly filled, old couples spending their pensions and young carbon copies of the tattooed man spreading Sun newspapers before them. He caught snatches of other conversations as he slurped his coffee staring at the menu. The typeface blurred and danced on the page pulsating in time to the dull thud of his head.

Just after the waitress had deliberately passed close for a third time, Jacob came in. He stopped at the door and looked as if he was about to leave when Micah raised his hand.

"Not easy to find." He announced by way of excuse.

"Sorry". Micah muttered.
Jacob sat staring waiting for Micah to comment. He didn't

"So, good night then?"

"Mmm" Micah grunted.
The waitress suddenly appeared. "Ready to order then?"

"Coffee please, black, ten sugars." Her anorexic eyebrow raised higher than before and Micah wondered if she would end up completely plucking it off and painting it on with an eyeliner pencil before she was thirty.

"Ten?"

"Or just bring the bowl." Suggested Jacob. She moved on to another table as the restaurant was now nearly full.

"Funny isn't it. Tell someone you're a heroin addict, and they casually nod. Tell them you take ten sugars and they question you like you're an addict." Micah nodded, fiddling with the menu; the corner was separating from the plasticote covering.

"So?" Jacob lent back stretching his hands behind his back.

"So, what?"

"Last time I saw you was just gone midnight in Chichester."

"Yeah" retorted Micah.

"And?"

"And what Jacob?"

He wanted to say, he couldn't remember. He wanted to say he woke up in bed with some chick and that he had no idea who she was and for that matter if she was alive and was freaked.

"Well you were on it. I mean, I couldn't keep up with you."

Micah placed his head in his hands and massaged his scalp. The waitress returned with Jacob's coffee and a sugar bowl, newly filled up.

"The boss says you have to order something to eat. It's policy."

"Best thing for a hangover." Said Jacob smiling and ordered for Micah.

They sat in silence. Micah nursed his head as he spooned sugars into the mug, hoping his friend would give some clues away.

"Jacob, don't laugh." He sat upright spoon suspended heaped with sugar.

"Go on."

"You promise?" He nodded, the nearest to a promise he would give.

"I can't remember a thing about last night after entering the Swan."

Jacob shuffled uneasily in his seat and began to study the grey flexes of the Formica tabletop.

"What? What should I know? What happened?" Micah felt nauseous.

"Well, I think that's my fault. The thing is, you were wired after the roof, you were knocking back the shots in the pub." He paused, looking for recognition in his friend's blank face.

"And you were asking for more drugs but I dropped them on the roof or when we were climbing the fence by the grave yard." He had a flash memory of being launched over the black railings of St Peter's churchyard as a short cut to North Street car park. More flashes of the High Street, a flurry of light and colour with noise, as faces loomed in and out of his peripheral vision, all smiling and laughing. He remembered the need for quiet but when he hid down a side ally the silence stalked him, like some growling menace. He could hear the growl turn to a roar a few streets away.

"I think your Russian roulette pill must have been acid. You needed to chill out. All I could get hold of at short notice was Flunitrazepam. I thought it would calm you down a bit."

Micah had a memory of running out of the pub garden. He had to get as far away from the silence as he could, yet the further he ran the darker and quieter it became. Jacob found him huddled in the backstreets in a bush in somebody's front garden.

"What the fuck is Flunitrazepam?" Micah hissed.

"It's Rohypnol." Micah slid back in his chair, rubbing his face, pushing the day old stubble against the grain.

"How many did you take? Silly question, too many obviously." Said Jacob.

"How many did I take? Fucking hell Jacob, what were you thinking?"

"Calm down." He snapped aware of the shuffling Sun readers and OAP's

"You wanted something. I figured it would help chill you out. I told you to take one each, it's not my fault you necked them both."
The waitress placed two plates of meat and carbohydrate in front of them, swimming in grease and motioned to the cutlery in a pot at the end of the table.

"Thanks, can we get some ketchup please?" Chirped Jacob rubbing his hands together.

"One each?" Said Micah suddenly realising what Jacob had said.

"Yeah you and Jim."

"Imogen, the girl was Imogen." Now Micah's head really began to spin. He tried to force the parting image of the flat out of his head. He wished he had taken the time to check she was defiantly breathing.

"She was on top form last night, a right bitch." Said Jacob.

"So what happened, how did I end up here?"

"No idea. I went to toilet, came back and you and Imogen were gone." Jacob slurped his tea.

"So where was the other side of the looking glass this morning?" Said Jacob cupping the tea in two hands.

"I have no idea, somewhere in Portsmouth. Where does Imogen live?"

"Chichester I think." Jacob tried to replicate a stern schoolteacher look.

"You didn't, like you know?" He raised his eyebrows sticking his tongue in the side of his mouth.

"How should I know, you gave me Rohypnol?"

The waitress arrived with the ketchup, this time there was no chat, no pause, she hardly even stopped long enough to place the bottle on the table. Her eyebrows were now tightly fixed in a v of concentration as she frantically hopped table to table.

"One day you are going to have to tell me why she is so mad. I mean you always tell me *Stay clear, keep away mind that one she's crazy.* But I have yet to see the evidence." He thought of hand-cuffs as he shovelled a fork full of fried bread and stared at Jacob in forced silence.

"Not much to tell really she cuts herself. Proper carving knife, slice the flesh hospital job." Micah swallowed and took a mug full of coffee, and said.

"Yeah but that's just a way to get by."

"All right Doctor Knight." Mused Jacob.

"So she cuts a little deep some times. I think Jacob's got a crush. I think you gave her the hot beef injection and she wasn't that interested. Left you wanting more." Micah shovelled another mouthful in but continued talking, moving the food around his mouth struggling to pronounce vowels.

"I think you are worried that I might be competition." Micah ribbed him a little. An older lady on the table next to them with a blue summer blouse over a white nylon petticoat looked flustered from the heat. She glanced over in disapproval, deliberately putting her cup down heavily. The lads weren't sure if she overheard or was appalled that Micah was eating with his mouth open. Jacob spotted the direction of her gaze and glared back, his thick black make up smudged and still crusted on from the night before. She turned away.

"Nothing interesting in their own lives. All they have to do is eavesdrop into other people's car crashes." Jacob spoke loudly and deliberately.

"So my life is a car crash then?"

"Figure of speech."

"That's what Freud said."

"Fuck off." Laughed Jacob.

"So it wasn't then?"

"Wasn't what?" Micah took another mouthful leaving Jacob with a puzzled expression as he chewed and swallowed. Micah thought about it. Thought about the flat he had left. The more he mulled it over the more he felt sure she had to be alive. He now wished he had un-cuffed her. He looked sideways at Jacob and tried to read his mood tried to think about all he had said before.

"Your relationship with Imogen?" Started Micah cautiously.

"There is no relationship." Snapped Jacob but Micah pushed a bit more.

"But there was? I mean you said you slept with her."

"When?" Jacob looked puzzled again.

"First night at the self-harmers anonymous." The old lady was frowning again, her thinning blue rinse hair moving back and forth over her scalp as she recoiled. Micah chose to ignore it but Jacob played to the crowd.

"I haven't fucked her. I mean, she is fuckable on your basic, physical level but, as I keep telling you, she is one to avoid." He was getting irritable now.

"But there is definitely something going on between you two." Micah broke the yoke that was still runny and soaked it up with the last of my fried bread.

"Not in the way you're thinking."

"So you haven't fucked her?" Micah reiterated his question. The old lady expelled a loud tut.

"No I haven't fucking fucked her" Jacob turned to the lady as he spoke "or as the older generation might like to say partaken of sexual intercourse but as it's my private conversation I like to use the perfectly legitimate, vernacular, vulgarism from the Anglo-Saxon "fach" referring to a tax, hence one gets taxed or fucked up the arse by the government something as a pensioner I'm sure you're aware of." The old lady went red in the face and stared at her plate.

"Why you got the bit in the teeth about me and Imogen anyway?" Said Jacob, turning away from the old lady.

"Just wondered. You have a thing for pretty girls."

"That's a stupid thing to say. Who'd have a thing for ugly girls?"

"True."

"Just don't go there. Micah it will be a nightmare it will be like Alice all over." Micah shifted in his seat, the past and the present mixing, as he remembered what went wrong when they were younger. He opened his mouth to speak but Jacob interrupted.

'I think we'd better go."

Jacob's little outburst had drawn the attention of a few chivalrous tattooed gentlemen in tracksuits who would consider it sport to kick the shit out of a bloke dressed in black with more make up than their girlfriends. They hurriedly took two more mouthfuls and headed for the door leaving money on the table. They didn't wait for a taxi but started to walk into town away from the beach and any slight breeze.

By the time they took shelter in the cool interior of the Victorian built Portsmouth Station they were stripped to the waist and sweating profusely. They had been silent all the way. Micah figured the girl must have been Imogen and was now pretty convinced he hadn't killed anyone as the drugs began to work themselves out of his system and full rationality returned. He began to feel guilty about having left someone handcuffed to their bed. He hoped she would be able to reach the key. They caught the 13.20 back to Chichester having to wait nearly two hours due to Sunday running times.

Pain and the pleasure

The itch pulled her from sleep. She could feel the familiar sensation beneath her skin, that sensation that only scratching could stop. The underside of her skin was alive, sparks of blue electricity jumping erratically. Almost pleasant. Her nipples were hard bullets, propping up the tented soft cotton of the faded green T-shirt she slept in. A warm sensation stirred between her legs. It always started like this she could distract her body with other sensations. As she rolled over, the cotton dragged across her skin rasping against old scar tissue. Each puckered keloid welt tightened as if cold. She wrapped her thighs round the bedclothes holding it tight against her crotch squeezing and releasing like an anaconda toying with dinner. She slipped her hand down between her thighs, rolling over on to her front. She closed her eyes feeling the sensation grow, the one she controlled. It spread slowly out enveloping her nerve endings as her body demanded attention. Her fingers worked, varying speed and pressure while her thigh tensed then slackened their grip on the near-knotted sheet. Her breathing deepened, her eyes rolled back as she forgot to breathe and then the sudden, golden, glowing rush momentarily eclipsed the itch like a morphine addict having received a hit. But it was respite and she lay still, enjoying it for as long as those endorphins swam around her blood stream chasing the inevitable away. She knew what was to come. She peeled the T-shirt off and threw it to the floor and stood naked. Sometimes she could fight it off, stop this low level irritation before it built into waves that were so powerful that she was forced to scratch, to dig deep till the hot sticky magma rose swelled and erupted. She screwed her eyes tight tried to think of Jane Eyre, distracting herself with thoughts of the two marriage proposals that Jane received from Rochester. The first one should have been perfect, in an idyllic garden on a warm summer's evening heavy with romance but he was already married and was imprisoning his mad wife in the attic. The successful proposal that led to their final marriage was on a rainy, dark day on a moor, with Rochester a broken man, crying. Imogen thought about this, wondered if a man ever proposed to her and it rained she would consider it a bad sign or an ironic pathetic fallacy. She crammed her mind with the plot, every detail she could remember, creating new details where she couldn't remember. The bathroom window was open and the breeze tilted the nicotine netting plucking at her skin.

"No no no." She shook away a hoard of imaginary ants marching down the back of her spine. Action was required, exercise to fire the adrenalin gland to overwhelm or distract her fidgeting nerve endings. Downstairs she dug the vacuum cleaner out from the back of the cupboard.

It was a 1950's 1334 Hoover, deep burgundy with cream dust bag and matching thick rubber trim round the bottom and a light bulb mounted on the front fascia. It had been a present from Imogen's father who had been a Hoover enthusiast, fully reconditioned and useless. These technical idiosyncrasies suddenly elevated the antique to useful. She hoovered hard, in the dark, steering by the sodium yellow bulb and the release felt good. She thrust and pulled the relic till her naked body was slick with sweat. The 1334 threw up dust that stuck to the thin film of sweat now pooling via rivulet on her flushed skin.

In the dark the phone jangled into life.

"Who is this?" She snapped. Only the back ground music replied.

"Well?" When she was like this her head would spin with thoughts and ideas as the mania rose. Later it would be difficult to establish what was real and what was imagined.

"Hello Imogen. I see you are in a happy mood. Did I interrupt something?"

"Fuck off you arse."

"That's a yes then." She could just imagine Jacob standing there by the back door with a beer or a spliff, hands waving as if he was conducting the conversation, the phone chord pulled tight. But she was tired and needed his help to play her games.

"I was hoovering."

"Are you alright?" She didn't reply.

"I mean I assume you were not actually doing housework at 3am?"

"Mmm" Imogen tried to hit the pitch just right, let Jacob know where the line was, let him know not to cross. She would not take any of his shit right now.

"So do you need to come round?" Jacob asked casually. How did he know? She must have phoned him, she certainly remembered considering it. She always phoned him. Always decided how and when and now he was phoning her.

"I, er, you phoned me?"

"Alright then, be that way." He changed the subject. "Me and Paul are sitting here and we've decided that a party is needed." Jacob continued to talk about possible dates, themes, fancy dress and some guy Paul knew who brewed his own beer that could hook them up. Imogen was not listening. She was repeatedly pulling her nail across the tender flesh of her areola.

"You rang at 3am to tell me that."

"It's not like you weren't up, and anyway…"

"Jacob," she interrupted mid-sentence.

"Yeah."

"I need to come round. Can you get rid of Paul?"

"Give me half an hour." He hung up. Imogen looked down a glistening crimson semi-circle had risen perfectly outlining the dark skin gathered like a walnut on top of her pale sun starved breast. She licked her finger and wiped away a thin trickle before getting a wad of toilet paper to press against the flow while she went upstairs to run the shower and wait for the hot water to work its way through the pipes.

She sat alone in the back of the taxi, showered and shaved all over. It was a trick she had learnt from a competitive cyclist who used to shave his legs as hairs in wounds easily caused infection. She had thrown on a pair of jeans, T-shirt, and flip flops, disregarding underwear and walked the two minutes to the taxi rank by the train station, deserted after the night club runs. She rapped her knuckles on the dividing window of the hackney cab and asked the driver to crack the window a fraction. A blast of cool air pricked her nipples pulling the T-shirt taut. The thin cotton clawed at the newly formed scab leaving a dark red crescent.

"You alright Love?" His had eyes roved, reflected white in the rear view mirror.

"Yeah." She crossed her arms confident that the orange strobe lighting of passing streetlights was enough to hide the sticky seepage.

The taxi pulled up. Imogen threw a hand full of coins at the driver and sprang from the cab to Jacob's door. Sorely managed privets crowded out the dim light seeping through the pulled curtains. Even before knuckles rapped on wood the door jerked wide and Jacob appeared leaning, barring her entrance, barefoot in tight black jeans with a cigarette hanging from the corner of his mouth.

"Evening." He smiled pulling his top lip high in one corner.

"Has Paul gone?" Imogen asked.

"Maybe." Jacob's shirt was undone to the fourth button and he rubbed his chest with the flat of his hand in wide circular motions. He looked like a poorly paid James Dean impersonator. Imogen pushed past into the dim lit josstick infused interior leaving Jacob to wink at the taxi driver, a salvage operation for his bruised ego. The cabbie was too busy counting his coins.

Imogen settled into the large red velour chair picking up Jacob's lighter and tobacco that were within easy reach. She scanned the low pine coffee table for Rizla papers. Though littered with other drug paraphernalia; a grinder, roach material, a chillum, and a home-made bong engineered from a Pepsi bottle but no lighter. Then she remembered.

"Only those in the know." She smiled at Jacob's little ways and slipped her hand down the side of the chair seat to find the king skins nestled where they always were.

"How you feeling?" He asked watching her hands as she tried to stop spilling the tobacco. She just shrugged.

"Here." He lifted the half formed cigarette from her fingers and twiddled it between his finger and thumb.

"Everything's ready. I've put the heater on upstairs for you." He smiled but Imogen was not focusing on him, goose bumps were running the length of her spine as if a gang of tattooists were needling her all at once.

"Diet or full fat?"

"What?" She looked confused. Jake was toying with a small wooden box.

"Spliff or fag?"

"Fag." She needed to cut to it quick. Jacob's tongue dabbed the translucent paper pooling enough saliva to gum together a perfect cone.

"Thanks." Said Imogen snatching the roll up from his hand and slinking away towards the stairs, peeling clothes as she went. Jacob waited rolling himself two spliffs. He tucked one behind his ear and followed Imogen up the stairs slowly so she could prepare herself.

Eateries of the Gods

There was effort gleaming from every primed pour of the clientele. Men in fresh pressed shirts with meticulously combed hair sat with close shaven jaws working over food or conversation. The ladies, the few that there were, wore garish outfits with exaggerated lapels and necklines. One lady sported a set of bright yellow beads large enough to keep a chiropractor employed. But it wasn't the sign that said "Champagne Bar" over the door that told Jacob this place was posh and expensive; it was the music. In the middle of the room a low-rise platform supported three violins and a double base. Of course Robert had chosen this place. He was paying so that was fine. There was nowhere like this in Chichester or Portsmouth or the South coast for that matter.

    Jacob followed two steps behind his brother. At the door they were met by a maître d' who smiled, his sad, cold eyes scanned. Then he spun on his black patented shoes clicking his heels and strutted peacock-like through the tables.

    "Good afternoon. Please follow me Mister Claremont. Your usual table is ready."

    "Cock" Whispered Jacob catching his brother's eye. Robert loosened his tie as he began to follow the monochrome dressed guide and lent in close to Jacob, his face set. When he was close enough that no one else could possibly hear he whispered back.

"Absolute cock!" Then winked.

Inside similar dressed peacocks flitted between plainly laid tables. Everything was crisp and white with a faint smell of paint in the air. This was a temple to the new optimism of the 1990's with its crystal glass and simple fine bone china. The maître d' sat them, tucking chairs in behind and snatching the ornately folded napkins, laying them in laps. Jacob suddenly wished he owned an iron. Robert talked, ignoring the peacock as he clucked around the table.

"I like this place it reminds me of change. The chintz of the last decade finally being swept aside with this new trendy design. But if you look carefully" Robert motioned upwards. "signs of the old opulence. Look at that marvellous domed ceiling. I'm not an architectural expert but a dining guest once told me that it was Byzantine style. And look at those columns." Jacob looked at the four columns that supported the domed ceiling. They were gold with azure crenellation top and bottom.

"Nice." Said Jacob.

"A bit gaudy but ten years ago it was high fashion. It's as if the next fashion in interior design is growing up under the feet of the old and pushing its older rival out of the way to take centre stage. Except if you look up the old still looms ever present over the new."

"Oh."

"Except the older style belligerently hangs on and over shadows."

"I see." Jacob wondered if this was metaphor or polite conversation. Either way he was struggling to follow the thread.

The usual table was a two seater tucked away in a corner next to a high vaulted sash window, south facing. Robert smoothed the brilliant white tablecloth enjoying the warmth of the sun on the back of his hands.

"As white as the grading tables at work." He said with a self-satisfied grin.

"Still grading diamonds then Robert?" He was always Robert, never Rob or Robbie.

"Oh yes, wouldn't change it for the world. Do you know what you want to eat?" asked Robert his fingers drummed on the unopened menu.

"I don't get it?"

"Get what?" Robert was looking around trying to catch the eye of one of the peacocks as they bobbed between tables attending to customers.

"All that money for such tiny little things. They all look the same anyway."

"My job in case you have forgotten" Robert raised an accusatory eyebrow. "is to grade the colour of stones and the difference between a colourless stone which we grade as a "D" in the trade and, say, a yellow tinged "M" can be the difference of thousands of pounds."

"So a pure clear stone is worth thousands and a piss coloured stone is worth piss?'

"Crude Jacob but yes." Jacob remembered his brother was an easy target to wind up.

"Except of course unless it's the colour of piss after a night drinking nothing but Irn Bru then that would be classed as a fancy colour and even more expensive." They both laughed.

"Besides, I can work all over the world in any of the Bourses."

"Bourses?"

"Diamond exchanges of sorts." Robert caught a waiter's eye and mutual nods were exchanged.

"Where are they then?"

"Oh, New York, Tel Aviv, Mumbai, Antwerp, Johannesburg, Moscow and London."

"So the fact that you only speak English narrows it to New York or London." The waiter arrived.

"Ready to order? My treat, of course. Whatever you want." Robert ordered without opening the menu. Jacob looked at the menu for the first time, ran his finger down the prices to the most expensive main and ordered.

"That's why I like this table." Said Robert brushing away imaginary crumbs.

"You said. Reminds you of the grading tables."

"That yes. But it's the light. At work we have massive north facing windows. Consequently, I like to dine in as much direct sun light as I can."

"I get that. It's like a chef who hates cooking at home."

"Yes I suppose it is."

"But Robert, why north facing windows?" Jacob wondered if he should already know this stuff. Was this a re-run of countless conversations from the past?

"I grade stones by natural light but the ultra-violet rays in direct sunlight can cause a diamond to fluoresce changing the colour enough to throw the price out by a good few thousand.

"Really that much?" Jacob found himself genuinely interested, though he nervously twiddled with his napkin.

"It's amazing. You would be surprised." Robert sat forward animated by the enthusiasm he heard in his brother's voice. If this was a repeat conversation his brother hid it well.

"There is a new trend that makes me laugh; badly coloured stones." He paused for dramatic effect. "Piss coloured and not after a gallon of Irn Bru, stones that are hardly worth anything being given exotic sounding names like 'Cinnamon' or 'Champagne' and then bumping the price up as if they were fancy coloured gems." They both laughed together for the second time, Robert somewhat louder. It was definitely a diamond graders' joke. Jacob decided the conversation was borne of ten years absence and his brother was not trying to force didactics. This was just a conversation. It was nice but it could not last.

Lunch was served in a dramatic flourish with three waiters. Robert made all the appropriate sounds, shooing them away before they could fuss any more.

"Wine?" Robert was pouring the Cabernet Sauvignon before Jacob replied.

"Beer would be better but hey, it's alcohol." Silence fell as they ate. Jacob listened to the stringed music. He didn't know much but he knew enough to hear that one of the violinists was playing the wrong note every now and then. He glanced over, keen to have something to concentrate on. It was impossible to tell which one it was. Maybe that was why there were three. Some kind of fraternal brotherhood of violinists looking out for each other, playing in packs, protecting the less experienced so that no one person could be fired. Finally the lack of conversation was too much.

"So what's all this brotherly stuff about then?" He sat pushing food around the plate with a fork. The other hand rested in his lap. He felt like a naughty schoolboy about to be scolded.

"Can't a brother treat his younger sibling to a meal?" Robert raised a half full glass, Jacob followed the rules of etiquette and touched a near empty glass to his brothers.

"Yeah and don't get me wrong this is very nice. But I haven't seen you for the last two years. Oh, by the way, thanks for the Christmas card." Jacob meant it. There had been one hundred pounds tucked in the envelope.

"No problem. I just realised I haven't been seeing you enough." They smiled at each other awkwardly. Jacob thought of the last time they met, him naked and bleeding profusely in the front room of their family home.

"Eat up." Chided Robert leaning across, spearing a potato with his fork. There it was, the familial link. Even in one of London's most exclusive venues Robert still resorted to habits remembered from meals shared in front of the television when their parents were still on the late train from work.

"Is this about Mum and Dad coming home?"

"No. Well yes. I mean they are back in six weeks and that house is a travesty. But that's your funeral Jacob. This is about me looking out for my little brother." Jacob smiled.

They ate their fill, pushing plates to one side for them to be pounced on by hovering staff. They engaged in small talk watching the gap open, reminding them of why it had been two years. By the time Jacob was scraping the last of his dessert out of the bowl with his spoon, they were back to silence.

"Have you been out to see the old folks?" Asked Jacob trying to resuscitate the conversation. They talked and it was convivial. Robert closed down and the obvious void in age and life became an odd, seat shuffling silence. Robert waved his hand in the air giving the universal sign for bill.

"This is for you." Robert abruptly pushed an unmarked envelope across the table. Jacob had seen enough stuffed envelopes to know what was in it and instinctively palmed it from the table out of sight as if instructing a novice.

"Thank you Robert though it's not necessary." Robert just smiled and paid the bill.

"Remember I'll be round next week as I need to measure things. I've still got a spare key so I'll let myself in, alright?"

"Might see you then." Jacob replied pretty sure he wouldn't. In the back of the taxi heading to Waterloo station of which Robert paid for, Jacob thumbed through the wedge of twenty-pound notes. A hand scribbled note stated *"To help pay for getting the house in order"*. Jacob laughed, stuffing the guilt payment deep in his front pocket. There was easily enough for one last big party.

The Box

"What is common and what is exotic, is all perspective." Jacob started

"I suppose." Agreed Micah, not wanting to be drawn into this too much. He was aware that the little mobile home was a thin metal can. Jacob could get a bit shouty when passionate and Mum and his brothers were fast asleep at the other end of the garden with window wide enticing any semblance of a cool breeze.

" You suppose? Tobacco and chocolate were once exotic. Privateers in the seventeenth century capturing Spanish galleons returning from the New World would throw sack after sack of cacao beans over board outraged at the lack of gold. Ironically pound for pound the beans were more valuable than any hoard of treasure." He stopped and downed the Jack Daniels Micah had poured him. Then poured himself another. He definitely got louder as he got drunker.

"Tea was once carried in locked chests shaped so that the owner could sleep with his head rested on top to deter thieves as it was so valuable. Pizza, when first introduced to London in the 1950's by immigrant Italians was haute cuisine. Then there's Rocket, a common weed dug out of flowerbeds by Victorians before it was rediscovered as the peppery salad." Jacob was standing waving the bottle about to pour a third.

Micah added. "Then there's the humble glass of water. It bubbles up through some extinct volcanic in central France and transforms into valuable bottled water, more expensive than a carton of milk." He spoke in hushed tones, trying to encourage his friend to be quieter.

"Exactly right."

"Sit down man. Chill out and show me what's in the box." The wooden box was placed ceremoniously on the table when Jacob had arrived for their second séance. Jacob had been keen to make up for last time. They had not seen each other since Southsea. It was like that with Jacob, floating in and out of your life without explanation. Micah had been glad of the break. He had needed time to think. He had been nervous of seeing Jacob again. He was not sure why but as soon as Micah had made the mistake of calling the box "a bit plain" and Jacob had begun his definition of exotic, Jacob's point was that to an Amazonian tribesman Gravesend was exotic, then Micah knew he did not need to worry.

The initials J.A.S were burnt or branded on. Every time Jacob opened it there always seemed to be something different inside. This time it was an economy box of cooking salt and a large jam jar with the label peeled off. In the jar were bugs. Mashed up bugs, a mess of wings, antenna and legs. Occasionally a piece of spider or daddy-long-legs was clearly visible in the melee. Of course there was the obligatory black candles and a box of matches.

"No knife?" Asked Micah.

"We are going to try a different method." Said Jacob as he began to busy himself around the room. He started by taking the packet of salt and pouring out a thin line round the table in the middle of the room.

"Have you turned all the mirrors around Micah?"

"Yep definitely. There's only two."

"No hand mirrors or highly reflective surfaces which act as a mirror?"

"Unless you count windows."

"No. Windows are fine."

"Why's that?" Micah was intrigued this time rather than sarcastic.

"I don't know it just works that way." Micah wondered what mirrors did and why they needed to be covered. He had asked Jacob several times about mirrors and had never got a straight answer.

"Alright" Jacob stood admiring his handy work, a slightly elliptical circle.

"The salt acts as protection. Kind of a barrier between this world and the next."

"Cool."

"Our last line of defence if things get crazy. So don't cross the line, alright?" Micah just nodded in agreement.

"Right, so following on from the last attempt. I thought I would try a different method." Said Jacob looking sheepish.

"I thought blood crossed the divide or some such thing."

"Sort of." Snapped Jacob defensively. Then catching hold of himself added.

"There are other ways it's more about life force than blood; blood being a conduit for the life force. Acts like a sort of electrical current to charge the connection."

"But it doesn't have to be blood I take it?"

"Exactly." Said Jacob tapping the large jar of desiccated insect remains.

Micah mused silently. His friend never got it quite right. Last time he had all the ingredients, blood, candles, and an air of supernaturalism but had turned up in the middle of the day. This time the séance was planned for midnight but he had shown up with a box of cooking salt and a jar of dead insects.

"Lights." Commanded Jacob. As the lights flicked off, he lit the candles.

"Remember the results of these things vary greatly. It's not like a television. You can't just turn it on and turn it off." That was Jacob's get out clause.

"Do we link hands or something?" Enquired Micah. Jacob emptied the jar out into the centre of the table, tapping it gently with his index finger to coax out the debris like a line of cocaine. His eyes were twinkling.

"No we just need to touch the pile of insects." Micah grimaced and Jacob assured him he only had to touch lightly. There was a light crunch as Micah pressed his fingertips into the pile. It reminded him of Rice Krispies.

"Now stare into the candle and focus on a memory of your dad. That'll act as a magnet." Jacob was beaming. With all the preparation complete he sat back down facing Micah across the table.

Micah sat silently watching the flame. The black wax dripped revealing red wax underneath, which ran down the side like blood. At first he struggled his mind wandering, thinking about work, about how he and Jacob had suddenly met again. The flame flickered from time to time responding to a tiny draft from one of the countless holes in the old mobile home. Micah looked up and saw Jacob glaring at him.

"You need to be thinking of your dad." He said.

"Alright then." Micah made a show of shuffling, relaxing and refocusing. Then he took a deep breath and stared at the candle. He searched his mind for a memory or a moment in time with his dad that he could hold on to. At first he jumped to the funeral, a procession of relatives dressed in black, umbrellas braced against the wind and rain, taking shelter in the lea of a hedgerow. Returning to the grave side when the rain passed. Hot tears began to fill Micah's eyes. He searched for something else. Dad's woodshed and woodwork lessons. Micah remembered the dry homely smell of fresh cut wood shavings littering the floor like whiskers in a barber's shop. Dad would hammer and saw, creating tables and chairs. The quality was professional but he was too slow to make a living out of it. He had been keen to pass on his knowledge to Micah. So Micah was tortured with dovetail and mortise and tendon joints. Suddenly Micah had the image of his dad forcing him to watch John Wayne movies while he stayed up past his bedtime waiting for mum to finish the late shift at the hospital. Why was Dad surprised when all he wanted to make were guns?

Micah was snapped from his thoughts by a sound. His eyes half blinded by staring into the candle flame struggled to penetrate the blackness crowding in.

"What was that?" He whispered.

"I don't kn…" The sound stopped Jacob mid-sentence. It was a muted clunk like a knock but not on wood. It was like someone knocking on wood when you were half asleep buried under a thick duvet and had water in your ears.

"Was that knocking?" Asked Micah glancing towards the caravan door. At this distance you would be able to see someone through the window.

"Yeah I think it was knocking." The sound resonated again and the two of them stopped breathing, straining to listen trying to pin point where the sound was coming from. As it started to beat a slow tattoo they tilted their heads.

"I can't work out where the sound is coming from."

"Keep your hands connected to the pile of insects." Said Jacob hurriedly. Micah snapped to attention.

"I think they are trying to make contact." Said Jacob.

"You know what you're doing though, yeah?" Micah's voice rose slightly at the end in that way that French people did when asking a question or Australians did whenever they said anything.

"Yes. No problem." Jacob reassured him, then lent forward as if trying to get comfortable or scratch an itch without removing his fingers from the insect detritus. The knock resonated again. This time Jacob sat up as straight as a coffin and called out in a loud voice.

"Who's there? Say your name." There was a searing whistling silence. Glances were exchanged. He tried again.

"Knock if you are a spirit trying to make contact." Both of them held their breath.

Thud.

"Knock twice if you are friendly."

Thud.

Thud.

"Knock if you are friendly? What kind of question is that? He's hardly going to admit to being Mephistopheles out to steal our soul and drag us to hell is he?" Micah half stifled a laugh.

"Who is Masterofleas?" Jacob looked blank.

"Faust, Méphistophélès?" Jacob was still looking blank.

"Just ask him open ended questions."

"How does that work if the spirit is answering with knocks." Jacob began to get irate. Suddenly he slumped forward and the knocking became almost a drum roll. Jacob jerked with the beat. Sweat beads pooled on his brow. Micah called over, not daring to lift his hands.

"I am John Smith." Said Jacob looking directly at Micah, his voice lowering four or five octaves.

"Fuck off." But his friend just stared vacantly forward, unblinking. Micah could now feel a pools of sweat forming in-between his shoulder blades. His arms felt heavy against the tabletop.

"What is it you wish to know Micah Gordon Buchanan." Micah shuddered. This miscreant knew his middle name. He faltered spitting out words, still unsure if it was Jacob mucking about.

"I want to know if my dad is alright?" And then something happened that could not have been Jacob, something that Micah could not explain or rationalise.

The hairs on the back of his neck jumped ridged. The room temperature dropped, and the candle momentarily flared burning like a Bunsen burner.

"What the fuck was that." Snapped Jacob snapped back to himself.

"I imagine it's the spirit we are contacting." Micah looked at Jacob who was wide eyed. He snatched his hands away from the table wiping them on his jeans. Insect pieces fell like snow.

"You said don't remove your fingertips" Protested Micah.

"What?"

"You said…" started Micah.

"I know what I said but that wasn't me." Slowly Micah nodded. His friend, white as chalk dust, hurriedly started to pack away the paraphernalia and got up to leave. Micah jumped up, quickly stopping him pointing to the circle of salt.

"Last line of defence." He echoed Jacob's words back to him.

Jacob stopped, eyes darting around the room.

"I would have thought this kind of thing was normal?"

"Normal are you fucking kidding me?" Plumes of warm breath clouded the air between them as they talked.

"Not the temperature change and the candle." Stuttered Jacob.

"Never?" Micah asked the question, the answer clear on Jacob's face.

"Never."

"Well something happened, turned up, crossed over."

They sat staring at each other across the table again. This time chairs pulled tight against the table, keeping as far away from the salt line as possible.

"How long till it's safe do you reckon?" Asked Jacob, trying not to imagine invisible grasping hands.

"You're the expert." He replied sardonically, eyes scanning the shadowed corners of the room. The light switch seemed so far away by the door. Slowly the room became warmer and Micah decided to risk it. Without warning, he jumped up and walked across the room trying to maintain a calm pace. He flicked on the light, an instant exorcism of their fears. Micah went from room to room turning all the lights on then opened the cupboard above the microwave pulling down the scotch bottle.

"Ice, neat or a whisky Mac?" He asked pouring himself a neat shot and downing it before Jacob could reply.

"Neat." Called Jacob. Micah poured two more.

"I think we might need help." Offered Micah.

"Possibly."

"I mean there must be professionals. No offence Jacob but surely the more heads the merrier?" He couldn't believe he was suggesting it.

"Hmm." Offered Jacob. Micah tried to read the sound.

"I mean I will always try a bit of DIY but if water's leaking all over the floor I call a plumber."

"I think I know someone." said Jacob.

"And I haven't upset you. I mean that was something." Asked Micah cautiously.

"Defiantly something. But what I don't know?"

"So we are fine then Jacob?"

"Yeah, we'll call a plumber." Jacob winked.

They finished what was left in the bottle, letting the alcohol chase away the stench of memories and bolster egos. By the time Jacob left stumbling down the side ally towards the purring diesel engine of a taxi, they remembered how they had been brave in the face of the unknown.

Wildman

They stood at The Cross. A sixteenth century clock tower, built for some long forgotten philanthropic reason. Due to its centrality, it was the obvious meeting place. The Cross was abandoned apart from them, a forlorn stone grey spider stretched up on tiptoe, as eight buttresses swept down supporting the weight of the clocks. They took refuge as the first rain in weeks struggled, spitting on the baked cobbles.

"Who are we meeting again?" Asked Micah.

"The Wild man of Racton."

"Does he have a first name?"

"Ray, but don't call him that."

"What should I call him? Mister Wildman sir?" Micah raised his eyebrows.

"Sir."

"Seriously?" His eyebrow pushed higher. "That's stupid."

"I don't make the rules." Retorted Jacob.

"I wasn't aware there were rules for meeting homeless mystics, never mind a committee that actually formulated rules." Micah's eyebrows now mimicked the arches they sheltered under. Jacob lifted a single middle finger.

"I just don't see the problem calling someone by their name."

"Just promise me that you won't alright?"

"Alright." Micah really wanted to meet this guy. So he sat down and lit a cigarette while he waited.

They sat on the stone seats at the foot of the market cross. From this vantage point they could see almost half a mile in each direction. Jacob paced checking the approaches. There were fun seekers starting the weekend on Thursday night as they weaved the streets between pubs. Those working early tomorrow were already heading home with meat kebabs held out in front like a compass, guiding them. Jacob tracked three women as they moved towards a cash machine, high heels exaggerating a drunken stagger on the cobblestones. He watched the short skirts and bare legs.

"Jacob?" A voice cooed in his ear making him jump. He spun round to face a man looking up at him slightly, the man seemed to shrink into his clothes. He extended his hand protruding from the frayed sleeve of his jumper.

"I'm Ray." The guy's face wrinkled into a smile. Jacob couldn't work out his age. He had a beard of sorts, patchy, scraggly whiskers that did not join up to his sideburns. They looked almost pubescent and ridiculous. But his face carved deep furrows as he smiled. He could have been their age or in his early forties.

"Yeah I'm Jacob."

"And I'm Micah." Micah eagerly shook his hand. "Nice to meet you sir."

"Ray. Call me Ray."

"On the account of it being your name yeah?" Said Micah looking at Jacob as he spoke. Jacob, half grinning, licked his finger and marked a one on an invisible score board.

"Err you guys are pretty weird. But if you are buying then we can nibble."

Minutes later they were at the Pizzeria they had chosen for its simple food at reasonable prices. Ray's eyes dragged his head left and right as he took in the tired interior décor like it was the Winter Palace.

"Better call me Jeffery while we are in here." Said Ray

"Is that your real name?" Asked Micah. Ray looked slightly bemused.

"I don't know. It could be!" Ray flashed a smile.

They stood, three unlikely characters in awkward silence. Ray was in a mismatched suit with enormous trousers tied with a piece of yellow garden twine. The jacket by contrast, was slightly too small and forced his arms to hang ever so slightly away from his body. Jacob looked menacing dressed in black, with silver piercings in his ears and nose. At least he no longer wore a chain connecting the two. Micah was wearing the banal uniform of a man who normally wears a suit to work, smart jeans and a polo shirt with a pinstripe suit jacket, which had never been part of a set.

The waiter approached them and Micah could see him trying to work them out.

"This way gentlemen." He said.

They went to follow but the waiter raised his hand to Ray.

"I am sorry sir but you know the rules." Said the waiter with an air of familiarity.

Ray opened his mouth to protest but Jacob beat him to it.

"This is my good friend Jeffery who I have not seen for years and we" Jacob waved his finger indicating the three of them. "would like a table now."

"Certainly sir." The waiter recoiled away to clear a table, leaving them standing at the door a while longer.

"What happened last time you were here?" Micah asked.

Ray shrugged his eyes roving across the far wall rammed with cheap repro art work. "This and that, things and stuff. Can't rightly remember details." The waiter returned to show them a little spot tucked at the back of the restaurant. Jacob stopped half way up then walked into the middle of the restaurant and sat down at an empty table announcing to the waiter that this was perfect in a clear loud voice. The waiter went to protest but thought better of it, handing out menus while avoiding eye contact.

"Order what you want, my treat." Jacob instructed Ray. His brother's voice echoed in his mind. They waited until Ray was immersed in the finer details of calzone.

"Nice one Jacob."

"Well the waiter was a prick."

"Waiter pinball?" Micah asked and Jacob smiled.

"Yes. Brilliant. I remember that family do your parents invited me too."

"Great Aunt and Uncle's silver wedding anniversary."

"That's it" Micah smiled the memories flooding back. "That funny old uncle Fred or Bob."

"Frank, Uncle Frank." Corrected Jacob.

"That's the guy, taught us waiter pinball. I reckon he was as bored as us."

The next hour was spent watching Ray shovel anything on the menu that vaguely resembled a soup, which translated to Salceci Al Forno, and a lasagne which the old boy spent ten minutes chopping up and about thirty seconds eating. Jacob and Micah spent their time nursing a beer, and sending the waiter off to get things. He would bring Ray's food and they would ask for pepper, then a jug of water, then extra garlic butter, clean knife and finally after sending him back and forth for ten minutes, look at him in annoyance and say, "No need to fuss" as the waiter smiled through gritted teeth. The trick was to send him back and forth just enough to annoy but not enough to be obvious, unless you wanted to be very rude and risk your food being spat in.

Finally, they turned their attention to Ray who had licked his plates clean and looked as if he would fall asleep. Jacob ordered him a big beer, which he guzzled like water

"Ray"

"Jeffery" he whispered leaning forward winking and cracking a broad smile showing his two missing front teeth and explaining why the meal had taken so long.

"Jeffery, how exactly can you help with these matters spiritual?" Jacob shielded his mouth with his beer as he spoke but it was clear that the two new tables were embroiled in directing sticky fingered children towards their meals.

"I can't help you." He replied, clicking his fingers at flustered waiter pointing at his now empty glass. Again a silence descended as the waiter appeared.

"Coffees gentleman?" He still couldn't bring himself to hold Jacob's gaze.

"No thank you, just another beer for Jeffery." Micah said, while facing Ray, staring intently.

Since the last séance Jacob had changed. His energy was channelled seeking professional help and that was Ray the tramp, now on his second dish, lasagna. Micah wasn't so sure but he could not deny it had been spooky. But he wondered how many drunken dirty souls would claim clairvoyance in exchange for food? The slums of New Delhi were probably a hot bed of paranormal activity.

Ray shifted on his seat feeling the generosity draining rapidly from the company. Micah could see Jacob's face darkening. Then Ray started to shake, as if he had choked on his food. Before they could grab him in a Heimlich manoeuvre, the shaking rose up until it burst out as a laugh, little pieces of lasagna sprayed out of his mouth, most of it catching in his unkempt beard.

"You should've seen your faces." He giggled.
"You're a good actor." Said Jacob.

Then added. "So you are capable?"

"It's true I have certain talents for those who wish to believe."

"Great, where and when?" Micah passed a mint from the tray placed quickly and quietly by the waiter as he moved past to clear another table. Ray looked uneasily around then threw his arms wide.

"Here" he beamed. The lads both got a clear whiff of his outdoor aroma. He lowered his hands and voice as a table close by glared.

"Or we could find somewhere quiet and private. That usually works better. I know which one I would choose." He said lowering his chin almost touching the table, like an excited child.

"Alright then." Jacob waved two notes in the air catching the waiter's eye for the first time since they had sat down.

"Oh not now. It takes a bit of preparation for these kinds of things. Poking the spirit world with a stick." The turn of phrase seemed familiar.

"Fine, so when? Full moon? It's only a week away." Suggested Jacob.

"Why not? Adds a bit of drama. But first, what about dessert?"
At that point the waiter appeared swiping away the notes and leaving a pile of loose shrapnel. Jacob shrugged looking at the coins.

"I'm pretty full anyway." Ray surveyed the two clean licked plates.

They left the change on the table, shook hands at the door and walked in separate directions. Ray carried away a scrap of paper with Jacob's home number on. The tramp would ring in two days with a plan and that was how it was left.

"Well." Said Jacob smiling to himself.

"Indeed, not what I expected. Do you reckon he's genuine?"

"We'll find out soon. Either way it's a good excuse to celebrate."

Micah nodded and turned towards the pub across the street. But Jacob stopped him and held his hand out. In his palm were two innocuous tiny squares of blotting paper. Micah looked puzzled.

"Microdot." Jake announced to no reaction. "Blue meanies, a Lucy, Lysergic acid diethylamide, L.S.D… acid man. A way to celebrate in style yeah?" Micah stared at the tiny little scraps of paper. He had always been wary of this drug. Stories of crazy trips, men thinking they were oranges screaming at police afraid that they were going to be peeled or squeezed into orange juice. But Jacob was grinning, hand extended, beckoning. He wetted his fingertip and touched one of the tabs then placed it on his tongue. Jacob did the same and they swallowed.

"How long?"

"Forty five minutes, virgin. Let's go get a drink." Jacob laughed pushing and teasing Micah as they crossed the road and slipped into the back door of the King's Head.

A Trip

"The tevelisions are on. I can see them."
"Television" repeated Jacob.
"Tevelision, that's what I said."
"NO. Television, television."
"Tevelision." Micah stumbled over the word trying to momentarily ignore the images projected from his mind onto the pile of broken boxes.
"Tele vision. Tele   vision" Jacob repeated elongated the word further and further.
"Yes I know but look at the tevelisions; they are showing, *The Waltons.*"
Jacob finally looked at the five cardboard boxes stacked one on top of each other totem like, the incandescent halo of a white fire exit door which was now phosphorescent in moonlight.
"No mate, it's just the acid." But Micah didn't listen to the reply, he was transfixed by the tevelisions. He could see John Boy's face and John Boy was speaking. As the apparition spoke, his surroundings began to materialise around him but he would walk off the screen of one television and then on to another, back ground following like a wave.
"John Boy?" Called out Micah. John Boy beckoned him nearer. Jacob's nervous laughter was rapidly fading, becoming distant and all Micah could hear was a fuzzy high-pitched hiss. John Boy was speaking, mouthing words that seemed important, but the meaning was lost in the static. He pressed

his ear against the screen felt the cool hard surface numbing his cheek and ear.

"John I can't hear you." He screamed shaking the tower of boxes which swayed menacingly. The static hissed louder, changing in pitch, snatches of words seemed to nearly form then fade. He thought he caught the word "father" as he noticed the edges of the screen begin to break down in a jumbled mosaic of pixels. John Boy's face began to distort then fade into the blizzard of colour encroaching from behind the 2D images.

"Quickly John what is it, what is it. You must shout louder." He screamed again shaking the tower as if it were a waking sleepwalker. Hands grabbed him roughly from behind, and pulled him away from the tower.

"No, no, I must speak to John." But the hands kept pulling him hard and hot on his shoulders, their presence so heavy Micah didn't know how long he could bare it. He kicked out feeling more hands on him, so many hands clawing and pulling him away. His foot made contact with somebody's leg and he kicked back twice before the hands swamped him, pushing him to the floor. He began to panic, he couldn't work out if it was the acid or Jacob or both. Then he saw Jacob's face loom into view. There was nothing else just a head suspended in the night sky but it was definitely him. Jacob smelt of beer and cigarettes, tainted with liquorice rolling papers.

"Micah, hold it together, it's a bad trip, hold it together." Jacob pulled him close hugging him tightly. Micah closed his eyes, the sudden swamping of warmth felt safe and homely. Jacob was whispering things in his ear but he couldn't hear. It was just the lulling tone dipping and rising melodically draining the fear from him. He opened his eyes and there was Jacob's face but this time neck and shoulders had materialised, then he noticed the white door less bright now, and the cardboard boxes scattered across the floor where they had toppled.

"We need to leave now, ok?" Micah nodded, agreeing and followed across the rooftops to the fire escape off the flat roof. He had no idea where he was or how he had got here. He could feel the cold breeze cutting across his back, the drugs causing the chilling sensation to feel like tearing. It was peripheral, when he focused the tearing stopped or hid. The Cathedral spire rose to the north a stone cold finger raised, volunteering a reference point. They took the fire escape down off the roof out of the strong moonlight and dropped back into the alleyway running between Marks & Spencer and River Island then down the alley away from the high street to the car park. Micah followed, forcing his steps on, trying not to notice the tearing sensation so that he could notice it. As they wound through the dark alleys Micah looked back and saw the old man from the séance following. He stopped. He blinked unsure if it was real.

"Can I help?" He blinked again. The man smiled and stepped back into the deep shadows.

"What do you want?" He followed, leaving Jacob behind. The shadows gave way to a narrower alley where red engineering bricks closed in. Past a rusting, Victorian down pipe mirrored by water stains where it had become blocked. Mr. Able-

Smythe was walking away quickly now, brogue heels clicking on the paving slabs.

"Sir, please wait." He didn't and Micah followed the path twisting and turning until it finally opened out to what was probably the fire exit of a high-street shop. He found Mr. Able Smythe sitting on a white, plastic picnic chair, tendrils of smoke from his cigarette curling slowly round his emaciated fingers in the still hot air. The old man was fully suited as last time.

"What are you doing here?" Micah asked rubbing his eyes.

"The question is what are you doing here young sir? After all it was you who followed me."

"But what were you doing in an alley this time of night?"

"Oh I don't know; taking in the night air, tasting the delights of the city. I like the darkness it is so calming, so welcoming don't you find?" Micah was beginning to remember why this guy annoyed him.

"I'm gonna go. Look after yourself old man."

"Mmm." Said Able-Smythe.

"What do you mean 'Mmm'?"

"Oh nothing, just the night is young. Cigarette?"

"Mmm do I want a cigarette, that is just weird." Micah mimicked the words back in a sneer.

"No, I was just thinking about vices and wondering how many you could get up to in one night. Sex, drugs and rock and roll." Able-Smythe snorted then spat thick mucus into the gutter and took another drag on his cigarette.

"Though I don't believe rock and roll has really been a vice now since the 1950's."

"O.K" Micah glanced over his shoulder at the way back. It looked narrower than when he came through.

"I can see you have partaken of one already."
"What?"

"Your eyes are dilated. Doors of perception isn't that what Huxley said?" Able-Smythe waggled his finger in Micah's general direction. Micah could feel the panic and paranoia rising again. He needed to go but stumbled steadying himself on the wall. The bricks were cold holding none of the day's heat down this manmade canyon.

"Your friend is on his way." Said the old man watching Micah slink away, hugging the wall for support.

Jacob appeared from behind.

"Where the fuck did you go?" He asked, a wild worried look in his eyes.

"I bumped into…" Micah looked around at bins, two chairs and a few bags of rubbish strewn across the floor. He was alone.

"You alright Micah, you look peaky?"
"This acid is freaking me a bit."

"That's cool, I'll take us somewhere we can chill out and get some orange juice down us." Jacob led the way, a firm grip on Micah.

They made their way back to the car park, Micah happy to let Jacob lead. He slumped against him, concentrating on his friend's feet moving one step in front of the other, struggling to hang on to reality.

"Jacob quiet. Don't wake them." He pointed across the car park to a dark corner over hung with trees from a town house garden. In the moonlight shadow, two hulking grey rhinoceros scowled; heads lowered, rounded shoulders jutting high poised to charge. Jacob glanced over at the corner where Micah was intently fixated. He rubbed his hand over his eyes but if he saw anything that concerned him it did not echo in his voice.

"Come on Micah, it's only the acid"
"No, it's Rhinoceroses."
"Well we won't wake them will we?"

Around the corner was the Hole In The Wall, a pub that's name expressed its geographical location. Thankfully the place was nearly empty. They found a booth at the back away from glaring eyes, whispering conspirators and mirrors. Jacob negotiated the bar. He ordered two pints of orange juice.
"Get this down you." Said Jacob.
"The vitamin C will bring you down a bit, take the edge off." They both chugged greedily at the slightly sour juice.
"It's nice here" Jacob picked his sentence carefully. Knowing that the wrong word could start Micah off again. If he commented on how quiet it was, they could be deafened by the hiss of the silence, warm and they might begin to take off too many clothes. Nice covered it safely without suggestions. The bar man approached to clear empty glasses and no doubt to check the bug eyed customers.

"You alright there mate?" He asked but all they could do was nod and stare at the table like dejected schoolboys up to no good.

"He's fine just had a migraine." Jacob managed to answer.

"I'll get him another orange juice then, on the house." As he reached down to pick up the empty glasses his shirt pulled back and revealed the beginning of a tattooed sleeve.

The Hole In The Wall didn't live up to its frontier namesake. It seemed pleasant and devoid of criminal element. It was an old building with lots of internal structural walls that had been worked round creating cosy hideaways. This meant they could sit listening to the low murmur of sedate conversation, without using anyone. Soon the atmosphere began to soak into them and they calmed, orange juice also worked its magic.

"I need the toilet." Said Micah.

"You alright?"

"I just need to splash some water on my face." He walked towards the bar and the tattooed man gestured a nod to the back of the pub, his eyes dark and fixed. Micah wondered if he was mind-reading and having to concentrate to unravel the acid induced mess. A large lady filled the space between the bar and the wall like a marshmallow in a vacuum cleaner. Micah did not want to look at her face. He could feel her hot, pallid skin radiating sweat and smell her stale, layered sadness. He felt funny, knew that if he looked up he was in trouble. So he looked down.

"Excuse me." He mumbled.

"Sorry love, I didn't see you there. Room for a little one…" She continued talking, the words blurring and lost. Micah smiled nodded and walked past. The toilet offered a haven. After splashing cold water on his face and checking he looked alright in the mirror he returned to the table.

"Where have you been?" Protested Jacob.

"In the toilet." Answered Micah bewildered.

"You've been gone half an hour."

"I literally just washed my face." Neither of them were wearing a watch so it was a claim difficult to refute or prove.

"You spent ten minutes grinning and nodding at the fat bird at the bar."

Micah looked more bemused and then with a smile he raised a finger in mock epiphany. "I think it's the acid."

"No shit."

They drank two more orange juices and, fearful of being too obvious, moved on. Urban legend had it that Chichester once held the world record for amount of pubs per capita. True or not, there were a lot of pubs for such a small city, plenty of choice as they wandered out into the night.

Ray the Tramp

A pattern developed as they began to spend more time together. The Saab 900 was not particularly cool. The front of the car streamlined, the back end clunky, as if it were the love child of an American Muscle car and a Volvo estate. Micah loved this car, not because of its aesthetic qualities, but rather the happy memories from time spent driving around with his dad. It had been his inheritance along with a donkey jacket and a collection of vinyl. It spent so much time at the garage that they knew him by name and he had his own parking spot when he booked it in for work. Tax and MOT was also a drain on his money and this led to the strange habit of having a tin box glued to the passenger side dashboard. Judging by pounds shillings and pence marked on the slots it was old. The idea was that if people had a lift they paid. The money helped keep the beautiful jalopy on the road. It also meant that Jacob began to think of the car as his personal weekend taxi service. He always faithfully put in money and Micah always took it out to use as beer money securing a slow but happy demise for the car.

    This weekend was no different. Jacob had phoned him on Friday afternoon while he was at work and left a message on the answering phone. Micah considered pretending he had not heard the phone. Or blame the technology, an older model prone to chewing tapes.

"The thing with these old tape versions is if the tape dies, warps or chews, you just replace the tape. These fangled new digital recorders break and you have to replace the whole thing." his Dad used to say. Jacob would only phone again at some ungodly hour so Micah phoned back and they arranged a jaunt to the country for Saturday afternoon.

This was how he found himself shifting gears, pumping the clutch and throwing the car into the corners as he negotiated the hedge-shrouded lanes. He knew the route enough not to ask directions from Jacob who sat transfixed in the passenger seat. He had rolled the window down and was holding the handgrip, arm muscles visibly tightening. With every lurch of every corner the coins that Jacob had deposited, jangled.

"So why are we going to Racton?" Micah accelerated hard into a corner braking at the last minute. He cleared it and saw a clear road ahead. He dropped gear to second, pushed the accelerator hard, the centrifugal force pushing them over the white line. He glanced over at Jacob as they cleared the corner.

"Well?" He asked.

"Err road" Said Jacob eyes transfixed on the road ahead.

"It's alright" the engine screamed, he pumped the clutch and jumped straight up to fourth crossing back on to the correct side of the road as they approached another blind corner. Micah was enjoying being a little reckless and scaring Jacob. He repeated the question.

"Why Racton?"

"Looking for Ray." Said Jacob.

"Wild man Ray?"

Irony seeped into his syllables.

"Yeah, wild man Ray. " Jacob looked surprised and deflated. These weekend trips were little magical mystery trips, Micah's insincerity drained any enchantment. Two weekends ago they had ended up in a random a little pub. Micah couldn't remember its name but it was down a dead end lane called Hooks Way. There was no village, nothing anywhere near. Just a pub in the middle of nowhere, lit by gas lamps and with straw spread about the floor.

"Changed every week" Jacob had assured him. They had a beer, real ale of course and then Jacob asked Micah if he needed the toilet, a strange request, after only one beer. The toilet was not obvious so Micah approached the bar and asked the Landlord.

"Tourist then?" The burly man snorted pointing to an unmarked door at the end of the bar. It had clearly been painted several colours in its life as Micah could glimpse red green and white through the current peeling top layer of blue. Putting his hand on the black wrought iron barn door latch and pushed. The few locals nursing their half empty pints were watching with mild interest. The landlord nodded encouragement. He opened the door.

Outside the sun shone ferociously on the flower studded meadow. It had been left to grow wild. Micah looked about but there was no out building to hide a toilet.

"Very funny." He ducked back in to a murmur of muffled laughter.

"So where is the toilet then?" He said shrugging off his embarrassment.

"No, that really is it. Mother Nature has provided this pub with one of the largest most beautiful toilets in all of England. I never saw the point of paying money to install plumbing. If you need a number two then turn the horse shoe round and there is a short spade and paper in the bin outside the door."

"Oh" Said Micah. It was now obvious why the pub was nearly empty.

"Mostly folks need a few more pints down them before they use the spade, but if nature calls." The landlord shrugged his shoulders.
Micah could see Jacob beaming over in the corner. Where had he found this place? He thanked the landlord with as much sincerity as he could muster and stepped outside to urinate.

"When did Wild man Ray ring?" Asked Micah.

Jacob had drifted away in his thoughts, a combination of tiredness heat and concentrating on the tight bends. He snapped back. "This morning."

This is how they came to be sitting, staring across a fire into the blood shot eyes of Ray. He offered them a seat by the fire and settled on the other side next to a pile of Tesco carrier bags tied together with twine.

"We have been looking for you." Said Jacob. They had been wandering around for most of the afternoon and had returned to the phallic looking tower for shade several times. But Ray was nowhere to be seen.

"And directly you've found me." He leaned back against the graffiti daubed walls. Cautionary tales of a "wild man of Racton" had clearly failed to keep kids away.

"Do you mind if I eat?" He did not wait for an answer and rummaged through his collection of bags unwrapping a round parcel triple wrapped in shredded Tesco carrier bags. As he peeled the layers off he talked; a skittish conversation, off on tangents.

"Anyone for Hedgepig?" Ray held up a dead hedgehog waving in the lads bemused faces.

"It's fresh." He sniffed it dramatically. As nimble fingers made quick work of gutting the little creature, Ray gabbled on. He mentioned Mary Wollstonecraft, William Blake, West African Green Mambas (the quickest acting snake venom in the world) and Corporal Edgar Worrall. A torrent of disconnected names, places and thoughts, followed by a toothless smile. Jacob managed pretty well, matching the conversation with his own random pieces of unconnected information. Suddenly it was like a Native American meeting a cowboy. Here they traded in obscure information rather than buffalo hides. Ray stood up tossing a handful of innards into the brambles, disturbing the candles places in the crumbling recesses of the flint work.
As dusk drew near they threw extra light into the darkening hollow.

"You live well for a homeless person." Complimented Micah.

"I'm not homeless. I am a tramp. A tramp is to the English what a Hobo was to the American psyche."

"Isn't a Hobo just a well-travelled homeless person?" Asked Jacob. Ray looked slightly offended so Jacob quickly countered. "More worldly, cleaner, but in essence still homeless."

"That my friend is where you are wrong. A tramp would choose to make his bed on hard ground under cold stars rather than forced by destitution. It is a romantic affliction." He gazed away into the middle distance demonstrating his pure "trampness."

"Fires a bit bodge but she'll come back." Ray stopped talking, poked and stoked turning over blackened charcoal until it began to shimmer red and white then continued.

"I have never begged or relied on hand outs. I'll busk" He pulled out an old nickel-plated harmonica and fluted his lips along it. "But most of the time I live off the land, snare coney and sleep rough. I know every bothy, barn, dell and abandoned shepherd's hut on the Weald."

"And you read tarot." Added Jacob keen to reintroduce the subject matter they had met for.

"Rightly but not for money, though if you feed me I'll thank you." In the half-light Ray became ageless again. He then threw on another log. Young, vibrant eyes sparkled dancing with the embers as they cascaded up. Crow's feet carved ruts around his eyes, made heavier by ground in dirt.

"I like it up here on the Weald so quiet and outaway." Ray nonchalantly tossed sticks onto the fire, his Sussex purr thickening as he talked about the landscape.

Clearing the flaming logs and re-raking the embers he rolled the hedgehog onto the edge of the fire. Instantly a cloud of acrid smoke engulfed the space, driving Micah and Jacob out of the tumble down shell of a tower. They stood at a distance sucking lungs full of clean air. Ray stayed hunkered low under the cloud, poking and rolling the hedgehog burning off the spikes.

"What is he doing in there?" Said Jacob struggling to hide his bewilderment.

"I have no idea. I guess he's hungry. It's the sudden Sussex bumpkin accent that I find weird." They looked back at the thick white smoke streaming from the eyes of the ruins.

"Will you partake?" Asked Micah mischievously hoping that by asking he was laying down a challenge.

"No" Said Jacob. "I mean a bit of squirrel or roasted badger, and I might be tempted, but hedgehog? It's just too gamey for me." Their laughter degenerated into a coughing fit.

"Sorry guys, the smoke has cleared now." Ray ushered them back to the fireside and they retreated into the safety of the wood smoke away from the midges circling like hungry sharks. Ray now had the hedgehog wrapped in tinfoil half buried in the fire.

For half an hour Ray busied himself getting an even cook. He produced a lightweight pan and then miraculously pulled out a selection of foraged foods mushrooms, and a type of long gangly moss.

"This stuff is common as muck, on any oak tree." Ray informed. It looked like a cluster of stag horns in delicate greens and greys. The lads watched transfixed as first Ray boiled the moss with water from a crumpled lemonade bottle, seasoned it with spices from an empty film roll case, and fried it. It gave off a nutty aroma.

"Oak moss bhajis? I made enough." The tramp offered.

Both lads declined and sat watching as Ray ate his forest delicacies in seconds then began in earnest on the hedgehog.

"Listen." He said, they did and could hear nothing but his knife, now carving the meat directly from the bone.

"You hear it?" He insisted. They shrugged. Ray got up and stepped out from under the protection of the tower.

Away from the flames the temperature dropped as the sun dipped. Heat leaked from the sky chased by a sea breeze. They were only six miles from the coastal inlets round Hayling Island. They followed as he hobbled out to the tree line where a cornfield stretched away. They could see the path of each gust of wind mapped out on the ears of corn. Ray stood in silence and they waited for him to show them or tell them something.

"Listen." He repeated and nodded towards a distant warbling bird.

"That's a thrush. Out here it's all in the distance. A bird over there, a dog barking in a nearby farm, crickets clicking in the long grass, the wind ruffling the treetops on the ridge. You can hear it all and you can hear it all at the same time. You can never hear all your surroundings at once in the town. Something is always drowned out. I can hear it all out here." He spread his hands wide like some messianic figure and closing his eyes said. "It's like I can hear myself living, the blood pumping and air moving in my lungs. I could happily die here." He opened his eyes and turned smiling at them, baring his sparsely populated gums.

"Out here it is easier to hear the dead." He turned to them, threw his arms wide again and the surveyed the scene.

"And that's what we are here for." Said Jacob getting excited that the conversation was finally getting somewhere. A fox barked in the distance.

"A fox." He said looking happy.
They walked back to the tower, now a dark finger denouncing the sunset. The fire-glow outlined the interior calling them back into the warmth.

As they made themselves comfortable round the fire, Ray conjured up a small metal hip-flask. He stood shaman like, tendrils of smoke wrapping around him as he cradled the flask in two hands.

"Now it's time for an open door policy." Ray said as he slowly turned the lid. He drank a sharp, quick swig before passing it on.

"Thanks" said Jacob following the tramp's lead. The liquor was a dark, viscose gruel of some kind. Bitter to taste and needing concentration to swallow. The flask passed on.

"What is it?" Asked Micah.

"Just drink it." Whispered Jacob like an over-fussing parent. Ray just smiled and began to sway.

Eyes watered from the smoke and Ray began to hum a low guttural tune. So it went for a while, the lads sat nestled as comfy as they could manage as Ray swayed and hummed then mumbled. Micah missed Jacob's theatrics as he watched the half illuminated figure. Mumbling turned to half chanting, finding a rhythm. Whether it was the smoke or drink or just heat and lack of sleep, Micah began to find his movements, hypnotising. Crouching he found himself swaying in time synchronising like a metronome.

Ray the Poet

Ray had insisted they chant.

"After me. Um Nuhm Chagh Um Nuhm Chagh." He began while staring intently at them until they began to mumble in unison. Only Micah wasn't sure of the words.

"Nunchanka wha the fucka Nunchanka wha the fucka." He softened the vowel at the end of fuck to fit the auditory drone. This went on for far too long. A half crumbled brick lodged itself into his left butt cheek causing pain. But something about Ray's absorbing stare made him not want to move in case he disturbed the tramp. He tapped Jacob on the shoulder and they shrugged at each other. Nothing was happening beyond the sun going down and the fire beginning to die. At least with Jacob there was a decent show.

"What shall we do?" Mouthed Jacob. Micah shrugged again. Then coughed loudly for affect.

"Um Nuhm Chagh Um Nuhm Gyre Um

Chagh Um Nuhm Chagh Um run Chagh Um Nuhm Chagh Um Nuhm Gyre Um Nuhm Chagh Um Nuhm Chagh Um Nuhm Chagh Um Nuhm Chagh Um Nuhm Chagh." His focus was impressive.

"Ray. Hey Ray." Micah whispered almost afraid of his own voice.

"Um Nuhm Chagh Um Nuhm Chagh." The words carried echoing round the cylindrical interior stretching up. As they whirled up, they grew in volume, until it sounded like multiple voices. Micah fixated on the flames lurching, fluttering and curling around the wood. The heat filled the recess, warmth seeping into the building till the walls felt like radiators. The mesmeric chant took a life of its own, as if it had travelled beyond the wall out into the now dark forest. Micah couldn't pin point where the chanting came from. He glanced over to Jacob who was staring at his hands. Then he looked up. The chanting outside was growing louder, separate from Ray. As the extraneous sounds grew Micah felt the hairs on his arms prickle. He clawed at his jumper, shifting in the spot where he sat. Prickly heat engulfed him and he was unable to concentrate.

"Can you hear that?" Micah whispered, but Jacob was waving his hands slowly in front of his face tracking the movement. Micah strained to listen. He could hear footsteps and a brushing sound like something being dragged. Shadows cast on the wall contorted hinting at images. He rubbed his eyes and looked again. Images of naked bodies writhing. The closer he looked the less he could pick out details, torture or sex he couldn't be sure. He looked up out of the natural recess through the window spaces towards the ever growing sound.

"Fuck." He said loudly. People had appeared, cloaked, faces hidden by cowls.

"Jacob, Jacob." He poked his friend who turned, gurning. Micah knew he was alone. His eyes fixated on the figures standing wraith like over them. They mimicked Ray in a soft murmur, an occult choir. Unmoving. Micah tapped Jacob and pointed up. Jacob's gaze followed Micah's outstretched finger and his expression changed instantly confirming the figures were there.

"Who are they?" Jacob asked. "Who are you?" He shouted. Stoically they remained still.

"They've been there a while."

"Are they dangerous?" Asked Jacob. "They're not being dangerous. They're not being anything." Micah shrugged.

"Ray thank you for your time but we're going to go. It's late and all that." Micah's mum had taught him politeness in all situations.

"Um Nuhm Chagh Um Nuhm Chagh." Micah tapped Jacob and pointed in the direction of the car. Thankfully Jacob nodded, the presence of the others had straightened him out. As quietly as brick rubble would allow, they began to make their exit. When they had half risen, steadying themselves against the building, they were aware of the silence punctured by the last crackling embers.

"Sorry to disturb you Ray, we did say but you were a bit caught up in the chanting." Micah's default kicked in. He looked over to Jacob for support who had dropped to the floor screwed his eyes shut and started chanting again.

"Um Some Some Um."

"Jacob." Micah kicked out hard.

"Yeah great chanting Ray but we need to be going thanks." Chipped in Jacob suddenly alert and rubbing his shin.

"Yeah, thanks Ray it's been good." Ray just stared. They both got up nodding and apologising all the while avoiding eye contact. Suddenly Ray leapt up and stood facing them over a smouldering fire. His eyes had rolled back into his skull, porcelain gobstoppers pitilessly gazing.

"YOU ALRIGHT RAY?" Micah raised his voiced waved a hand in front of him.

"Do you think he is having some kind of fit Jacob?"

"What like being possessed or something?"

"I was thinking more like epileptic fit."
Jacob shrugged again. It was becoming a tick this evening. "More like he took some heavy duty Mescaline." Jacob leaned across waved his hand in front of Ray's face and changed his diagnosis.

"Ketamine"

"Do you think he's alright?" Said Micah, concerned.

"There is a reason he lives out in the middle of nowhere. I'm sure he does this kind of thing all the time."

Ray Lurched forward, grabbing Micah tightly one rough hand on each side of his face. He pulled Micah forward like he was about to kiss him. They were engulfed in the suffused haze whirling above the fire, like a man recovering from a larynx operation, he whispered.

"Anarchy is loosed upon the world. Beware the rough beast. Beware the blood-dimmed tide. It will drown all innocence." Micah could feel Ray's hot breath on his ear, and couldn't bear it. He pushed him away and instantaneously Ray's eyes rolled back and he sat down to re-stoke the fire, leaving Micah standing bemused while Jacob looked down from above with a similar expression on his face. The sentinels retreated as if gliding on ice.

Micah Chirped "So we're going now." He had questions, but his compulsion to leave was stronger.

"Righty, then close the door on the way out." The wild haired man was now engrossed, chuckling to himself. He didn't even acknowledge the two lads as they climbed out.

"Where are they, the men in hoods?" Said Jacob.

"So you saw them as well?" Asked Micah, checking.

"Yeah." They both stared into the now pitch black tree line. There was no sign. All the way back to the car they stayed close to each other wary of the shadows and over hanging hedgerows. They reached the car parked in a muddy lay-by chewed up by tractor tyres.

"A great story to impress the ladies." Said Jacob as he fumbled with keys in the lock, still glancing over his shoulder at the now distant, wooded ridge.

Driving back towards the distant glow of civilisation, away from the darkened hills, Jacob began to pester Micah.

"What did he whisper in your ear?"

"I thought he was going to kiss me at one point."

"I thought you were breaking up with him when we were trying to leave." Chided Jacob as his beams illuminated a scraggy fox picking at carrion in the road.

"Manners cost nothing my mum always said." Retorted Micah, then fell silent. Jacob continued to talk trying to cajole answers out of Micah but there was no reply. He didn't speak again until Jacob dropped him home.

"Thanks, catch you later."

"Cool. Pick you up tomorrow night." He lifted his open hand to his mouth mimicking a pint.

"Sorry busy. Catch up Tuesday maybe?"

It had been an hour since Jacob had dropped him home. Whatever Ray had given them had been mild but he couldn't sleep. He sat in darkness watching for satellites, the tiny pin pricks of light speeding across the starry sky. Then he would shift in the camping chair trying to induce comfort. He was waiting. The lights in the house were finally out. He would wait a little longer. It was crazy to think a small lump of metal, probably no bigger than his caravan, was circling the earth so high that it still caught the sun's rays and twinkled bright enough that he could see it. He traced the arch of four as he waited.

When the house was cemetery quite, he sneaked in, his footsteps muffled by the carpet and furnishings. Dad's books were in the lounge, the only real problem being the squeak in the door. The trick was to open it quickly and decisively. He counted under his breath.

"One, two, three." Then pulled the door sharply to the three quarter position. Then stopped, still listening for sound upstairs. Nothing. He continued even more cautiously as this room was directly below the twins. He stepped as if in a minefield gently depressing every foot. Thankfully the light from street lamps at the front of the house was leaking enough light to guide his way. He reached the bookshelf.

"Shit". He couldn't see enough to read the titles.

"Shit." He said quieter, realising he'd cursed too loud, then stood poised listening again. Silence. He knew that Mum wouldn't mind him looking at Dad's stuff. Some conversations were just best avoided.

Mum had cried once for Dad's death. At the funeral, as the coffin disappeared behind heavy velvet curtains. A single, uncontrolled sob escaped loud and undignified. One hand immediately shot to her mouth the other hand encircled the twins. To the twins the day passed much like Aunt Matilda's fortieth birthday party but with less laughter. All the family got together and stood around drinking and chatting. Mrs Stokes nee Lavior, from number 17, drank too much and sang a sad French song like she always did. Dad was absent now as he had been at

Aunt Matilda's fortieth, although last time it was because he had apparently eaten some rich food. Since the funeral his mother had a puffy red face most mornings, though he never saw her cry. She could be crying right now as he squinted at the unreadable book titles. He rummaged in his pocket and pulled a lighter and sparked it up. The small flame gave him just enough light to locate the volume of W.B Yeats' verse. Laying the book on the coffee table he flipped hard cover and read the inscription on the inside cover. *"To my darling husband, not as good as your poetry but I hope you find some inspiration. All my love XX."* He found the contents and ran his finger up and down the list of poems, trying to remember the name of one of them. None seemed familiar. Slowly, he became aware that the lighter was heating up in his hand. He started flicking through looking up those he recognised.

He muttered to himself as he laboured "*Lake Isle of Inisfree* page 87. No. *Easter 1916* page 122 unlikely and…" He read a few lines "No. *The Second Coming* 139. Bingo. Ouch fuck." The lighter seared his thumb. He let go and was plunged back into relative darkness. Patiently, he waited for the lighter to cool tapping the top to check then sparked it up again and read out loud trying to imbue every word with passionate intensity. He re-read the second stanza twice Micah closed the book, replaced the lighter in his pocket and slipped the book back into the perfect sized space on the bookshelf.

"No idea what that old fool meant." Micah slept uneasy that night with shadows slouching through his dreams.

Ray woke shivering, flames had long since deserted the hearth. He raked over the coals with his feet coaxing out as much heat as he could then tossed a handful of kindling. Moving was slow and painful. A stone, rubble from the slowly degrading tower, had jabbed his ribs while he slept and the sensation remained after he had sat up. He rubbed, stretched and yawned, chasing away the stiffness of sleep. Then hunkered down over the fire blowing at the base of the sticks.

"Just leave it." Said a voice from the gloom. Ray sat bolt upright, his left hand scrambled for a weapon, stick or stone.

"Calm yourself." The voice purred. "Violence never gets you what you want."

"Who are you?"

"A perpetual question, not easily answered." There was a cough like a deep rumble.

"Do you have a cigarette?" The voice asked.

"No."

"No matter I have enough to share." Ray shook his head.

"Don't be silly. I know your vices." A hand reached out. Withered old hands, skin pulling back puckering at the edges of long manicured nails. Ray plucked the cigarette, careful not to make contact.

"Light it from the fire." Said the voice and, as if on command, the bundle of stick burst into flames.

The light thrown up illuminated an old man who immediately sank back into the now shrunken shadows.

"I have many names. Which one would you like to use?" He asked, his face momentarily flushed with the warm glow of a flame leaping from his cupped hands.

Ray had been about. He had plotted paths through the geography of the world and of the spirit. When he was young he had chosen to drop out of education and head to India on foot. Armed with a dog eared copy of Colin Wilson's 'The Outsider' and a smattering of clothes, he took seven years and he crisscrossed North Africa, the Middle East and the great Subcontinent itself.

He had lived with Monks, Sadhu's and Afghan tribesmen. He had stared at castles made of sand in Morocco, rode bareback through the Khyber pass and followed Mother Ganges to her source; a rather unimpressive dirty glacier at the foot of the Himalayas. He had met and sought the advice of every seer, wise man and incarnation of God along the way and it had taught him enough to know when a strange man with hands like a corpse tells you he has many names, you need to be careful.

"I don't care for names. I'd rather know what you would like?"

"Astute." The old man sucked hard on the cigarette, inhaling to the point of passing out.

"I want you to perform something like this for a friend of mine." He waved his hand casually at the surroundings, exhaling a cloud of smoke as he spoke.

"I am happy to provide for anyone who asks." Ray smiled the cigarette untouched in his hand.

"He will not ask. He doesn't know he needs to speak to you yet. It will need..." He paused leaning forward. His eyes narrowed as if in concentration. "It will need a tailored service. He needs to be convinced of something. Do not worry about the details. Just perform" Again he waved his hands at the surroundings. "And I will do the rest."

"How do I contact you?" Asked Ray. The old man just laughed and lent back into the darkness which enveloped him and pulled him from sight. The fire rekindled suddenly throwing up light chasing away all shadows. Ray was alone staring into the renewed fire, the man had vanished.

Speed date

The pub was half empty, a fug of stale cigarette smoke hung like a drug den hotbox. On weeknights the place was populated with old men running away from old wives. They propped the bar up, shoulders hunched, eyes down, lips pursed round the rim of a beer glass, chaser on standby. Imogen seemed out of place, a lithe snake slithering through a cornfield of fattened field mice. Their heads lifted at the sound of stilettos on flagstone, transfixed and fascinated. They could sense danger, twitching on their bar stools but her skin shimmered as she slinked up to the bar, hypnotic. The bar man moved over slowly shifting his weight with every step.

"What you having?" He asked.

"Pint please." She pointed to one of the pumps not paying much attention. The man lifted his arm up to pluck a clean glass from a shelf above his head, shirt pulling out from his jeans revealing a matted weave of dark wiry hair across his distended belly. Imogen stacked the coins neatly on the side, took her pint and retreated into a corner seat at the back of the pub.

The King's Head was one of a dying breed of pubs. The front of the building had three doors, one door for the saloon and one door for the lounge bar. In the old days the saloon was for gentlemen, looking around, it seemed little had changed. The lounge bar was where gentlemen could bring their women folk for polite conversation. The third door was sealed shut. One hundred years ago this door opened onto a barroom just big enough for two people to sit in. It was designed for workers on the way home, dirty and smelly they could use the special quarantine bar to have a few swift pints before going home. Now it was an extra storage space stacked with glasses and beer mats.

Micah was waiting in the cubby hole fiddling with a beer mat bolstered by several pre date shots. He had finally decided to act on the phone number and in a buoyant mood he had miss dialled an old lady. She was keen to talk but clearly had never heard of Imogen. Second time he got through and was now sitting opposite her in a pub. She smelt great.

"I'm not very good at this." Micah mumbled.

"I wasn't expecting Casanova."

"That's good because I can't paint." She looked blank sipping on her drink trying to fathom the joke.

"Caravaggio, Casanova?" A smile politely flashed across her face revealing perfect, white teeth, apart from a left canine sitting high, flush with her incisors. He had not noticed it at first but when she laughed, the slither of white extended up into the gum line like a beacon for dentistry. While staring at her tooth, he decided that explaining the play on words would only make things worse. He let it go.

"Anyway it's been a long time that's all." He was now staring at his feet trying to avoid the gaze of her hazel eyes as she relished in his awkward shuffling.

"Well then lets speed date?" She suggested

"If it involves drugs, I'm still recovering from last time." This time she laughed, head back, crooked tooth on full show. When he had rung her it had quickly become apparent that she was definitely the hand cuffed girl. She had assumed it was a one-night stand and was surprised to hear from him.

"No really, I have no idea what speed dating is?" She laughed again and he wanted her to stop. Better this than sitting in silence, he thought.

"I mean, I know it's not amphetamine based dating or romance while jogging but.." He continued, and suddenly they were having fun. She leant forward, stretching her arm across the table, olive skin holding the memory of distant Mediterranean ancestry, set pale against the dark mahogany table. Her scars were hardly visible in the dim lit booth.

"You tell me about yourself for ten minutes. Sell yourself, like why should I go on a date with you?" she sipped her drink winking as she watched him over the rim of the glass.

"If I had known I would have brought my C.V"

"Speed dating is difficult, like philosophy students asking you to explain yourself in three words." She looked like she had dated a few of those.

"School of hard knocks, majoring in philosophy of self-important bullshit?" He said wanting to make her smile again. She looked lighter, prettier when she smiled.

"More like self-impotent" She chided. Now he laughed.

"So you've speed dated." He asked. There was something alluring about the idea of Imogen sitting in a room holding court over a sea of testosterone, trying for a chance of intimacy.

"Yes" Her eyes lowered for the first time.

"I am surprised that someone like you would need to go speed dating" He tripped over his words and took a long swig from his beer, giving him time to gather his thoughts.

"I mean, you are really pretty"
She tugged on her sleeves, gripping the cloth between thumb and fingers and stared out of the booth.

"So ten minutes to sell yourself. You ready, you're up for it yeah?" She said abruptly like an Alzheimer sufferer in a sudden moment of lucidity.

"Err O.K"

Micah babbled, she laughed. He remembered an article he had read discussing New York dating and ten questions a woman should ask before she even considers going out on a first date. The questions were:

Question: What do you do for living?
Answer: Pack books for a mail order company at the moment, though last month it was a cleaner at the hospital.
Question: How much do you earn?
Answer: Not enough
Question: Do you spend time in the Hamptons?
Answer: No, unless they mean Southampton and then only for a gig.

So it went on with questions that were in favour of millionaire bachelors. He wondered if Imogen was judging him. He decided his only strength was humour. Micah told her about one first date where he had affectionately leant across to remove a stray hair from the woman's cheek, and the horror when the hairs removal tweaked a mound where it was attached. She sprayed beer over the already sticky table.

"And that's ten minutes up?" She beamed. "How did I do?"

"Well you can have a date" she clapped slowly, still giggling.

"I'm sorry about the Sofia Lauren thing." Had he really finished by telling her how his perfect woman was probably based on Sofia Lauren in a film he had seen when he was very young? He assured her it was on a subconscious level, how that in some ways she reminded him of her with her Mediterranean skin.

"Makes sense, my great granddad was Spanish."

"I think it's your turn." Micah ventured but she shrugged.

"I think I'll buy the drinks to celebrate you successfully winning a date."

"What's this then if it's not a date?"

"This was a pre date assessment." She said standing up with great gusto and slipped away through two check-shirted lads leaving Micah wondering what would have happened if he hadn't passed. He watched the two younger men dressed head to toe in Burberry like urban clansmen. Their eyes followed Imogen's legs as she sashayed past them. Micah took the beer mat and began to peel at the edges ripping little sections off, placing them in a pile. He wondered how Jacob would feel if he knew if he was on a pre-date assessment with Imogen.

Imogen returned with her bright smile that had forged an instant bond with the barman; advantageous when trying to get served quickly.

"I didn't ask what you wanted so I got you Fosters."

"Thanks. So you and Jacob?" Micah ventured tentatively.

Imogen's brow furrowed as she placed the beers down "I told you he is my dealer." She whispered the last word

"Really? He seems to think it's more."

"Look if you want to self-sabotage that's fine but let me know and I'll go." She gestured to leave but her hand stayed firmly on her pint. Micah could see her mulling over what to do.

He offered her a cigarette; a straight, he was trying to impress. "By way of an apology?" She took it and used her own lighter.

"Did Jacob say we were a couple?"

"No. Seriously no, he kind of hinted I suppose."

She rolled the tip of her tailored on the edge of the ashtray, deliberating. "The thing with Jacob is he likes to make up stories. It's not so much lying. That's too far. But he'll self-mythologise and let you fill in the blanks." She shot a look of collusion as if Micah would understand. He did not; yet gave a warm encouraging smile.

"I need the toilet." He announced standing abruptly. The beer went through him really quickly. He half expected Imogen to be gone by the time he returned. At least then he would know whether or not she was actually offended.

The floor was white with black square tiles arranged like a chequers board. Micah could feel the dimpled grips pushing through the bottom of his flip-flops like the soles of his feet were trying to read braille, a warning from the floor that his footwear was not ideal for a public toilet. He checked the row of urinals and selected one. The half corroded blue cubes dammed up pools of yellow; a soup of cigarette butts and chewing gum. Puddles of wet dotted the floor like a minefield. The strip light overhead burbled and stuttered like a drunken bee as the starter motor struggled. He removed his cigarette before he unzipped, and placed it where the browny yellow burns lined the edge of the windowsill. The urinal stared back at him with its cycloptic drain, an eye, protected by the browned cage. He tried to piss, staring ahead, staring at the celling. He couldn't even go with the pressure in his bladder. He switched to the cubicles, confident anyone sober enough to be paying attention would assume inebriation rather than shyness. The smell of swollen chipboard bloated with piss filled his nostrils as he carefully pushed the door open with his elbow. The laminate was peeling away round the hinges and handle. His head was spinning, he was beginning to regret the pre-date shots.

The sounds of the toilet echoed around the cubicle. He heard other punters come and go, hand dryers and taps starting up. The background noise distracted Micah allowing him to start. Then the sounds would cut once the customers left leaving the room quiet but he could hear someone still out there shuffling. Poor guy sounded like a victim of a stiff lunchtime drink. Micah heard the cubicle door next to him creak open then the sound of the bolt draw shut. Suddenly Micah couldn't urinate again. He forced images of streams and waterfalls through his mind trying to engage a muscle somewhere deep in his groin.

The laughing started as a slow guttural chuckle, like a lawnmower engine trying to catch until it built into a full laugh. Micah gave a sideways glance as if the man were next to him, then he tried to refocus.

"Could you pass me some paper I seem to have found myself at a bit of an impasse." Said the voice next door as it stopped laughing. Micah stood silent. Who found that funny? The silence reverberated, pulsating in his ears.

"I can hear you breathing in there. Help a fellow out would you?" The voice purred. A hand thrust under the divider. The veins on the hand were vivid violet-blue reminding him of electric cabling and tracking across the back of the hand. Micah stared. How could a hand look familiar? Micah pushed a roll of toilet paper into the hand being careful not to touch it. The hand disappeared and as soon as it was gone he remembered. Remembered Mr. Able-Smythe's hands when they first met as they hung in the air waiting to shaken.

Quickly and quietly Micah pulled his trousers up and, without flushing, he sneaked out. As he debated washing his hands or exiting hastily, the door bolt and flush simultaneously sounded behind him.

"Good day Micah, a fortuitous surprise to meet you." Micah nodded a cold, curt response and grunted a reply.

Able-Smythe moved up to the sink. "Don't forget to wash your hands. A dirty sin that."

"Oh yeah." Flustered and embarrassed he conformed, taking the only other sink. Six urinals four cubicles, yet only two sinks told you a lot about the expectations of the pub landlord for his clientele's hygiene. Side by side they wrung hands under cold water. In silence the old man preened and smoothed his hair, scrutinising his reflection as if it were a novelty.

"Was it you with that pretty little thing out there?" He didn't wait for a reply. "She looks like a handful." He ran the flat of his palm over his thinning strands of hair forcing them to stick close to his grey scalp.

Leaning forward, baring his teeth at the mirror, he added, "I would be careful there if I were you. End in tears or worse, blood."

"What did you say?" How did this guy get under his skin so quickly?

Able-Smythe turned for the first time. "But if I were you, I mean, if was actually you, I would get what I could. Enjoy it as much as I could and get out before it got messy. You know?" The old man winked un-salubriously.

"Yeah. Got to go, nice to chat." Micah wiped his hands on his trousers as he went.

Back in the bar Imogen was still sitting in the booth. She had continued where Micah had left off, shredding the beer mat. It was now reduced to a pile of slithers. He picked his beer and in one movement emptied the glass chugging enthusiastically.

"You should know I don't go for your normal macho beer swilling man." She giggled.

"I'm Thirsty. You fancy going somewhere else?" He asked. It was clear that he was leaving and she could follow if she wanted. Imogen sprawled back, her hands elegantly rested on the top of the banked seating.

"Well hello Micah. I didn't realise you were so..." She searched for the right word. "forceful."

"I did handcuff you to a bed."

"Doesn't count if you can't remember." She laughed again partly at her joke partly at his, but she downed her drink aware of his eyes nervously watching the door at the back of the pub. They pushed out into the warm evening she took his arm leaning in and bumped into Paul.

"Alright. What you up to?" Asked Imogen.

"Meeting someone. You?" Replied Paul

"We're going to the..." She looked at Micah.

"The Swan." Added Micah taking the cue. They stepped out waving to Paul. Imogen pushed into Micah and they fell into walking closely bouncing off each other like magnetic pinballs.

"What was all that about?" Asked Imogen.

"I think Paul's got a date judging by how cagey he was."

"Not that. Earlier in the pub." She poked playfully at his arm.

"Just someone I'd rather you didn't have to meet. For that matter someone I'd rather I'd never met." She shrugged the comment off. They both carried scars and she had enough of her own to worry about.

"Where to next then mystery man?"

"The Swan. Definitely the Swan; it's Karaoke night."

The Vale

Paul stashed the moped in the far corner of the car park against the hedge under the shadow of a tree. It would be dark very soon and his little Vespa would become invisible. He looked around, the carpark was empty. He glanced at his watch checking off a mental list.

"10pm." He read the time, twenty to. Enough time to walk up into the vale.

"Bring a knife, a candle and bottle of water." He checked his ruck sack; a bottle of water, a candle and a cheese knife, it would have to do.

"Follow the path up right into the nature reserve." He looked beyond the bin with plastic bag full of dog excrement hanging like bunting round the rim. There the gravel path cut of across the open fields towards a distant clump of woods already in shadow as the sun dipped behind Bow Hill which encircled the vale.

Twenty minutes later he reached where a once great elm had fallen over during the Great Storm of 1986 and was now carved into a sculpture marking the beginning of the reserve. One side were crude cuts representing a radiant sun, on the other side a moon. The cuts were so deep the sculptures met in the middle, a liminal space in the heart of the wood. At this point, open field gave way to densely packed forest. Under the canopy the days baking sun had not reached and it was noticeably colder.

"Through the woods to the old oak." He knew the oak. An anomaly amongst ancient Yews. It was so unusual that the rangers had placed a plaque explaining the biodiversity of the tree.

Paul saw the old man's drawn mouth, wrinkle lines radiating out as he formed his words in a clipped sharp accent that could not be placed. That mouth had given direction had been precise, so far. He had not expected this treasure trail when he had agreed to meet the gent in a Chichester pub. The idea of trekking off into the middle of nowhere sounded exciting, mystical even, in the familiar surroundings of the King's Head. After the oak, directions were less specific. From the oak he had to turn right and walk through the yews. Keep going until you hit the edge of the wood, from there Paul was informed that he would be able to see the mystic he was supposed to meet.

Moving into the ancient woodland the noise was sucked away, muting his footsteps. He glanced ahead through a mess of gnarled branches. Here the yews were over a thousand years old. They splayed their boughs like a grove of exhausted giant spiders. With the branches reaching to the floor, the path became diluted. He picked a rough route, stepping over and ducking under. He made the deer glades where the forest opened out before crowding in even denser. Natural light had now leached from the sky and moon wasn't due up for another hour.

"Torch." He said loudly at the trees, pulling it from his bag. But the torch lit the path ahead plunging peripheral trees around into pitch black. He turned it off and stood blinking hard trying to reacclimatise. As his pupils dilated he saw another yew, branches reached out towards the path like tendrils grasping at space, crowding in on human scar of a path.

"Through the yew trees. Check. All the way to the edge of the forest." He momentarily used the torch to locate the route forged by successive ramblers.

The smell of earth filled his nostrils as he stepped into another world. This part of forest was the oldest. Yew trees supposedly planted to commemorate a battle fought one thousand years ago against marauding Vikings. Here the majestic giants had rotted from the inside becoming hollow shells. He picked a route aiming for the next twisted trunk and then the next.

"I'll know it when I see it. What does that even mean?" He grumbled out loud.

"Spooky tree, another spooky tree." He flicked the torch on and off locating the next point to walk to then regaining night vision before moving forward.

"And why did that old man insist on it being here?" Able-Smythe had made promises, hinted at possibilities, and made it clear there would be a cost. Like a true sales man he had not demanded payment up front. He had not even talked about it. All Paul knew was he had to meet this mystic. He spotted a light twinkling through the trees. Like a moth he walked straight toward it, the beacon burning on to his retina, throwing the clawing woods into pitch black. The tree line broke and he climbed a low barbed wire fence leaving the vale and stepping out on to farmland. The ground glowed an ethereal white from the furrowed, chalky soil. The light was a storm lamp hanging from a caravan perched half way up a gentle slope, nestled under a small clump of hawthorns.

This had to be it, thought Paul. Although exactly what this was he still wasn't sure. He was beginning to doubt himself. Beginning to wonder why he would listen to a ranting old man. But there had been something in his eyes. Able-Smythe had gazed into his Paul's eyes, into his soul.

Cautiously, Paul approached. The uneven ground negated him sneaking up. He glanced down wanting to secure a decent foothold and when he looked up again there was a figure standing outside the caravan. Paul raised his hand and waved, the figure remained stationary. He trudged uphill under the eye of his watcher. The man wore ill-fitting clothes; trousers too big, jacket and a trilby hat with a collection of feathers jammed under the band. He stood listing slightly, eyes fixed at the distant tree line.

"Hello, I'm Paul. The old man sent me." He extended a hand which was left untouched. He was looking beyond Paul who just waited looking back trying to work out what the guy was trying to see.

"The king has lost his head. Seven hundred and twenty six." The tramp muttered, still fixated. Had Paul heard right? How did this tramp know? Did he understand what he said?

"What was that? What was that?" Paul shook the tramp who roused suddenly as if from a dream.

"I have a message." The tramp said.

"A message? From who?" Paul insisted, letting go of the man. The tramp readjusted this clothes.

Then, flustered, added "Sorry, where are my manners? Chairs." He disappeared into the caravan, a small tourer whose original colour was obscured by an intricate array of daubed patterns and scenes, all in lurid paint. Returning from the interior, he found space for chairs between piles of wood and the remains of a skinned rabbit. He brushed one ceremoniously, placing it close to the small, smouldering fire.

"Here, for you."

"Thank you." Paul replied studying his surroundings as he sat slowly.

"You understand what is required?" Said the tramp.

"Not exactly." Paul studied the designs as he spoke.

"He can give you power, success, all you want." The tramp spoke slowly adding kindling.

"He? Who is he? I thought you were the man to meet." Said Paul sitting. The camping chair creaked as he did so.

"The old man, John Able-Smythe he calls himself."

"I'm confused. The old man in the pub is the one who can help. Why am I here?" Paul looked around. From up here there was a sense of space, the field stretching away on both sides. Below the tree line of the forest was dark and watchful.

"He can open up doors, give you a window into the unknown. He has true power beyond our understanding. He sees all and shapes the world to his liking, shapes people's thinking. And all he asks for is obedience." The tramp poked at the fire haphazardly as the kindling caught.

"So I ask you again, do you know what is required?" Repeated the tramp.

"Not really, I just want power, like spiritual shit. I don't want to be the one standing there asking questions. I'm fed up with being the dumb fuck in the corner. So if obedience is what is required, then yeah, I'm in."

"Consent will do." Said the tramp pulling a crumpled paper bag from his pocket. Balanced on his lap, he gently rolled down the top to reveal the contents. Then held it out for Paul like a bag of sweets.

"Thank you." Said Paul picking a handful of the black, dried substance. He stared, not sure what to do. Then put it in his mouth and chewed. The noxious substance stuck to the roof of his mouth. He struggled to keep chewing, struggled not to gag. The tramp watched every move, frozen bag still proffered. Then reached in, taking a pinch and threw it on the fire. There was a huge plume of thick smoke with a strange smell with a hint of some kind of herb. Paul spat out the gunk and snatched at the water canteen offered.

"Can't imagine that tasted too good." The tramp said still watching with fascination as Paul now paced around the field swigging rinsing and spitting.

"I thought that was the price. I mean I thought it was some kind of drug. An initiation." Paul scraped his tongue on teeth then rinsed again. The tramp threw another pinch on the fire as Paul sat again.

"You are local, yeah?" The tramp asked

"Yeah, Bersted, over Bognor way."

"You hang out in Chichester." He said it more as a statement.

"Yeah."

"Thought so." The tramp rubbed his chin. Paul rinsed again.

"You can tell. It's that confidence, even when it's forced confidence, to paper over insecurities." The Tramp drew a pinch and sprinkled. The wind had now dropped so the scented smoke hung in the air like incense, thick opaque white cloud.

"Yeah Chichester is a bit like that I suppose. Big city mentality in a small town." Paul breathed in the fog, it was nice. He leaned forward filling his nostrils. It was very pleasant.

"I wouldn't live there. I mean it's nice, really nice. And it's clean, except for the bubble gum on the pavements. It's everywhere. Like I wonder if you can identify the bubble gum flavour or brand by the consistency. Like it all turns grey, doesn't it?"

"What turns grey?"

"The bubblegum, so you can't identify it by colour." Paul stopped himself babbling and positioned himself to be engulfed as the tramp cast a palm full of black onto the hungry flames.

"What did you say earlier? Said Paul, flopping back, stretching out his legs.

"When?" The tramp was now leaning forward on his chair gazing into the fire.

"You said something about a king and seven hundred and twenty six." Paul stared up at the sky trying to place the smell. It had a strange sweet after tang.

"That was what the old man said to say to get your attention."

"But?"

The tramp interrupted. "You don't need to say. I don't need to know." Paul wasn't going to say. He had kept his crime a secret for a long time. Jacob had never worked it out. He had stolen seven hundred and sixty pounds from the safe, gone straight to the casino over in Portsmouth and lost the lot in minutes on a roulette wheel. No one knew and everyone suspected Jacob as he was shift manager. The police were never involved but Jacob lost his job.

"But" Paul repeated, "how did he know?"

"Occult. It means to hide or conceal that which is secret. What can I say? The old man is the best. If you keep something secret he knows. It's like a sixth sense. Put him in a brothel or in Thatcher's cabinet room and he would know all the nasty, dirty secrets." Paul nodded agreement, inhaling from the cloud that still hung around them. The cloud seemed to be swirling around them an ever tightening gyre, refusing to disperse, like flies having discovered road kill.

"Opium." Paul shouted. That smell, the gradual feeling of detachment and a propensity to talk rubbish, it all added up to one drug.

"Loosens the mind, prepares the soul." The tramp laughed and threw the rest of the bag; paper and all, on to the fire. Suddenly everything was obscured. The caravan, the tramp, field and distant woods vanished in a swirling mass of white.

"Embrace it, breathe deeply and surrender to his will." The tramp's voice drifted out of the mist. Paul made a show of breathing in and out deeply and loudly. The fire reappeared with the tramp now hunched over it. His eyes, fixed on Paul, were blood colour where there should be white and black portals where his irises once were.

"They are coming. Take this you will need it later." He thrust a knife into his hand. Paul gripped it then saw silhouettes moving from the tree line, advancing slowly up the slope towards the caravan.

"Who are they?"

"The faithful they will have your answers." The tramp nodded and then retreated into the caravan in a blaze of now fully animated, vivid colours. Paul tried to stand, to run or hide or at least meet figures now in open field. They wore inky, black robes with hoods covering their faces. They drew close, spiders picking a line across the web towards the centre, towards their prey caught defenceless in the centre. Stuck fast in a tangle of opium fug.

They reached him and his doped mind still tied him to the chair. Fear crept into every pore, his shirt, wet with sweat, scraped coarsely against his skin as he struggled to get up. A hand rested on his shoulder.

"Come with us." A voice whispered.

"O.K." Was all Paul could think to respond. Then, instantaneously, he could move again and stood up with a jolt. He looked back several times at the caravan and the fire smothered by excesses of opium as he was bustled away by the hooded monks. Their whispers grew in his ear without specific source. The words repeated instructions. He imagined boney mouths, lipless, moving ceaselessly. They talked of knives and sacrifices they mentioned a name. He imagined black tongues bloated like a dead corpse by the side of the road, a constantly moving surface, bubbling away as fat white maggots burrowed and fed. He imagined it and as he looked into the depths of one of the hoods, he saw what he imagined and screamed.

The sound echoed across the vale, empty apart from nocturnal creatures beginning to stir. The tramp entrenched in his caravan shuddered, and closed the door.

Redemption

This time the date was formal; he was wearing an ironed shirt, the first time since his Dad's funeral. Not the same one though. This was a slimming black shirt, strangely more sombre than the starched white Van-Husen he had worn to the ceremony. Funerals had an easy dress code, a simple uniform to communicate grief without too much public embarrassment. Women could streamline wardrobe selection: black and understated, demure, not slutty, elegant and not ostentatious. Rules that led them to an egalitarian uniform. Except of course for Micah's Auntie, Hilda the dowdy Scandinavian who never really seemed to live up to the exotic expectations. Suddenly, at Uncle Bob's wake she flourished into a grieving succubus with a cleavage to lose finger food in.

Imogen wasn't wearing anything so inviting but by her own standards she had adhered to the dress code laws of dating, with a flash of deep purple glittery eye shadow to complement the heavy gunk of eyeliner. She wore jeans, a pretty blouse with floral print and a scruffy, mock leather jacket nonchalantly employed to mask any effort. Micah had considered a T-shirt, but was now glad of the shirt as the waiter hovered presenting the label of an inexpensive Merlot. He swilled the blood red wine around the glass and sieved the tannins through his teeth.

"Hints of blueberries." He said. The corners of her mouth lifted as she mimicked his smirk.

"That's fine, thank you." Micah took the bottle as the waiter tried to pour and the man withdrew, a consummate professional.

"Well, first proper date then?" He poured her a generous first glass.

"What did you count the last date as?"

"An interview I seem to recall." He finished pouring his wine and placed the bottle to the side.

"Isn't life just one long interview?" Micah shrugged politely unsure how she wanted him to reply.

She continued. "I mean if you think about it, we're rarely ourselves" she raised her hands making speech quotations, "in front of adults or strangers. You get a job in a...a..."

"Restaurant?" Micah threw his left arm wide.

"Yes. A restaurant, learn how to be nice to people. *Can I get you another drink sir? Would you like cream with that sir? How would sir like his arse wiped sir?* When all they are thinking about is the tip or *They just worked my fingers to the bone.* Or *Please shut up you pompous twat, I don't fancy you, and I don't like you looking at my tits.*"

"Or making Penis jokes about the pepper grinders." Somehow Micah found a mote of amusement in the fact that the pepper grinders here were over a foot long and were ceremoniously brought to the table with each course.

"We have game face façade."

"Is this about us? Did I miss something?" He wiggled his finger between them both as an indicator.

"Don't get so hung up on yourself. I'm just saying we are all things to all men."

"Deep." He said.

She shrugged and picked up the menu turning straight to the desserts. He followed her lead, unsure how to play it.

He scanned the menu for keyword like "local" and "farmhouse". "Wild" mushroom soup would almost always be more expensive than fresh mushroom soup. God forbid there would be anything "foraged" on the menu. Luckily everything was fresh or delicious and the rib eye steak was a "choice" rather than "local" cut managing to stay at an affordable price.

"Food looks good." He commented.

"Yeah, they've got eight flavours of ice cream."

"Posh. Do they have pistachio?"

She scanned the menu.

"No."

"Shame, it's a crazy green colour." He went back to scanning the menu though he had already decided on the steak.

"You look serious?" He said.

"My game face." The corners of her mouth turned down oddly as she smiled and he felt her shoeless foot, stroke his calf under the table.

" I don't play poker." He admitted picking up on the oblique reference.

"You should" Her foot began to work in circles. He raised an eyebrow waggling it like some over eager dog.

"What am I thinking now? Read my tells then." He challenged her keen to see where the game would go.

"O.K, you are hoping tonight goes well. Wondering which face to put on, so to speak. And you're wondering if you're going to get lucky, but you will deny that. You are a bloke so that's expected but you are thinking it and you will deny it."
He had definitely thought about it earlier that evening while getting ready. No one spends that much time shaving, brushing and preening without some hope of a naked encounter. Though he had not considered it much since entering the restaurant.

"Close." He said.

"That's as good as a denial."

He shrugged. "What about you? What are you thinking about?"

"Surely by the rules of the game we have just established you have to work it out from my game face." Her face muscles went limp and she stared expressionless and hollow eyed.

" You're worried about tonight. How you look, how I think you look. You are not sure if you want it to go well. Because if it goes well, that means you have to see me again. More time more complications." Her eyes suddenly snapped into focus.

"Jacob is not a complication I have said before."

"You are wondering if this is a traditional affair and I'm paying for the meal, or should you stand up as a feminist and go Dutch regardless of whether I offer or not."

"Psycho-babble. I was thinking about whether to skip main and just order dessert." Micah got the feeling that this girl would make you cross an ocean for her while not even bothering to step over a puddle for you. She leant closer.

"Do you want to play a different game?" Her eyes twinkled in the low lighting.

"Twister? Monopoly? Tennis? Yeah, any game that two can play." A clumsy remark but she was still smiling as she pulled her chair round the side of the table to draw alongside him. She leaned closely, her lips pressed to his ear.

"Try to order normally when the waiter returns." He could feel every annunciation, her pout brushing his lobe. Imogen's hand wormed its way under his shirt working its way up his side, up his chest finding his now pointed nipple. Her cold finger and thumb gently held it hidden by the billowing material. He could see the waiter making his way towards them with his pad and pen poised. Goose bumps were running up and down his back.

"What can I get you?" The waiter asked smiling, his eyes scanning the nearby tables.

"Order me a salad with the dressing on the side and a vanilla ice cream." Imogen couldn't face the waiter with her hand resting on Micah. With her spare hand she reached out for her wine glass trying to affect more normality. The waiter seemed to not notice.

"I'd like a salad for the lady." He could feel Imogen rolling his nipple between her finger and thumb. He picked up the menu and scanned across the salads.

" Chicken Caésar or avocado?" He asked Imogen. She leaned close and whispered into his ears, the vowels catching. He shivered.

"Chicken Caésar." He felt her thumb and finger pinch, pain seared for a second followed by an intense sensation spreading outwards from the now throbbing whole alveoli. It was not unpleasant.

"Chicken Caésar please with the dressing on the side." She pinched again and he just managed to get to the end of the sentence.

"Don't forget to order my ice cream." Eyes glistening she put down the glass with her spare hand and pointed to vanilla on the menu.

"Could I" He felt her digits slowly tighten. "A vanilla ice cream, and could I get a steak; rare please."

"Is that all?"

"Thank you" Micah handed over the menus the pressure under his shirt now beginning to peak again. As the waiter spun on his heals turning to the table behind him and cleared their plates Imogen released her grip gently stroking his chest,"Well done Micah I'm impressed." She removed her hand. He noticed her strange smile; all in the eyes while her mouth turned down at the ends.

"With my threshold for pain, I nearly remembered your order." He was aware of his over sensitive nipple rubbing against the starched cotton of his shirt.

"You are funny." She didn't laugh.

Micah straightened up in his chair pouring himself another glass of wine from the bottle, taking his time to drink some. Taking time to look around. Taking time to look at Imogen as she people watched. She sat perched on her chair somehow not taking up much space. Her wide, skinny shoulders extenuated her skinny waist and her legs double wrapped around themselves. The kind of shoulders you only saw on swimmers or child athletes. Sitting was an art form for her but when she walked it could look awkward and disjointed as if the top half of her body was ever so slightly out of kilter with the bottom. Micah guessed that was why she often wore layered clothes to hide the strange gait, that and the scars.

He wondered whether she was secretly thinking about him in the same way.

Wondered if he really fancied her or just the idea of her.

He wondered if she would hurt him in bed.

Wondered if he would like it.

Maybe he had. He couldn't remember.

"What you thinking about?" Imogen asked, she was studying his face with intent and, lost in thought, he hadn't noticed.

"I... that ... I wondered whether they used fresh ingredients, what percentage of food is pre-prepared and how long we would have to wait if it was all completely fresh." Not bad, he thought to himself.

"You?" He countered.

"I was thinking about those people over there." She gestured vaguely.

"Which ones?" Micah asked looking in the general direction.

"The old couple. They have been sitting there the whole time I have been watching and hardly talked. It just seems funny that people would pay money to sit in public and not talk to each other when they can do it at home for free."

"Unhappy extroverts. What can you do?"

"Funny." She didn't laugh.

Micah didn't consider himself a success in matters of the heart. He had a serious young love at sixteen. She had led him by the hand, metaphorically and literally to the bedroom and taught him the ways of the world. At the time they had talked of love and read poetry naked while smoking cigarettes. They spoke of marriage and even bought each other teddy bears that they invested emotionally to the point that they became pseudo-surrogate children. Thinking back he cringed. For five months they had been inseparable. Then one morning Micah woke up and wasn't in love. As quickly as he fell in, he fell out. It seemed so cruel that he phoned his lover and told her it was over. Of course there were no real answers to the questions through the sobs. He did not know why? Alice Magreaves was a name that still could still not be spoken out loud. She had chosen Jacob as her next boyfriend. Micah's best mate obliged of course. If she was offering then he was going to take full advantage. Alice made sure everyone knew the comparisons. Jacob always came out better and she paraded around her new man like a poisoned trophy. After that Jacob and Micah drifted apart. Jacob and Alice didn't last. Every relationship since seemed to be paying penance for that one girl. Maybe here was a girl who needed saving, a girl who could finally clear the debt.

The waiter arrived with all the food at the same time, as requested. He laid out the random feast; ice cream steak and salad without showing the slightest concern.

"So are we a couple?" Ventured Micah once the waiter had retreated.

She kissed him on the cheek. "You are sweet." Micah wasn't sure if it was a compliment or a dismissal. Picked up his steak knife and began cutting.

"Thank you." He topped up her glass.

The wine began to work its magic. As he relaxed, Imogen seemed to relax as well. He dared to wonder if he was in for a passionate night. A night he would remember. They paid the bill: Imogen went Dutch splitting down the middle even though Micah clearly spent more, she thanked him for a lovely evening and asked if he would walk her to the train station. They kissed passionately while he waited with her for the 10:58 to Portsmouth and Southsea. Her tongue twisted hot and frenetic inside his mouth. She pushed into his embrace as he stiffened and then suddenly with no ceremony she pulled away and jumped on her train.

"Ring" She called forcing the window down as the train pulled away. Micah was left on an empty platform: drunk, confused and with a raging hard on.

He looked down and noticed a splash of red wine like a stab wound.

"Nice look." He muttered to himself as he slipped through the barriers and cut across the carpark in the direction of home.

The Deal

Micah walked into the bar, student territory. It was like being in a foreign land, a tourist separated from the masses by their extreme youth. Maybe that was why Jacob had chosen the University bar in the first place. No one knew them, they were all freshers.

Micah ordered a drink, a coke in a highball glass. At the bar three young men were partaking in what could only be described as verbal rutting.

"I got this one falling off my bike when pulling tricks off a ramp." Micah glanced over half interested. The young man was flexing his bicep to showcase a dragon tattoo, the ink newly wet and colours vibrant enough to have been drawn on by felt tip pens. The dragon's tail curled down the forearm just missing a paltry white scuff he paraded like a war wound. Micah caught the eye of the girl: bored and intent on obtaining her next free drink. Micah scratched his chest gently so as not to dislodge the scab on the latest burn. They always itched as they healed, as if reaching out for attention; desperate to be played with, poked scratched and reopened to give new life.

Micah spotted Jacob as he walked in. He was wearing no makeup and mixed his usual black wardrobe with a grey thin cotton jumper over the top. It looked really familiar.

"Sorry Micah I'm running a bit late. He hailed the bar tender with a five pound note.

"Same as him please." He nodded at Micah's' half-finished drink. "Have you been waiting long?"

"Only five minutes." Replied Micah.

"Cool." The bartender placed Jacob's drink in front of him taking the proffered note.

"You took your sweet-arse time Jacob."

"Please don't refer to my arse as sweet, it makes me uncomfortable." Jacob gave a wry smile and took a sip from his drink then spat it out as if it were cleaning fluid.

"Coke-a-cola! What are you tee total?"

"Fuck off Jacob you ordered it." Jacob just shrugged and shifted his weight from one foot to the other. For the next ten minutes the two of them propped up the bar, constantly re-adjusting positions. This was like paranoia without the cannabis. They knew logically that no one was watching them; a crowd of 300 sweaty students were more interested in dancing and drinking. Micah glanced back at the rutting lads. The bicep-popping one and the drunken girl were locking faces with an unnatural vigour.

"Right, drink up. We got people to meet." Announced Jacob. He had not mentioned meeting people, the phone message had said cheap drinks at the University student bar. Micah wondered if it was to do with Imogen, as he had not heard anything for a few days.

"This isn't illegal right?" Micah asked.

"Illegal? No, not really." Jacob grinned leaning back on the bar, people watching. The DJ swapped from Salt 'n' Pepper to Chesney Hawkes. It was the wrong call and the crowd thinned leaving a clear view across to the seating on the other side of the dance floor. There was Imogen sitting at a table with a man, leaning close speaking into his ear.

"Imogen!" Jacob shouted, his voice drowned by the warbling tones of *'I am the one and only'*. He waved trying to catch her attention.

"Leave her." Said Micah turning back to the bar. Jacob's eyebrow arched, his mouth dropping open slightly.

"She's bringing a friend of her brother's here to meet me."

Micah tried to not sound too surprised when he said, "I didn't know she had a brother."

"There is a lot you wouldn't know about that girl." Jacob mumbled. Micah looked away.

"Wait a minute. What was that look?" Said Jacob.

"What."

"That?" Pushed Jacob again.

"What! Nothing." Insisted Micah.

"Oh yeah. Something has been going on."

"Leave off."

"I warned you." Jacob said downing his coke no vodka.

"Warned me what? Seriously."

"All right then, but I did warn you." Jacob walked away across the dance floor waving in Imogen's direction. This time she saw them, Jacob all arms and smiles, Micah a shadow following.

Imogen introduced her brother's friend and they shouted pleasantries in each other's ears, inaudible to anyone else. It was clearly going well by the handshakes and back slaps. The guy was older and looked even more uncomfortable than they did. He wore green, ill-fitted combat trousers with a zip up leather jacket covered in studs and straps, but the single most outlandish item in his wardrobe was his hair. He had thick dreadlocks, he twisted a dark natural coloured dread with a peroxide blonde creating hairdressers' candy cane. Jacob was clearly throwing all his charm at this guy who was smiling, flicking dreads from his face. The front one dangled down emblazoned with random beads. This was the first proper New Age Traveller Micah had seen and he was struggling not to stare. Imogen winked and Micah waved then, feeling stupid, put his hand in his lap grasping it with the other hand to stop himself repeating such a ridiculous gesture. He considered going to sit next to Imogen but that action was not conducive with the denial he had just furnished Jacob with. So they sat facing each other like personal assistants while their bosses made deals.

Jacob turned his attention to Micah. "We need to go out to the car." He shouted in his ear.

"OK. Why?"

"I left something in it." With that, Jacob got up and left, walking to the door in a straight line cutting across the dance floor as if it did not exist. The friend of Imogen's brother followed lolloping with a strange gait caused by his large German paratrooper boots only half done up.

Jacob and the guy walked quickly across the car park, weaving between parked cars, not waiting for Micah or Imogen. Micah took the chance to speak to her.

"You alright?"

"Yeah, you? Nice to see you, I was just expecting Jacob tonight."

"Did you get home alright the other night?"

"Sorry about that. I had to shoot off early. I had to catch up with a friend who has some stuff going on. I would have rather stayed over. I mean, if that would have been fine."

"Yeah. Another time maybe." He tried to sound cool, casual but he was aware that he was grinning as if one of the Kray twins had just given him a Chelsea smile.

"Oi love birds, hurry up." Shouted Jacob from where he was standing at the boot of the car.

"So you told him?" Teased Imogen.

"No, but I think he has guessed."

"Maybe." Sarcasm dripped from her voice. They reached the car. The two new friends were standing smoking and shuffling feet. As soon as Micah unlocked the boot they both threw away the half smoked cigarettes. Jacob pulled a plastic carrier bag. A carrier bag that Micah had not known was there.

He passed it to the urban hippy. "It's all there."

"I'm sure it is and besides I know where you live." He still wore the same congenial smile but the eyes clouded. Like a magician performing sleight of hand, he stuffed the carrier bag down his trousers that suddenly seemed to fit a little better.

"And for you, as promised." He was looking around constantly as he spoke. Then he reached into his jacket pocket and handed over a tiny see through zip lock bag with what looked like Tic Tacs inside.

As soon as Jacob's hand was on the bag the dreadlocked dealer turned to Micah.

"You." He pointed a grubby finger in Micah's face. A strong smell of camp fire and petunia oil filled the air. "You've seen nothing." Micah just nodded. Then he winked at Imogen

"Thanks gorgeous." He said. She blew him a kiss and he marched off between the parked cars towards the open fields, gone from sight in seconds.

"Nice bloke." Said Jacob smelling the package.

"It's Ecstasy dipshit it doesn't smell."

"I know Imogen, I am smelling the sweet success of the party to end all parties."

"Seriously, Rome burns and you are planning a Bar-B-Que." Micah rubbed his head slowly trying to comprehend how Jacob had put the money in his car without him noticing.

"I blame the Christians." Retorted Jacob, a smug grin spreading across his face.

"Historical references aside guys, what the fuck?! That was a drug deal!" Both Jacob and Imogen turned and stared at Micah. Imogen stifled a little laugh.

"You are aware that is what I do?" Jacob's eyes flicked around nervously in a similar manner to their recently departed acquaintance. The car park was pretty remote but he never liked talking about stuff in the open.

"Well, yes, I had kind of worked it out but I am complicit now." Imogen stifled another laugh.

"We've smoked together dropped acid together. It's drugs, the free market economy. We are Thatcher's children after all, so what else am I going to do but make money from a commodity that people want?"

"Besides" Imogen chipped in "It's E, it is completely harmless, makes you love people. It's the new wonder drug. Seriously you are going to love it." She was smiling now, standing by Jacob's side like a new lover, unsure what to do.

"You can't involve me in stuff like this without telling me, it's not right." He spun round and began heading off in the opposite direction that the dealer had, full of indignation.

"Micah" He heard Imogen pleading.

"Micah what about your car?" Called Jacob. He walked back, locked the boot then said. "I'll get it later." All without looking at Imogen who was still pleading. He was beginning to feel foolish for his outburst. But he was too angry to stay. Not because of the deal but because of Imogen, the way the dealer had been so familiar with her, the way she had responded. The way Jacob and Imogen were like a married couple, the shared knowledge, the coded language, he hated it, he hated his jealously. He hated the tone in her voice that echoed the sentiment that he was being a fool.

"Micah. Come back, let's go for a drink. Please." She called and his shame flared hotter than his jealously, fuelling his legs. He kept walking.

Imogen Discovered

Jacob barred the door. He knew he shouldn't have answered. Micah's knuckles were red from hammering the blue painted door and he was squaring up, jutting out his jaw and suddenly speaking two octaves lower than was natural, trying to suppress the frenzy that had been building the last two hours.

"Let me in." He said as he climbed the front step so that he stood eye to eye.

"Micah you don't want to go up there. Trust me."

"Trust you? Trust you? You're fucking Imogen," said Micah, his face flushing crimson.

"It's not what it seems," protested Jacob.

"Really Jacob? Really? Because it seems like my girlfriend is upstairs in your bed." Micah looked into the dim lit interior confirming that Imogen wasn't down stairs. The couch and chair were empty and music was emanating from upstairs.

"Really? Girlfriend? I didn't realise you guys were that serious?"

"What, otherwise you wouldn't have fucked her, is that what you're saying? If you knew we were an item then you wouldn't have spread her legs, sunk your torpedo?" Micah pushed forward using his weight to force Jacob out of the way. Jacob threw his hands up pleading. In the restricted confines of the doorway Jacob couldn't move, he couldn't even turn, he fell and Micah went too. They scuffled Micah trying to get past, Jacob trying to stop him. They rolled in a tangled flailing embrace. Music from upstairs, some kind of scream rock, leaked down in jagged bass rifts.

Micah had watched them leave the car park from a far. He had seen Jacob put his arm round her as they turned the corner of a road. He had seen her not push him away. She had tilted her head, rested it on his shoulder as they walked the last stretch to Jacob's door. He had sat outside across the road, out of sight behind a bush in someone's front garden like a peeping tom. He waited for a taxi that didn't come. The lights downstairs had gone off and lights upstairs had gone on. Micah caught a glimpse of Imogen as she pulled curtains shut as faint music started up. She looked intent as if her mind was set on something.

"Fucking whore." He had whispered under his breath. Then he had waited half an hour, as long as he could stand it.

They both struggled to their feet separating like prizefighters sizing each other up. Jacob had lost a button from his shirt.
"Get out of my way Jacob or I'll ..." He pulled his clothes straight and pushed his hair from his face.

"Or you'll what?" Jacob sneered, his tone a hard verbal jab. "You can't go up there. You don't want to go up there."

"Telling me what to do again. Things don't change I see. This is Alice all over again isn't it?" Micah was aware of tears running down his face.

"The fuck are you going on about?"

"You were full of advice for me about Alice, telling me how she wasn't the type of girl I really wanted. It would never work, you said." Micah was sobbing and shouting, his voice horse.

"What?" Jacob's face clouded with confusion and anger as he remembered Alice Magreaves, such a pretty first name, such an ugly last name.

"WE ARE NOT FIFTEEN ANYMORE MICAH, GROW UP!"

"You were the one acting like a child taking what you wanted not thinking about others. Spending most nights round her house."
Jacob couldn't believe it. Some girl from school, some girl Jacob had dated after Micah. Some girl that clearly Micah had been sweet on. Jacob couldn't remember much about her: blonde hair, a love of candy-floss and blue nail varnish, beyond that she was just a name now.

He gave up "You can go up. See if I care." Jacob stepped too one side. Their noses touched as they passed.

"It's not what you think." He called up speaking to Micah's back.

Micah marched up the stairs shouting Imogen's name but there was no reply. He burst into Jacob's bedroom not sure what he was going to say, not sure what he was going to see. His blood was pumping, the adrenalin leaving a tinny taste in his mouth. The bedroom was empty, no Imogen. No candles, no sordid scene with discarded contraception, nothing, not even the music he could hear. He followed the sound to the second spare bedroom, chasing nagging questions, saliva to glue. Why did Jacob choose aggressive music? Why not his bedroom? Was he covering for a friend?

"Imogen!" He shouted again as he pushed the door and stepped into a wall of sound. His eyes scanned the room trying to take in the scene. The matching velour chair sat in the middle, a lonely sentinel. On the chair was a pair of purple lens novelty glasses. It faced a thin white bed sheet hung like a curtain dissecting the room in two; obscuring what was beyond. The music drowned out his footsteps as he walked over and pulled it to one side. He saw Imogen, her back to him, curled foetal in the corner lying on a plastic sheet. She was naked and shivering or crying, the loud music making the distinction impossible. Then he saw it and stopped. There was blood. Not quite a pool, there wasn't enough for that. But dark red smears layered over with fresher brighter more recent streaks. Micah could see, at the corner of the plastic sheeting, a sharp kitchen knife, a razor blade and a bread knife neatly put to one side. Bread knives always inflicted instant pain when they cut, more of a burning sensation rather than the delayed sting of a neat sharp slice. Imogen lay motionless in the middle. She turned, just her head and as she moved he caught a glimpse of the latticework gouged into her arm, chest and abdomen. She saw him, hollow, staring eyes, swollen and red began to well with yet more tears. But the storm had passed and she was docile, allowing the pain to swallow her, calm her, a familiar friend that she could control. She mouthed something. He moved closer still, feeling that with every step he was intruding more.

"Go away." She mouthed. Then she rolled back leaving him staring at her heaving, alabaster white shoulders.

Jacob was sitting when he got back downstairs, flicking his cigarette end into the over flowing ashtray still smouldering with remains of the last cigarette.

"Well?" Micah demanded. "What the fuck was that about?"

"You do remember where we met her. I mean you do know this girl?"

"Yeah I know but what is all the plastic and sheets and chairs." And then it dawned on Micah. "You sick fuck. You watch!" Before the words had fully left his mouth Jacob jumped up. His leg caught the table sending a flurry of light grey dust floating like fallout. They were both shouting at each other, at the same time. Up close.
Close enough to touch.
Close enough to swing, too close to land a decent punch.

"Do you get your kicks out of it? Does it turn…"
"You are always jumping to conclusions aren't you? You never listen. You think it's…"

"I mean is it someone hurting themselves? Do you like watching people in pain? Do you jack off? Is it a sexual thing? Do you…"

"All about people trying to hurt you or get one up on you. My Dad was shagging Alice's mum. Extra-marital affair and…"

"What has Alice got to do with this? Was that power games too? Is that what this is a power game? You have control over…"

"I was doing you a favour, and Imogen you judgemental dick. Of course she cuts herself, she goes…"

"What's in it for her does she like being watched. Is it her…?"

"I fucking was watching so that she didn't over…" The volume of their voices was escalating. Micah's face was red with rage as he tried to shout Jacob down.

"She's nearly killed…"

"Or do you help does it only work if you are actually…"

"…herself three times cutting too deeply…"

"…causing the pain? Have you got control of her, like some sort of secret that you're blackmailing her with?"

"Blood makes me faint you dick. I sit and watch from behind the sheet, make sure she is safe with red shades that help."

"You join in don't you? Seriously it's sick. You sick fuck."

"Are you listening to anything I'm saying?" Jacob's face changed, the aggression leaking away.

"How can I listen to you? You pervert. I need to leave."

"Good. Leave then. Fuck off and don't bother coming back." Jacob retreated to the other side of the room, and was pulling at another cigarette, his back facing Micah.

"Well I will."

Jacob pointed at the door. "I am really not stopping you. Please feel free" His voice monotone.

"Fuck you Jacob."

Micah stepped outside and a slight breeze suddenly chilled the sweat that had broken on his brow. He tasted salt as the sweat ran down his face and his eyes stung, casting rainbows as the light from the street lamps refracted through his welling tears.

As the door closed, Jacob, back still to his departing friend, spied the pale bone-white button he had lost off his shirt. It must have pinged across the room when they grappled earlier. He picked it up rolled it in-between his thumb and finger then dropped it in the ashtray.

Crises

He was naked apart from his boots. His bloodstream was filled with dangerous levels of chemicals. Yet he felt more alive like this. Maybe it was being naked, shouting to the amphitheatre of terraced windows twitching with silent observers. In one hand he held a bottle of Jack in the other a cigarette.

"I am alive."
Alive.
Real.
More than real. He felt like he was standing on top of the world. But the world was spinning on its axis one thousand and forty miles an hour, and moving through space at sixty seven thousand miles an hour. Standing still while speeding towards destruction. Jake could feel it as he could feel the slight breeze prickling his skin. Or maybe it was the gram of amphetamine in his blood stream.

Somehow in this state he had the foresight to put on his Doc-Martins, though the laces trailed precariously. The summer night air was damp and cool as sea mist travelled up the brooks and streams from Chichester harbour, a break from the relentless, muggy heat. Goose bumps traced the breeze as it cut across the tight packed gardens and then his back. He inhaled deeply, exaggerating slightly and smelt the remnants of a B-B-Q.

"I fucking love this shit." He spoke loudly to himself as he stepped onto the chair and table, using the garden patio set as a staircase to the back wall. He placed both feet squarely on the crumbling brickwork and stared at the moon, full but for a slice.

"I am alive." He shouted arms wide, legs apart like a sumo wrestler.

"I am fucking alive." He bellowed. Curtains swished, sash windows closed or opened dependent on the level of intrigue from the people hiding behind their curtains.

"You are all asleep, you boring people, and I'm alive and no fucker can kill me."

"Go and be alive quietly somewhere else." Came an angry shout from a few houses down. The gruff northern twang reminded Jacob of a neighbour who was a plasterer. They exchanged pleasantries occasionally but he couldn't be sure of the accent. He pulled hard on the cigarette tasting the harsh tang of the fibrous butt as it burnt too low. He flicked it away across the dark alley below his feet. Then he checked his pockets for a packet, and laughed.

"And I'm completely naked you bastards." He glanced at the backdoor. At the glittering splinters, remnants of the Ouija board, chair, and mirror that he had worked his anger out on earlier. The stark glare of the florescent light from the kitchen blinked into life as a blond haired lad stepped into the room. Paul had let himself in the front door.

"Jacob get down you idiot someone called the police. There's a car parked out the front. I had to wait to till they stopped knocking and went round the back before I let myself in."

"Fuck the pigs." He shouted, still clutching the bottle in his hand. He faced away from the house towards the cool unquestioning darkness, hiding from dozens of inquisitive eyes seeking entertainment. He swigged the Jack Daniels neat, stinging his gums. He had no recollection of phoning Paul and wondered who else he had phoned. "I am the Lizard King." He was alive but too drunk to notice the frenetic spinning weaving beams of light that marked the slow approach of PC Maynard and PC Foster as they negotiated dustbins and rusting padlocked bikes in the alley. They had not yet seen the 5.9ft naked man standing on the wall. Paul could see the beams, he could see Jacob, now quietly drinking from the bottle, staring at the sky. He knew he wouldn't talk Jacob down and persuade him inside away from any witnesses.

Micah had received a garbled phone call from Jacob. In between the stream of consciousness, verbal vomit were apologies and tears. Micah knew him well enough to know that he must be in a bad way and had come straight round. He had seen the direction the police had headed off and ran to the other end of the alleyway. Obscured by the gloom of the moonlight shadows and the kink of the twitten, he moved rapidly avoiding the obstacle course. He could hear the two officers trying to work out their bearings in relation to Jacob's house. The electrostatic background chatter of headquarters from the radios slung at the hips, masked any noise Micah was making. He saw Jacob ahead and flinched from the sight of his drunken friend's shrivelled penis protruding from a bush of scraggly hair.

He saw the shadows of men looming from beyond the kink and without time to talk or time to think, he jumped up launching himself off number thirty-two's dustbins. He hit Jacob squarely in the midriff knocking him off the wall with such momentum that the pair of them fell clear landing hard on the grass, Micah's clothed body covering the reflective pale skin of Jacob. Seconds later two torch beams scanned the back of the house.

"Can I help?" Called Paul from the back door.

"We have had a complaint."

"Noise I expect?"

"Yes, a naked man was reported to be shouting in a back garden."

Micah could feel Jacob's hipbone digging into his shoulder. They did not move. Winded and dazed they remained perfectly still.

"Yeah I kicked him out a while ago. A complete nightmare sorry."

"Can you open the back gate?" Micah and Jacob heard the latch rattle.

"Sorry lost the key to the padlock. If you come round the front I'll let you in." Paul could see the two men flat against the grass in his peripheral vision.

"What's your name?" Paul gave Jacob's in case they checked. There was a silence maybe as they contemplated how much paper work they wanted to do this evening.

"Any idea where your friend went?"

"Home I hope."

"Where's that?"

"Parklands Road I think."

"And his name?" Paul could hear the other officer who was out of sight relaying the information down the radio. Paul gave Micah's name. Thankfully he didn't know his last name.

"Alright then, thank you. Have a good evening. Oh and keep it down."

"Certainly officer. Good night."

They waited a couple of minutes and then Micah rolled off Jacob.

"Thank fuck for that Micah, any longer and you might have given me a hard on." Paul walked over and stood redundant with a pair of jeans in his right hand, scooped from the kitchen floor where they had been discarded. When they composed themselves Paul suggested they go inside to avoid any more attention.

"Hold my trousers for a second." Jacob instructed Paul and rummaged in his left pocket pulling out a packet of cigarettes and a lighter.

"What's with the knife?" Jacob quizzed Paul as he noticed a kitchen knife in his friends other hand.

"Oh um. Just in case." Paul stuttered moving the knife behind his back.

"Stabbing a copper. Not smart." Micah chided.

"Those trousers are dirty." Said Jacob as he lit his cigarette and walked inside to find a clean pair. His sallow muscles tensed in his spindly legs as he climbed the stairs. Micah wondered if he had been eating regularly.

"You know where the door is boys, show yourselves out." He shouted down as he began clattering about loudly.

"Thank you would have been nice." Said Micah, aware it had been the first time they had seen each other since falling out two weeks ago.

"I would have settled for a beer." Added Paul calling up.

"Don't worry, I have pissed him off."

"For sure."

They left quietly by the front door heading towards town avoiding the main roads sticking to cut-throughs or alley.

"How did you get in Paul?"

"Spare key under the gnome in the front garden."

"Good job Paul." Micah injected as much sincerity as he could without trying to sound patronising. It still sounded slightly condescending.

Paul was unbothered. "Sorry about using your name Micah, I panicked." He said.

"Thank god you don't know my last name." Paul shrugged as he checked a major road intersection before crossing.

"What is your last name Micah?"

"I think we'll go with Smith for now, just in case."

They reached the Clock Tower in the centre of town. Four roads marked the four points of the compass and the four quarters of the city. This was always the point where people headed in different directions.

Tension with Tea

"Cup of tea?"

"No thanks" Micah knew it was a mistake as soon as he answered. So he was relieved when Jacob offered again.

"You sure, I have just put the kettle on? That's why I didn't hear you knocking at the front door." He already had his hands on the mugs.

"Go on then, cheers."

Micah struggled to believe he had been in the kitchen all that time. He had hammered at the door for five minutes pounding so hard, listening to the echo inside. He had pressed his ear to the peeling paint and caught the sound of the television, a low murmur of car crash chat shows where the lie detector test served as an arbiter. He thought he heard movement but couldn't be sure. He decided to go round and try the back door. He had smoked enough cigarettes on Jacob's small patio to be able to recognise the back garden. The trouble was a high wall hid the long rug of unkempt lawn and the rusting barbecue. The gardens protruded at an oblique angle placing the back gates in strange relation to the houses. He scanned for hints, eliminating two houses immediately by their Laura Ashley curtains. Even as he sat balanced awkwardly on a wall, one leg dangling garden side, he had a split second doubt it was the right garden. There was a barbecue and a patio but the lawn looked longer. If all the houses looked the same why would the gardens be any different? It was only the puzzled face of Jacob coming out the back door that confirmed his decision.

"I hope you don't mind earlier, the whole wall climbing thing." Said Micah.

Jacob just shrugged and placed the mugs on the side. "Grab the milk."
Micah opened the fridge with a contents that bore striking resemblance to a drinks cabinet. The door shelf where he expected to find milk was full of vodka, vodka with a hint of citrus, vodka with a hint of toffee and vodka with cucumber.

"You've run out of milk."

"Cupboard top shelf." He pointed without looking up from the kettle.

"Coffee-mate with tea?"

"It's that or black tea." Jacob shrugged again. Micah must have put the Coffee-mate down with more force than he realised as Jacob softened his tone.

"I used to forget about the milk and leave it out. Rancid tea with lumpy milk. Not nice."

"Coffee-mate sounds like a good idea." Said Micah agreeing.

"Funny thing is I don't drink coffee."
Micah nodded thinking of something to say to keep the momentum of this genial conversation going.

"I nearly didn't recognise your garden the grass was longer than I remember." Fuck, he was talking shit, next thing we would be discussing the weather.

Jacob had his back to him, an unmoving vigil on a boiling kettle.

"You know what they say? A watched kettle never boils." He said.

Jacob laughed, a little one-syllable chuckle, over before it started.

"When was the last time you used that barbecue?" Keep it going thought Micah.

"Not for ages. The rain's rusted it to shit."

And there it was the weather. It has been said that if a discussion began to compare things to the Holocaust or the Nazi's then the discussion had strayed too far beyond redemption of sensibilities. Micah viewed the mention of weather as a similar territorial marker, indicating a conversation had slipped into polite fake small talk. Farmers were possibly the only exception to the rule. Jacob ran the spoon round the edge of the tin breaking up solidified milk powder.

"One or two spoons?" He asked.

"Coffee-mate, one or two spoons?" He repeated.

"Oh, one I suppose."

They stood silently sipping tea, leaning against the kitchen side looking out of the open back door. Scuff marks were clearly visible on the fence where Micah had climbed over.

"What you up to today then?" Asked Micah cupping the mug in his hands and blowing. Jacob just shrugged. This wasn't working.

"Nothing much."

"Mmm."

They stood like mirrored images leaning back on the kitchen side as far from each other as they could be in the confines of this small kitchen. Jacob, with his home advantage, stared at Micah over the rim of his mug through wisps of steam. Micah inspected the ceiling noticing the radial cracks from the extractor fan. It looked out of place as if it was meant more for a bathroom, one of those annoying fans that continue to whirr and hum for twenty minutes after you turned the light off. It was placed up against the outside wall away from the logical spot above the cooker, awkward and unsure of its purpose. He studied the cracks realised some of them were spider webs coated with fine dust and grime. All the while Jacob had not looked away once.

"Assuming you have not come to check out my plastering shall we talk?" He placed his mug on the side like a judge's gavel.

"That would be good." Another silence as Jacob stared.

"O.K. then Jacob. I'm sorry." Started Micah.

"For what?"

Micah shrugged and his eyes drifted to the celling again.

"I mean if you are saying sorry for climbing my wall then you've already apologised for that, and that's fine, I'm over that. But if you are apologising for something else, something that might actually be big, something that might actually matter to our friendship, or break some unwritten friendship code, now that might be something you would need to be apologising about. But a simple 'I'm sorry' might not cut it. You might want to think about what you want to say." He picked up his tea again and took a sip then added.

"But if it is about the wall?" He shrugged. Micah's head was racing with a hundred words in a thousand combinations, none of them fitting together into an audible coherence. He had known that Jacob would not be in a good mood.

"I…but." He spluttered.

"All ears." Jacob reached for a biscuit without offering Micah one.

"Well?" His arms that remained stoically folded, unfolding briefly to take a snap at the bourbon.

"I am sorry, I genuinely didn't realise." Jacob cut across him before he could get a head of steam up. "Didn't realise what, that you hadn't listened, that you hadn't trusted me?"

"Well I wasn't sure what was going on at the time. It was all a bit sketchy."

"I'm not fucking surprised it was a bit sketchy." He tossed the half-eaten biscuit into the bin and Micah knew he needed to get to the point soon.

"I was sketchy, not thinking because, well I guess I was not sure where I was with Imogen. She is always so…well mysterious and I thought maybe she was like that because she was seeing you." He tried not to raise his voice. Whether it was the tone of the statement or the words, it seemed to calm Jacob and he blew his tea but his eyes still bore into Micah.

"What about just asking me then?"

"Yeah good point." Micah could feel himself recoiling like a slug from salt.

"And when did you two start going out."

"You know that girl from a few weeks, back the one I can't really remember? Turns out that was definitely Imogen."

"So you've been dating then?"

"If, by 'dating', you mean a chat over a meal and a few drinks."

"Did you fuck her again?" There was an odd tone to Jacob's voice.

"No" He decided not to mention the hand holding or kissing.

"It's still a date though Micah, whichever way you cut it and memory or no, it was a second date." Radial cracks ran away from Jacob's pursed lips.

"Fair comment, it just seemed rude to fuck and run once Imogen had reminded me of the details of the night."

Jacob fell silent. This time he reached for a biscuit with the intention of eating it and offered the barrel to Micah who rummaged, hoping for a chocolate digestive but pulled out a rich tea. He made do.

Jacob moved from the kitchen to the lounge and sat on the couch. He began to roll a cigarette, spilling tobacco as he did. Then he retrieved the waste paper bin overflowing with empties from last night's session and brushed the flakes into it. Micah followed Jacob, sitting opposite.

"So were you two a couple then?" Asked Micah

"Never really, it's a little more messy than that."

"How messy?"

"Let's just say don't trust her, she is a crazy wild one. You saw the scars yeah? Oh right, memory loss. But you must have got a glimpse upstairs the other night. Skin like a ploughed field. The girl makes things up as well."

"So she dumped you." Micah shot him a cheeky smile as he said it.

Jacob calmly picked up the rolled cigarette, tapped the end securing the roach and lit it with a flourish of his zippo.

With head tipped to the side he spoke in a drawl as he exhaled his first drag and said "Fuck off."

It was too early for humour. Micah wondered how long ago they had been a mess together.

"She is off limits as far as I'm concerned, but if you want to go there then that your business."

"Yeah whatever. Thanks for your permission." He replied

"Just watch yourself, she is nuts." Jacob leant forward moving through a plume of smoke and tapped his head.

"Of course."

"Promise me." Jacob extended his hand.

"I promise." Micah shook it.

Jacob slumped back satisfied, blowing the cherry so that it glowed red like an ember from a coal fire.

"Good, now that is sorted we can celebrate." Jacob disappeared upstairs and Micah heard scratching in the ceiling above him like a giant rat famished and gnawing at the rafters. When Jacob returned he was rolling a little black rock between finger and thumb. A sixteenth thereabouts, Micah surmised from the brief flash he got of it before he was handed a conical pipe.

"Chillum. For special occasions."

The clay pipe felt cold in his palm and he inspected the unassuming dark blue glaze. In the wide end he noted a little stone, which he loosened and popped out onto his hand. The pear drop-shaped stone had a cross deeply scored in the top that ran down the sides, channels for the smoke.

" The Rastas use them in the celebration of Groundation Day, to reach a spiritual awareness." Micah shrugged, forgetting that it was better to nod when Jacob began to proselytise.

"Oh yeah, Rastas" He quickly added in a vain attempt.

"Yeah, though strangely they were not the first to use the pipe as part of their rituals. Hundreds of years before Haile Selassie was even born there were these Sadhus holy men.

"They even had dreadlocks." The lump of black, impaled with a dressmaker's pin, was being tickled with the tip of the flickering flame issuing from his Zippo. From another lecture, Micah remembered that the black resin was Moroccan in origin unless it was malleable and not in need of a flame to tease the lump into smaller lumps. The "squidgy black" could be rolled like dough and laid into the joint. But they weren't rolling a spliff.

"Who has dreadlocks? The Sadhus?" asked Micah who was involved now so figured he would kill time while Jacob prepared.

"Yeah, strange, naked, dirty men living lives with no personal belongings and amazing dreads. They know how to truly push the limits."

"Sounds like you would get cold."

"In India, a sub-tropical sub-continent?" Micah refrained from pushing his point though he thought about a recent story he had read about a group of pilgrims in the foothills of the Himalayas in August. A freak snowstorm blew down from the high mountains and three hundred people died on the footpath outside the little shrine.

Jacob sprinkled the crumbled hash like burnt bread crumbs on top of the stone until it was full up to the top of the recess.

"The trick" he said "is not to pack it like a weed pipe but let it sit loose to allow the oxygen to circulate." At least they weren't talking about Imogen.

Micah was happy that the further time stretched away from the awkward conversation, the more he could convince himself that he hadn't lied, he had just omitted certain truths. Not quite truths even. A feeling between two people is not an act, it's a feeling and anyway he may have misread the situation. Even if he saw her again he just wouldn't tell Jacob. Anyway the chances she would want to see him after he had walked in on her cutting herself was remote.

"Ready?" Asked Jacob.

"Ready" Micah wasn't ready. His mind was still racing, justifying, trying to counterbalance betrayal with dismissive passivity. He needed to find that place where this chillum was not going to mess with his head. Jacob paused, lighter in one hand, loaded chillum clenched in a fist in his other.

"To friendship." His thumb rolled over the flint wheel and he lifted the lighter up to the top of the chillum which he held vertically above his head and craned his neck underneath like some half mad calf at the teat of his mother. Eyes closed, hands steady, he sucked hard drawing down the flame and then passed the pipe and lighter over the table. Micah copied the actions and the sweet, sticky, resinous smoke hit the back of his throat, hot and thick. Then they sat, seconds ticking, lungs bursting, holding down the white wisps for as long as they could, then they were hungrily snapping breaths of fresh air before quickly returning for another hit before the bread crumb coals burnt away. By the time Jacob passed the chillum for the third hit Micah's senses were independent of thought. His eyes focused on radial cracks on the lounge celling. He had never noticed them. He was not sure if they were really there. He dispatched thoughts about structural integrity before they nested in his mind. Ears were hearing imagined sound, and minds galloping from random thought to random thought. They needed to lock in on something positive.

"Come, I'll read your Tarot. Find out if we will be friends forever." Suggested Jacob, picking up.

"Music" Micah suggested standing up and passing the pipe over again.

"I reckon there's one more hit in it." Jacob held back playing the good host. Years ago, when they smoked together, they would watch each other with the scrutiny of an anthropologist ready to catalogue the cardinal sin of joint hogging. This change was nice, a sign of maturity.

"No, you have it." He took them from Micah's outstretched hands leaving him to scan the music collection. He looked past the tapes scrawled with illegible handwriting and rummaged through Jacob's records. Zeppelin, too heavy, Fleetwood Mac, didn't get it, Ned's Atomic Dustbins, Flowered Up - both too random. Stone Roses, perfect. He slipped the record from the sleeve; there was growing selection of electric dance creeping into Jacob's collection. On the whole He disapproved but the Stone Roses was enough in the middle ground to sound new and exciting without making feel old and out of touch at twenty four. He heard his friend exhale heavily behind him just before the crackle of needle on vinyl.

The father of Nyx

Paul woke with a shudder. The darkness pulsated, outside the air was perfectly still, stifling all sound. For the last week Able-Smythe had been there, haunting his subconscious. His dreams were different from normal dreams. They were tangible and solid though the background details shifted without warning. The one constant was the old man. Paul would be walking down the high street then suddenly walking through a restaurant, an amalgamation of his childhood kitchen and a restaurant in town. Able-Smythe was the waiter, or a passerby, a distant relative or a train driver. He was always there and always wanted to talk. The dreams were not scary. He knew where he was and no one was chasing him. He looked around the dreamscape and saw the impassive faces round the restaurant refusing to take a solid form. But he couldn't shake a feeling of dread from his gut. In every room, every taxi rank, restaurant or swimming pool there was a darkness, a shadow that grew from the cracks filled out the hollows or corners. An insipid slow growth eating into his subconscious. Every time he tried to look directly at the shadows they shrank into his peripherals, ever out of reach. So he turned his attention back to Able Smythe whose words formed, as if audible, whispered from outside of the dream state. His words purred, vibrating their poisonous idea into every synapse. As that voice continued its nightly drone it was rewriting his thought patterns. He could never remember the words once he woke but he was aware that he was changing. The abhorrent became mundane and his propensity to anger and violence grew in the secretive recesses of imagination. The first time it spilled out into the real world, with calculated precision, he dissected his gold fish while he flapped helpless on the chopping board. These new sensations followed him back to his dreams, an ever widening loop. When he woke there was always the sense of the message sat heavy on his chest, a physical weight pushing down. He shifted in his bed, the feeling rising up, he felt sick. That idea, so alien just a few weeks ago in that field by the tree line, was now an idea lodged deep in his mind.

    The room spun into focus. He immediately reached for the light at the side of his bed, knocking over a glass of water. He looked around checking that everything was real, everything was normal. He checked the walls, especially the corners, scrutinising the shadows for any trace of some hidden horror that could spread. The sickness had vanished as he opened his eyes. He sat up and considered mopping up the spilt water but decided to go to toilet instead. After the toilet, he stood in the light of the fridge door glugging a half full bottle of wine. It didn't matter what it was, he needed the drink. He hadn't been sober really since the field. Anything would do; sherry, cider, wine, even Cinzano. When the house was dry he would get high and, failing that, he smoked oregano. The resulting asphyxiation had resulted in a high of sorts. So, for the third time that night, he stood barefoot at the fridge door drinking from the wine bottle. He placed it back then picked it up again took one more big swig before replacing the screw top lid and closing the door.

"Whoah. You scared me." Paul jumped. Able-Smythe was there standing silently, grinning behind the fridge door. He wore his suit but his tie was noticeably loosened around his neck reminiscent of brat packer returning after a night of champagne. He nodded, tapping an umbrella on the floor. Paul nodded then moved to the sink. He ran the tap cold and cupped a handful of water, splashing his face. The tap, tap like a metronome stick rang in his ears. Able-Smythe was real and somehow in his kitchen again. But he wasn't talking, he just stared, smiling, tapping, and blurring the lines between Paul's waking and sleeping moments.

"I can't do it." Paul sobbed, tears leaving slicks on the cold tile floor. A hand rested lightly on his shaking shoulders.

"Shush." The soothing sound hissed like a snake from Able-Smythe's mouth.

"I just can't."

"We are all capable of so much more than we dare to believe." It was the first time the old man had spoken outside of his dreams in a week. It startled Paul and he raised his head wiping away the stream of snot pouring from his nose. There was no old man, no umbrella tapping on the floor. He could still feel the lightest of touch on his shoulder, yet there was no hand. He threw another handful of water over his face, and went back to bed via the fridge and one last big swig of wine. He knew what he needed to do. He had known right from the beginning. It was the only way this stopped, and he needed it to stop.

"Paul? Is that you Paul? Are you up? Could you bring me a drink?" A voice called down the stairs. He checked the kitchen clock. His mother usually woke around four in the morning, as regular as her waterworks. He found her as he had left her, propped up in her bed. The glass which he had filled with water earlier was empty. Removing the straw he went off to refill it in the bathroom.

"Not in the bathroom Paul. The water tastes funny from the bathroom." Her ready voice chased Paul back down stairs towards the kitchen tap.

"Thank you darling."

She said regarding him with her watery eyes. It was a look of expectancy.

"Where do you want me to put the glass?"

"On the bed side table. Oh could you get a fresh straw please. Then take care of me." She smiled.

"I'll get the straw and we will see."

"Now Paul, you know that's not fair. I can't do it myself." Again she was calling after him as he returned to the kitchen to rifle through draws to find the straws.

"Do you think I like this? I'm your mother it's not easy for me." Her voice was rising in pitch, tinged with impatience, the same tone she used to scold him as a small boy.

"Where are you? Why are you taking so long? I need to go to toilet."

"Just go then!" He shouted back, leaning against the fridge grasping two straws too tightly. "I can't it's full."

"Paul. Where are you?"

This would change. He just wished there was a different price to pay. The law of economics dictates that currency under stress, is cheaper. He opened the cutlery draw and rummaged until he found what he needed for the party. It needs to be sharp enough to do damage but not big enough to have him arrested for concealing a dangerous weapon. He settled on a glorified butter knife, putting it in a plastic bag pulled from the clutter under the sink and put it in his coat pocket for later.

"Here." He called back up, lingering a moment longer. Upstairs his Mum had thrown her duvet off, revealing the job at hand. Popping the two straws in the glass, his eyes followed the plastic tube from under his mother's nighty as it wound its way down to the bulging bag hanging from a convenient hook by the bed. They fell into a silent routine as he tapped off the full bag and attached another. He double checked his work before disposing of the first bag's contents. Finally, he went back and checked the catheter bag again, just to be sure.

"Saturday night is Twin Peaks." She said it as a statement but Paul knew it was a question. She wanted real company not the domiciliary nurse who swept in and out within a half hour window.

"I'm busy Mum. I did say."

"But it's Twin Peaks darling."

"I did say Mum."

"Did you darling? I don't remember."

"Well I did." Said Paul as he left the room to go wash his hands. "Oh." Her utterance hung in the air until Paul returned, shaking his hands dry.

"Can I get you anything else before I go?" He smiled, his teeth bared like a portcullis guarding his emotions.

"Where are you going?"

"Out. See you later." The rehearsed, sickly smile dropped as he stepped out of the room.

Grave Intent

Jacob had been forgiving. Much more than Micah thought he would have been if the situation was reversed. Though it was noticeable that the smoking of the chillum had sealed all conversations about the past. No further discussion was had either about Imogen or about Jacob's dad having an affair. Micah had so many questions but with the smoking of the peace pipe came complicity to silence. At least they were friends again and with that Jacob had shown a new vigour to investigating the creepy Mr. Able-Smythe. A pass time that, since they had met Ray, had been discarded.

Micah cut across the allotment following the raised path edged by tufts of long grass as no one rushed to claim this no-mans-land. The wild seed from these grasses and accompanying weeds were indiscriminate as they infested.

Micah could see the high Victorian red brick wall that backed the cemetery, giving provenance to the burial ground beyond. A strategically placed pile of breeze blocks was still obscured by a precariously leaning shed cobbled together from old doors and an arched roof, the rusting remains of an Anderson shelter. The wall had been there from the day the cemetery was sanctified. In those days the land to the east of the city was pock marked with gravel pits, the wall stopped the daily migration of workers from St James' Road traipsing over other people's newly deceased, loved ones. Now the pits were flooded and used by those who could not afford a bus fare to the beach.

He found the blocks neatly stacked against one of the ornamental buttresses and vaulted the wall. He dropped heavily, both feet landing simultaneously to steady his balance. The graveyard was empty, shut at least an hour ago. Jacob had said the mausoleum would be easy to find *"like a little gothic house."* But as Micah purveyed the regimented lines of marble, white stone markers spreading out uniformly from a central memorial cross that rose above them, and beyond them, the grey granite markers refusing to conform to size or shape, nowhere was there a *little gothic house*.

Micah read snatches of lettering from the gravestones as he headed towards the administrative building at the far side. He noticed the dates were getting older as he got nearer the buildings. Slowly, like some Wellsian dial on a time machine, the numbers gradually plummeted to 1791 and the headstones flowered with yellow lichens. Micah reached the administrative building and stood under the archway that looked out on the ornate wrought iron gates. It was clearly an old building constructed of knapped flint with the corner work in limestone contrasting with the dark flattened edges of the flint. Two Siamese twin churches were conjoined by the archway he now stood in. Micah looked both left and right down two windowed cloisters to large oak doors. He wondered if they were both little chapels allowing two funerals to happen at the same time. After all, burying people was a business. The vaulted archway offered respite from the lazy late heat of the sun and Micah waited for a while enjoying goose bumps.

Late, with no sense of hurry or concern, Jacob appeared vaulting the front gate following the rucksack he had pushed through the bars. Micah stepped from the shadows of the archway revealing his hiding place. There was no point in a reprimanding Jacob who neither cared nor knew he was late.

"Found it then?" He chirped cheerily before ducking out of sight of the road.

"If you mean the crypt? I can't find it." Jacob gestured for Micah to follow pulling two stubbie from his ruck sack and passing one to Micah."

"Twist top." He instructed with a gesture that indicated any rift was truly forgotten. Micah hesitated, eyeing the green, French style beer before Jacob pushed it into his hand.

They cut back towards the wall at far boundary. Back to where the World War One memorial graves were, then picked their way through irreverently ignoring the path circling wide. Here the graveyard entered a little cul-de-sac, an area the size of a football pitch. The gravestones had returned to the grey granite teeth and in the centre to the left was what they were looking for. The building was the size of a small shed but constructed of the same flint and limestone. The windows were adorned with mottled red jasper and apertures filled by ornate scrolled ironwork giving an affect that Bram Stoker would be proud of.

"The crypt, or mausoleum to be technical." Said Jacob, arm spread wide in dramatic repose.

"What's the difference?"

"It's subtle but quite complicated." Jacob shrugged off the question as he pulled a blanket out from his bag and spread it on the ground.

"Isn't a mausoleum, a cenotaph without a crypt?" It wasn't of course. It was a surreptitious question.

"Yeah, that's right. I see you've been reading up." Clearly Jacob had not and was confusing his underground burial chambers with empty ones. Micah nodded, smiled and savoured his private joke. They spread themselves out over the blanket, drank beer and wondered what to do. This had seemed the right place to come to.

The grass was baked to a dried brown by four weeks of continuous sun and prickled like thistles through the blanket. It required strategic rolling to find a comfortable position. Apart from that, it was an idyllic summer evening in an empty graveyard; no more or less scary or supernatural than an empty supermarket car park.

"How are you and Imogen?" Asked Jacob casually, eyes fixed on the sky, head tilted back.

"She hasn't really spoken to me since the night she was at your place making a mess. I mean, I've seen her but I get the cold shoulder." Micah remembered the few times he had seen her out and wished it had been a cold shoulder that would have been something a few drinks and a messy liaison with a stranger would have driven away. In truth, she had been acerbic, glaring, snarling and unpredictable. She had emptied two drinks on him and any attempt at conversation was met with a hail of diatribe about infringement of privacy. Her words lancing out into the public like bombs.

"Pervert."

"Sneaky."

"Invasion of privacy." The screamed words drew veiled whispers and accusatory eyes until Micah was driven away embarrassed.

"Nice euphemism." Said Jacob.

"What was a nice euphemism?"

"Making a mess, it sounds so much more… I don't know creative, than hacking yourself up with a bread knife."

"Was it a bread knife?" Enquired Micah his mind still transfixed on the image of Imogen's eyes ringed with thick, black eyeliner, fierce and glaring.

"Yeah, strange choice. The serrated blade burns, more painful, more cathartic. Personally I'm all for the clean razor slice. Neat, quick, easy to stitch if it goes to deep." Jacob rummaged in his bag pulling out a Tesco carrier bag containing two Marathon bars and a book. "A little snack." Micah unwrapped one and begun to eat the gooey half melted chocolate, caramel and peanuts cementing on to his teeth.

"Thanks. I get the bread knife thing. Pain of choice for me is a cigarette burn." Confessed Micah. He had never told anyone that.

"You could make good money letting people do that. If you want I know a few people." Jacob wasn't grinning and appeared to not be joking. He simply sipped beer and stared skyward lackadaisically.

"No thanks. Have you heard from Imogen?" Asked Micah as he worried the label of the beer bottle.

"Yeah a couple of times." Jacob swigged his drink and Micah waited patiently but Jacob lowered the bottle and resumed staring at the sky. By the time Jacob spoke again Micah had pulled half the label off in tiny strips and piled it on the grass next to the blanket.

"She doesn't mention it." Said Jacob answering the question Micah had not asked.

"Oh." Micah said forcing indifference.

"Look, if you are still interested, and god knows why you would be, the trick with Imogen is to completely ignore her. Look like you don't want to know. Better still, look like you're having more fun without her. Just watch and see what happens."

"I thought you said to leave it." He forced his voice to remain disinterested, eyes on the label still tearing piece by piece, placing each little slither of destruction on the ant size pyre.

"Yeah I did and you should. Believe me you should. She is a dizzy, swirling mass of destruction but if you really want to go there then I wouldn't be a friend if I had stipulations on that friendship. So if you are interested, ignore her."

"Really? That sounds a funny way to go about it." He wavered in his disinterest knowing full well the masquerade was not fooling Jacob.

They sat silently, the twilight throwing a strange light across the graveyard as the shadows lengthened till the little patches of sunlight looked like some ancient Mayan pre-literature codex written in binary. They sat propped up against the mausoleum. Their faces soaked in the last vestiges of the evening sun. Jacob pulled out the Rizla, tobacco and a lump of resin wrapped in Clingfilm. He constructed a cone shaped smoke with the calm automated control that denoted regularity. The steadiness of hand indicated this was not the first of the day, as Jacob had notoriously shaky hands until he managed to toke. As Jacob finished, Micah broached the subject.

"So what's the plan?"

"I'm going to get you a little drunk and stoned and then read your tarot." He raised an eyebrow then laughed loud and it echoed in the gaping maw of the tomb behind him. The heat leaked from the ground as they sat, now facing each other. Micah pulled more tricks from the bag: a few candles, the type that look like they suffered from stigmartyr when they burnt. Micah was thankful he had seen them before as the smoke was beginning to shear the edge off reality. Aldous Huxley had suggested such states actually opened doors of perception. The problem was sometimes you could be so fucked you weren't sure what you were 'perceiving' so to speak. He suspected this was why most of Jacob's rituals involved some kind of drug. Either that or he had a problem.

Candles lit and nestled in little jam jars to shield them for the breeze, Jacob produced the Tarot. Wrapped in silk.

"To keep away the negative energy." He explained though he was at a loss to explain the mechanics behind how silk had repelling abilities.

"Alright, now remember, cards are not like Ouija boards; they are less specific"

"I don't remember Ouija boards being that specific if I'm honest." Countered Micah.

"What I mean is with a Ouija you are trying to pierce the veil. It's the interference that blurs the lines of communication. With cards they read the vibe, the situation. It's more of a holistic picture rather than a specific answer. Make sense?" Micah nodded firmly though he had no idea what Jacob was talking about.

"Right then." He spread the silk scarf on the grass then shuffled the deck. With the expertise of a card shark, he fanned them out.

"Pick one." He gestured looking away as if it was a card trick. Micah was expecting more but did as requested. Finger and thumb nimbly plucked a card.

"Do I memorise it and put it back in the deck?" Asked Micah.

"Funny man. No just give it here and then pick another two." Micah followed instructions trying not to think too much, trying to let the cards pick him as Jacob encouraged. Once three cards were picked they were laid down with flourish and pomp. Jacob paused reflectively with every turn. First was the four of cups, then the two of swords and finally, the lovers. Micah shuffled forward, anticipating a good read at this point but Jacob held the tension of the moment splaying his fingers deliberately across all three cards and uttering one word.

"Interesting." Micah opened his mouth to speak but Jacob silenced him holding his hand up then rearranged the cards so that they were in a triangle rather than in a row. The Lovers were at the top with the four of cup and two of swords underneath.

"Very interesting."

"What?"

"Well the Lovers means ..." He stopped, tapping the Swords card.

"There will be love in my life?" Chipped in Micah.

"No, they are upside down so it means love lost." Micah looked at the card, he couldn't see upside down from right way up.

"But" Jacob tapped the four of cups card.

"Yes?"

"This card reads well. Cups for drinking out of, for abundance a good thing, wealth, it cancels out the inverted Lover card especially as there are four they are paired off not singular. It points to a relationship."

"And the swords? Are swords bad or good?"

Jacob spoke slow and deliberate. "They can mean both. Either good, as in cut free, a new start or bad as in, cut apart and broken but in the context of the other cards I think it is good. I think the cards are saying you will have a new relationship out of the ashes of an old relationship."

"You think?"

"I told you, more of a reading the vibe but yeah, I reckon it looks good." Cards aside, they chinked beer bottles and laughed, Micah trying not to smile too much

"I'm going to have a party. A really big party, celebrate my parents return and the end of my freedom." Said Jacob as they finally wound their way through the gravestone towards the entrance.

"Your parents are returning? You haven't said a thing about that. When? How? Why?" The question stumbled out. Micah was confused with this poleaxe. Jacob's parents had always been distant when they had been friends growing up but since reacquainting with each other Jacob had hardly mentioned them at all. He had eradicated any trace within the family home. It was if they had died in some tragic accident and the pain had been too much to bear. Of course, the truth was far more humdrum and now that they were returning from working in Singapore they would be pulling all the furniture out of storage and resetting life in England to what it had been six years ago. Except Jacob was not what he had been and the house - shit, the house! thought Micah. There were no carpets, the walls were nicotine stained and there was a thick crust of grime on the kitchen cabinets that would take weeks to scrub off. The furniture that had been left for Jacob had mostly been sold or broken.

"What are you going to do?" Asked Micah.

"Have a party, I've told you."

Micah shifted, uneasy with his friends flippancy. "You know what I mean. About the house."

"Have a party." He repeated in the same tone. "That's what the drugs were for."

"A BBQ while Rome burns." Mumbled Micah suddenly understanding something Imogen had said the other night.

"I am probably not going to bother with catering." The wild gleam was in Jacob's eye.

"You will come Micah? Imogen will be there I expect."

"I'll be there, for you and then after everybody's gone I'll help you clean the house."

"You're a good friend Micah. Too good."

Fandango

Jacob's place was lit up like a Mardi Gras parade. Micah could see the multi-coloured glow bouncing off the rooftops two streets down as he made his way from the corner shop. Jacob had outdone himself and Micah wondered if the party would make it to midnight. Neighbourhood tolerance levels lowered with every flash. As he turned the corner he could hear the throb of music. The house had vomited people out onto the pavement, leaning against next-door neighbour's walls and cars. One or two people had strayed to the other side of the road watching like sociology students. Already a collection of cans and cigarette ends were collecting and a strong herbal smell permeated the air. There in tight black jeans and shirt undone, with a large silver pentagram dangling down over his white, hairless chest, was Jacob. He held court with a fat joint waggling from the side of his mouth as he shouted his welcome over the music. He hugged Micah and then held him at arm's length, his pupils wide black pools with bloodshot rims.

"*It's the end of the world as we know it and I feel fine.*" He sang.

"A bit obvious don't you think? The police are bound to turn up." Micah spoke the voice of sanity. But clearly looking past Jacob into the throng of bodies packed tightly, he knew the voice of sanity would not be heard tonight.

"I said spread the word." Jacob threw his arms wide knocking a guy standing next to him round the head. He didn't apologise. The guy hardly acknowledged the blow.

"I don't even know most of these people. And if the police turn up? If the police turn up? You and me" His arm circled Micah's shoulder in collusion. "we jump the wall at the back and scarper and I'll claim I left hours ago and had no idea. The game is up anyway." He referred, no doubt to his parents' imminent return.

Jacob led them both through the crowds pushing through the dance floor melee. Micah recognised no one. He ducked under the point of a stiletto from some overzealous girl mounted on the shoulders of a lad. She was waving her hands in time to the music, grasping a glow stick in each hand. An expression like granite behind yellow sunglasses, jaw working like a cider press. This was Acid House. Micah focused and followed the fast disappearing Jacob through the throng. The kitchen was chaotic with bottles strewn over every surface. What wasn't being drunk from, was instantaneously transformed into an ashtray. Micah placed his beers down as was the custom. Instantly a guy snapped off two and waded off into the garden. Micah picked them up again. Opened one and put the other in his pocket.

"Garden." Jacob pointed with both hands raised above his head as if directing an airplane into land. "There are some people I want you to meet." Micah followed Jacob like the Pied Piper out into the garden. It was drenched in soft twinkling fairy lights.

They manoeuvred past a couple close to copulating in the door way, oblivious to a small group standing swigging beer and throwing match sticks at them trying to get them to fall between their close pressed grinding hips. Micah didn't recognise them.

"Do you know anyone here?" He called. Jacob shrugged then bowed in front of three people all in combat trousers, paratrooper boots and khaki vests with long matted dreads smelling of petunia oil and bonfires. There was little to distinguish between male and female. Though the two girl wore bikinis clearly visible under their loose fitting, man-size vests. Lithe, bronzed limbs, pretty, angular faces with keen eyes welcomed them with smiles.

"Hey guys." Jacob hugged them. They hugged him back with almost as much gusto.

"Hey man." Said the guy.

"I like your hair." Said the taller of the girls, and began playing with it. Micah caught snatches of conversations.

"No seriously the sixties were over after Altamont concert."

"I understand what you're saying. The spirit of the sixties did die then, but technically there was another month until it ended."

Two guys wearing berets and military jackets a little too tailored to be the real McCoy, pushed a flyer into one of the dreaded girls hand. She glanced at the paper emblazoned with the class war skull and crossbones symbol, then screwed it up and threw it on the floor. The pseudo soldier shrugged turning back to a group of guys who were either Two-Tone fans or skinheads but Micah had seen these guys (they were always guys) proliferating public places with tiny stickers proclaiming, "Rights for whites".

Micah turned his head to catch the conversation.

"The poll tax riots were a necessary evil."

"Generous mate! How standing up for the rights of the little people could be seen as an evil…" A cheer went up from the dance floor drowning out the end of the sentence. Micah strained as much as possible without looking like he was eves dropping.
"The police were out of line."
"Unprovoked violence." He knew one of the guys talking, he had seen him after a few beers, having to be held back by three bouncers having just prized a brick from his hand. Somehow he couldn't imagine the chap standing quietly not provoking the police.

Jacob lent close, shielding his mouth with a hand, focusing Micah away from his eavesdropping.

"Real Crusties. They live in buses and all Micah. They're stoned and they believe in free love. I think the tall one likes you so make love man." He made the peace sign, leering, then raised his fist as a faux phallus. Micah was sure his friend had spoken too loudly but before he could say anything else Jacob was gone, merging into the crowd. Micah was left standing with three grinning bronze statues, one of which twiddled his hair.

Micah attempted conversation for ten minutes but became convinced that they were an acting group in role, practicing for some play. Everything was groovy, cosmic or far out and Micah was getting twitchy about this strange woman touching his hair and his neck and commenting on what she liked. She liked a lot of things. No amount of alcohol was going to put him in a frame of mind where he was going to want sex with her. The last thing he wanted was Imogen to turn up and see him standing here being fawned over. Micah made his excuses and slipped away to sit by the four-way plug with multiple adaptors stacked and buzzing like baritone mosquitoes.

He people watched, it was a strange mixture of people. There was a massive cross section of different sub cultures here and they were looking young. Time passed slowly drinking alone. He chain smoked till his lungs ached then smoked some more. Socially acceptable self-harming. After finishing his beers he wandered back to the kitchen to quench his thirst with spirits, looking out for anyone he knew. He thought he caught a glimpse of Paul disappearing into the crowd but when he looked again and he was gone. Micah set up residence next to a fridge full of water bottles. Thankfully, a bottle of Lemoncello had been overlooked, wedged in the freezer compartment. The sweet sharp taste instantly forced his taste buds to salivate, chasing the stale taste of ash away.

The tall traveller girl appeared at his shoulder. She leant across taking the bottle from his hand purposefully. Her eyes locked on his as she went to take a swig, missing and pouring it down her loose fitting T-shirt. Her gaze did not drop.

"Oops." She smiled. "Seems I have spilt my drink. I'm going to go upstairs and take this wet top off."

"You do that." Replied Imogen who had stepped from the crowd at that precise moment. She eyed the soaked girl up and down slowly, the corner of her mouth lifted on one side into a sneer and then nodded her head once sharply in the direction of up.

"Now fuck off." The New Age Traveller raised her hands as if in surrender and backed away, having to physically push through the crowd. Micah snatched the now half empty bottle of Lemoncello from her hand as she was enveloped.

"Really?" Quizzed Imogen.

"No, really not." He necked the liquor and Imogen reached across snatching it from him mimicking his actions. Twice.

"Can we talk?" Micah asked. She nodded and took his hand, pulling him back out into the garden. They threaded their way past swathes of people sitting on the lawn. Imogen pulled the rusty bolts on the back gate and pushed Micah through. As soon as they were alone in the alleyway Micah took a deep breath and began to explain himself.

"Look, I know I mucked up a bit. I got jealous. But, to my credit, the only reason I got jealous was because I really like you. I honestly had no idea about the other stuff." Imogen interjected as she tried to pull the gate closed.

"I don't want to talk about it. That's why I avoided you for weeks because I do not want to talk about it." Micah gathered his thoughts and changed tack.

"The thing is, I like you. I really like you and I want to give us a chance." He gesticulated using his whole hand pointing, straying into Imogen's personal space.

"I'm not good with this kind of love stuff."

"Love stuff… big words." Her tone was curt. He knocked the remark to one side and continued.

"I can never seem to say what I want to say. But I know that you intrigue me. I know that I think about you when you are not around and I know spending time with you excites me. I feel stupid and clumsy around you and I'm not used to that." She turned and Micah could see the corner of her mouth turn slightly. She stepped closer, rocked on her heels. This was working, he thought he just needed to keep going, make her see how it could work.

"I know I can be an idiot. I know I've upset things but I've talked to Jacob and he is fine with it. He said if I want to go for it then he's cool." Micah smiled a wide smile, all teeth. He went to hug Imogen to vanquish the ghost of Jacob.

"What?" She said, pulling away, arms crossed.

"What?" He recoiled like a bungee chord over the precipice. The feeling growing in his stomach. He was about to drop again.

"You and Jacob have decided who is going to fuck me. I'm glad you worked that out."

"I didn't mean it like that." He stuttered. She did not pause for breath. She didn't pause to listen to his stammering apology.

"And referring to me as "it", well I'm not an "it". Emily Davison didn't jump in front of a horse for you to refer to me as a…a possession." Micah's bottom jaw was flapping trying to catch vowels and form sounds round them before Imogen moved on but she was quick.

" I am not another notch. How does it work? Is it another notch? What if you got a second shag or did that not count cos you can't remember. Are you just keeping your stats up?" She was nearly shouting, muscles tensed in her arm, tendons popping through the skin. Micah thought he was going to be punched. If she did, he would not flinch.

"I bet you and Jacob are in competition racking up notches. Are they physical notches? I mean is there a bed somewhere with deep gouges hacked out with a Boy Scout Swiss army knife? Or is it more a metaphorical score you keep in your head? That fucking slime-ball Jacob I bet he claimed me as a notch."

"I don't understand I thought you guys were friends. I mean that night he was looking after you." The vowels formed, the words slipped out and he closed his eyes knowing if he saw it coming he would flinch.

"I TOLD YOU I DON'T WANT TO TALK ABOUT THAT." She was close, he could feel her hot breath. Each word was punctuated with a rain of spittle. Then quiet. He peeled his eyes open slowly. She was still standing close, eyes fixed, scowl slung low.

"Ok." He whimpered, then shrunk back against the wall pulling himself in. Arms folded, legs folded and his mind now seized. He couldn't think of anything to say that wouldn't make it worse. Imogen mirrored him and they pushed themselves against either side of the alley trying to keep as much distance as possible. This felt like splitting up, though they had never really been together.

"I'll see you around Imogen. I'm sorry." But before he could leave Imogen pushed open the gate and disappeared back into the garden. The clatter and the thrum of the party now repulsed him. He sunk back against the wall. Momentarily he considered searching out the New Age Traveller girl, instead, he punched the wall.

Panic

By force of will, Paul had made it to the party. The hedonistic joviality that greeted him was jarring. He stood a sentinel across the road. Watching people coming and going. The house pulsated with strangers, younger and brasher. They spilled out and continued the party outside on the road unafraid of locals or police. His eyes stayed fixed on the door looking for the host. His mind raced like he had done a gram of speed, noticing every detail. How people stood and talked to each other, how the shadows thrown against the curtain distorted the revellers so it looked like a fight. He saw a familiar face moving slowly towards the house, holding a four pack of beer. Still, he held back, tracing Micah's approach. Sure enough, Jacob appeared. They briefly chatted and Paul wondered what they were saying. He wondered how close he could get to Jacob. Then what? He had not thought this through.

Paul stared pitiless at the open door as they disappeared inside. He now focused on the cavorting bodies inside, fixed on the point where they had vanished, oblivious to the milling drunkards occupying the small patch of shingle at the front of the house. He could feel the edges of his concentration beginning to tatter. The feeling swelled then receded like a tide, and with every rush he felt physically sick. The voices drifting across the road became muffled and incoherent and Paul was suddenly aware of the thrum of his heart, beating like war drums in his ears. Vision began to blur, then worse, pulsate, disorientating all before him. The muffled thump in his ear grew to a gallop. A beer bottle smashed on the pavement his side of the road, too far away to be a missile aimed at him. But he snapped back and immediately walked over, careful not to look at, or engage anyone. No one noticed or cared as he stumbled in.

  Inside the heart of the party his vision began to distort again. This time a crystalline mass of sparkling filaments, moving like ferocious bacteria distorted his vision. It was like seeing everything from his peripherals. He was aware of people but could not focus. He managed to negotiate the front room by bumping and pushing through, hands in front, forcing his path. Making it to the kitchen, he realised that it was impossible. He didn't know what was wrong. It had started like a panic attack, but now he was in uncharted territory. The harsh kitchen light now stabbed at his eyes causing searing pain. He needed darkness quickly but did not want to leave the mission, so he headed back into the front room scrum cutting across to the stairs. He lifted the rope with a crude 'Do not enter' scrawled on a ripped up cereal box and slipped upstairs. He made it to the top of a flight of stairs and sat, head buried in his knees trying to calm his senses. Ears whistled and eyes felt as if they were trying to jump from their sockets in time to the music. He pulled the kitchen knife from his pocket and toyed with it digging small holes in the bare wood of the top step. He wasn't sure what to do. Even if he could see and think straight, he still wasn't sure he could go through with it. Able-Smythe had said blood was needed. Paul replayed the conversation through in his head, unsure if he was remembering real conversations or dreams of conversations had. The elasticity of his memory allowed him to remember in a way that could work.

"If you want blood then you can have it." Paul's face screwed tight as he placed the knife to his wrist and he drew it. He imagined how easy chicken breast butterflied. Finished, he looked down at an angry, red scratch. No blood, no sacrifice, just an angry red line like a child had attacked him with a felt tip, almost invisible in the low lit stairwell. So he decided to switch to plan C. Blood was blood after all and he thought it unlikely that some weirdo in the woods would have blood testing equipment to identify the difference between cat and human.

The Score

Jacob materialised through the crowd flitting from one person to another. He found Micah slouched by the kitchen sink, bottle of Limoncello back in hand.

"I forgot I had that. I think my parents must have left that when they went to Singapore. The irony."

"What's ironic about that?" Quizzed Micah.

"You know." Said Jacob chinking his beer against the half-drunk bottle without answering the question.

"Hey, they're not back yet."

"One last blast, one last big fandango. Then my brother comes at the weekend to take the keys."

"Are you mad? That's barely enough time to tidy the house."

Jacob shrugged. "It's all gone to shit, so might as well go to shit in style." He shrugged again like he was developing a tick.

The seed of self-destruction had taken hold. Now with conditions right, that seed could multiply. His bloodshot eyes dilated, engulfing nearly all colour, sucking in all light, and all sanity, projecting madness everywhere he looked. Micah saw the chaos burrowing, the gyre spinning and the centre wouldn't hold much longer. Micah needed to get out. He checked his watch, it was eleven thirty. Pubs weren't shut for another hour. He needed to leave before the surge of people.

"Where's Imogen? I saw you two talking." Asked Jacob.

"We fought. She left."

"How long ago?" Jacob's eyes seemed to clear and he looked at his watch.

"Do you know where she went?"

"No."

"Did she say anything? Any clue where she might be." Jacob's voice was getting higher and speech pattern faster.

"No."

"Come on we need to find her." Jacob did not wait for a reply, grabbing Micah by the arm and leading him, as he barged through the front room. An understudy for Motley Crue stood in the open front door, his blonde nest of hair so pumped full of product that it blocked the entire doorway.

"Jacob." He bellowed, arms wet with fresh tattoos, spread wide. Jacob ducked the embrace and pushed the rocker to one side.

"Later Alvin."

Only Alvin noticed the host leave his party. Everyone else was gurning, grinding and waving limbs in ecstasy to the electric throbbing from Jacob's overworked speakers.

They walked quickly down the road, breathing in lungfuls of air, free from smoke and stale sweat. They kept walking fast until they cornered the road and the sounds dulled to a heartbeat. Jacob leant against the wall and re-gathered his thoughts.

"She'll head for the train station but she might stop on the way. So if we check the pubs en route then we have a chance."

"Is it really that serious?" Asked Micah, unaffected by the dramatic tone.

"She rang me earlier in the evening and - yes it is."

Micah shrugged his response, after all he had only known her a few weeks. He leaned on the wall next to Jacob, listening to the distant sounds. He could hear laughter and glass smashing.

"Must be a riot going on somewhere else, keeping the police busy." He said.

"Most of the reprobates were at the party. Come on let's get moving."

As they walked through the near empty streets with the smell of baked Tarmac filling the air, they became aware of the sound. The low murmur was everywhere like it was inside their heads. Micah stood in the street tilting his head, cupping his hand to his ears trying to pinpoint where the sound was coming from. He could not pinpoint the sound because it was coming from everywhere. In the gloom of the dusk now swallowing the streets, he could see the static glow of television screens in front rooms.

They made for the train station noticing that the pattern continued all the way. It seemed every single house had a glaring eye gazing out. They had to walk through the industrial estate. On one side of the road the large corrugated warehouses crowded in, on the other side of the road was an old gravel pit, which had slowly filled with water. Those that hadn't, became landfill sites. Most of the housing estates on the peripherals were built on dumps. The train station they were heading towards was an unusually large station for what was no more than a market town. Like archeological architecture it hinted at the massive amount of aggregate moved through sixty odd years ago. The gravel pit bordering the road they walked down now, had been flooded and used for fishing. Even here he could hear the strange murmur. At first he dismissed it as an audible equivalent of staring at a bright light then seeing the afterimage, but the tinny sound persisted. He glimpsed through the bushes and saw, lining the lake, small groups of men sitting huddled around radios neglecting their rods, beers in hands, faces screwed with tension. Whatever they were listening to, it was gripping them. They made it to the first pub at the end of the road, an old, thatched house with benches thrown up by the side of the road. Inside, access to the bar was easy. Jacob indicated for Micah to buy a couple of shots while he checked the other end of the pub which was packed by a large group of men gathered around a wall mounted television. Then it dawned on Micah, it was The World Cup. Judging by the abbreviations at the top of the screen, England was playing Germany. Micah was not orientated towards football. He had only ever watched one game on television. This had been on a family holiday to France when his dad had been alive. The owners of the campsite had invited his family to watch a match. England were playing and the soccer crazy campsite owner couldn't bear the idea that Micah's dad would miss the chance to cheer on his nation's team. Language had proved difficult and "no" translated too rudely so Micah's dad said 'oui' and the whole family sat mustering as much enthusiasm as they could for 90 minutes. England lost and the French man consoled his dad with lots of free alcohol.

"Two shots of tequila." Micah proffered a five pound note and the barman tentatively poured extra-large singles, his eyes not leaving the distant screen.

It was a draw; one all. The commentators were babbling on, quoting statistics as footage of the game was spliced, backing up their summaries. It was the lull before the penalty shoot-out. The pub watched transfixed, as Lineker ran towards the ball. There was a sharp intake of breath as his foot struck the leather sending the ball left. The German goalkeeper rolled right in a moment of misjudgement and it was a goal. The roar from the television distorted the speakers and the pub whooped as one. The bar tender forgot payment in the excitement and Micah pocketed the note and moved away from the bar, drinks in hand.

Jacob left Micah guarding the drinks as he did a sweep of the pub, picking his way through the transfixed punters.

"She's not here." Shall we?" Jacob necked the shot while standing ready to go. Quickly they made there way to the next pub a minutes walk nearer to town and the station. The scene was the same. Men standing statue like, feverish brows creased as, Brehme began his preparations in his head, psychologically trying to get himself in the right space. Shilton, the England goalkeeper, light on his feet, was dancing on the white line. The commentary reminded all who listened that this battle had been played out before in 1985. He shot, he scored, and the atmosphere in the room tensed.

"Two shots of tequila please." Ordered Jacob, glancing at Micah.

"Your round." He said. Micah hoped they found her soon for the sake of his liver and pocket. This time Jacob guarded the drinks as Micah searched the premises, half aware of the drama played out exquisitely on the faces around. With every penalty England took they looked as if they were in a moment of rapturous ecstasy that peaked at the moment the ball hit the back of the net. Micah weaved his way back to Jacob. The pub hissed and contorted as Germany put a penalty away.

"Not here then." As if in reply to Micah the pub let out a long gasp. Pearce shot too straight and Brehme saved it. Lineker ruffled the young lad's hair and the group let out a groan then a string of expletives. Some wandered back to bar preempting the result. The friends took it as a queue to leave

"Have we lost?" Micah asked to the bar tender, who silenced him with a shush sounding more like a hiss.

"If we score the next goal we still have a chance." Came the muffled reply as he chewed his nails to the quick.

Chris Waddle placed the ball on the penalty spot and walked away, trying to keep his nerves. Trying to muster the strength physically and emotionally to score. Pearce stood at the side looking away. He knew this shot could redeem his miss. t Then Waddle ran at the ball, the crowd surged with anticipation as his foot struck the ball. A solid kick, the sound lost in a roar. The ball missed completely sailing over the bar and it was all over.

"Well that was shit." Announced the Barman, springing to the pumps and pouring multiple pints in rapid succession as the orders were shouted over, but Jacob and Micah were already out the door and marching on to the next venue.

And so it went for the next three pubs. They walked in, Micah ordered shots while Jacob looked around. Everywhere was drunk, miserable football fans.

They reached the White Horse, a particularly townie pub, the kind of place that repelled goths and punks with violence. With heads spinning, they agreed before entering that they would not drink here, rather a quick search and out. Thankfully, their way was barred by two barrel-chested. bomber jacket-wearing bouncers, keen not to work hard pulling the two lads from a rain of fists.

"Please we're looking for a friend." Jacob pleaded. The shorter guy without the scar and still with hair, rubbed his bristling chin.

"Skinny, pretty thing, highly strung, with a mouth?"

"Yeah, sounds right."

"That way." He pointed down the small side road that slipped into the tightknit back streets of the Pallants.

"Right." Said Jacob marching off. "Thanks." Added Micah following, pleased they had avoided the White Horse.

The punch

"You fucking bastards, you touch me and I'll cut myself." Came the screams as Jacob and Micah were desperately trying to work out what to do. They had found her perched on a wall outside one of the few businesses amongst the well maintained town houses. The two policemen, the target of the abuse, were clearly running out of patience. This was not their normal Saturday night brawl. The panic on their faces reflected the image presented to them. A woman, arms thrown wide with blood running down them. Parameters of choice were rapidly narrowing.

"We need to do something soon or they are going to lock her up." Said Micah. The police had given her the choice; get in the ambulance or they would have to arrest her for criminal damage. The lads looked over to wild-eyed Imogen, standing in front of the full-length window of Jonathan Thomas Design Company. The window was shattered and she stood guarding it, grasping a broken shard like a dagger. She was holding it threateningly against her arm where she had already sliced, shredding the blue blouse she was wearing. Crimson droplets splashed Jackson Pollock-like on to the grey, chewing gum speckled pavement. The police officers had realised that she was not a direct threat to them and were trying to calm her down but whenever they moved near she would motion to cut again. So they retreated, calling an ambulance. Thankfully the alarm that had first informed the police had been remotely silenced and the ambulance had turned off siren and lights all in an attempt to keep her calm. The medics wanted to take her to hospital where she would be assessed given anti-psychotics and possibly sectioned.

So there was a stand-off. Jacob was looking away, scared the sight of blood would instantly make him another casualty. Micah stayed with him, away from Imogen and the gathering huddle of uniforms. One of the Police officers came over.

"Gentlemen, we need to get her into the Ambulance or I'm afraid we will have to restrain her and take her in." His fingers twitched nervously on his pepper spray.

"We're working on it mate give us a second." Said Jacob and then looked at Micah not sure what to do. For a second Micah enjoyed the moment. It was rare that Jacob didn't know what to do or say.

"If you hadn't have told her about our conversation then she wouldn't have gone off at the deep end. I told you she was volatile."

"No shit."

"So what are we going to do?" Jacob's hand had slipped into his pocket and he pulled his lighter and began to flick the lid and run his thumb nervously over the flint.

"We're going to have to let the police deal with it." Replied Micah equally clueless.

"Because they are clearly dealing with it." They both looked over at the two policemen standing almost on the other side of the road trying to talk to Imogen who was leaning against the frame of the window, reanimating every time they moved. Jacob quickly lowered his eyes feeling dizzy. One of ambulance crew came over to talk to Jacob and Micah.

"Don't fucking touch me don't even come near." Shrieked Imogen, her tone was becoming more erratic.

"Look lads she needs medical attention and we need to get her into the ambulance. Now we can't force her but if she is not in there soon the officers are going to deal with it in a way that is not in the best interests of the young lady."

"We know that mate, tell us something we don't know." Snapped Jacob, flicking his lighter in his hand, making sure his eyes were fixed on the floor averted from the horror scene.

"Don't mind him. He faints at blood." Micah added. The ambulance man lowered his tone and levelled his gaze.

"The thing is, we" he gestured to himself and his partner standing at the back of the ambulance, "cannot force a patient into the ambulance. Do you understand what I'm not saying?" Micah nodded.

"Give me a minute."
He pulled Jacob close and explained the situation though he could tell from the glazed look that he was not really listening or understanding as he fought to stay conscious. He knew then that this was his decision alone. He left Jacob, arms out, pushing against the wall trying, to extract some of its stability from the brick work.

Micah walked over to the police officers and called them away, leaving Imogen rocking from one foot to the other, unsure what her next move could be. He explained his plan and though they could not agree to it, they stepped away and let him know that they would be looking away at the opportune moment. Then Micah approached Imogen.
He took one step towards her.

"What the fuck do you want?"

"To talk. The police are backing away so we can chat Imogen" He held his palms out in a non-threatening manner.

"So did you and Jacob have a conversation to decide who was going to talk to me. Like you had a conversation about who could fuck me?"

"You know if Jacob came over here to talk to you he would pass out at the first glimpse of blood." He tried to inject as much humour as he could. He took a second step closer.

"Oh so you get to be the big hero, well done, congratulation Micah. Why don't you come and rescue me? Is that it? Is that your thing? Damsel in distress?" She was flailing her hands around. Blood was now pulsing from her hand as she tightened her grip on the shard.

"You're hardly that Imogen. You're having a Mexican stand-off with two policemen and an ambulance crew."

He took a third step closer, moving to one side. Imogen responded by mirroring the side step. He shuffled again corralling her away from the broken glass scattered across the floor.

"The police have agreed not to arrest you which is good news, yes?"

"I don't fucking care. Fuck them. Fuck the police they're cunts." The angry beats of NWA popped into his head.

He took a tentative half step, he could almost reach out and touch her.

"But you do need medical attention, look at your arms." Imogen looked down at the rivulets of blood coursing down her arms from the multiple gashes. He took his chance, moving quickly across the final metre and, before she could look up again, he swung and landed a punch squarely on her jaw.

"You arsehole! You bastard. I'm going to have you…" she lunged at him in a rage and lost her footing on the blood slick. He reached out to catch her but she smashed her head on his chin, knocking her out cold.

Micah stepped away as the paramedics swarmed with a raft of medical paraphernalia.

"All taken care of." He called to Jacob as he walked back across the road. Jacob looked up, spotted a smear of crimson across Micah's white shirt and slumped down in the doorway of a town house. He passed out from consciousness, half propped up by a topiary box bush, his chin pushed down on his chest. The two Police officers helped Micah put him in recovery with a blanket from the ambulance under his head. Imogen was out long enough for the two ambulance crew members to secure her in the van and drive off leaving Micah with a bruised fist and chin. Facts about keeping wrists straight while punching learnt from Bruce Lee films were pointless after the fact, but Imogen was safely on her way to the hospital without a criminal record. He sat and rolled a cigarette waiting for Jacob to come round. By the time his friend seeped back into consciousness Micah had removed the shirt. He looked like a stripper with his dark denim jacket done up, bare flesh peeking from his midriff as he half carried, half dragged his friend home.

The Second Punch

Passing out always exhausted Jacob. It drained him, as if the very thing that scared him to unconsciousness, emptied from all capillaries near the surface of his skin leaving him a sallow pasty colour. An hour later and three medicinal brandies followed by a medicinal Jack Daniels and he was beginning to feel normal. Micah had helped him home and, carefully hiding the blooded shirt, had changed into one of Jacob's T-shirts. He now sat across from his friend studying him. Jacob sat hunched on the sofa wrapped in his duvet, only his underpants on. Just his head and one hand protruded like a claw grasping the half-filled glass. They were definitely not pub-sized shots. He was gazing at the glass, swilling the content trying to clink the two ice cubes against the side. Neither had spoken for ten minutes.

      Micah turned over the last few weeks in his mind trying to make some sense of it all. Finding Imogen upstairs, Ray, John Able-Smythe, the party and Imogen losing it. The cards had said that things were going to be good. He tried to place some narrative on it to make sense. Somehow it seemed connected in a way where he should be able to draw a life lesson from. That circumstances were not circumstantial, but nothing would line up. The cards had been vague, as promised. They picked up on situations, but he couldn't fathom how the last few days were good to anyone but a dyslexic clairvoyant. Were the cards wrong? He thought back to the name John Able-Smythe. The old guy had called himself that name and then disappeared. That had to be something. There had to be something beyond this. If only it were love. He looked over at Jacob wrapped up like some Incan mummy perched and serene.

    Was it the power of memory that kept the dead alive? Were they just little electrical impulses hardwired in? Somehow Jacob's shenanigans could have acted like steroids to half forgot neurones, firing off deep in his subconscious, vomiting up memories that became real. Though it didn't explain Able-Smythe. Micah entertained the possibility that maybe they genetically inherited trace memories at a sub-conscious level from parents. Able-Smythe could have been a Great, Great, Great Grandfather jumping out of the cerebral cortex. It would explain people believing in past lives. He thought about sharing his ideas with Jacob. He thought about his Dad. He remembered strong, impossibly hairy arms holding him high out of the water at the seaside. He remembered blinking furiously trying to get the sand and salt from his eyes, shrieking with fear and delight as his dad tossed him into the sea, a human catapult. Then Micah would protest "No, no Dad please no" while he stood shivering waiting to be picked up again. He remembered crawling into bed, burrowing down between Mum and Dad, prizing them apart. Then he remembered lying there awake listening to their snores while playing with the lumpy scar tissue on dads elbow. There had to be something beyond. Heaven, the afterlife were ways people used to describe the beyond. Words ascribed to give meaning. Once the Earth was flat and when you died you ascended above the firmament. Of course, the stars were little holes in the firmament. Dante went down and, ever since, bad people have always gone in that direction, a phenomenon in most cultures. Micah wondered why. The only things above the firmament now were satellites in blasphemous degrading orbits. Reminders of the science that had dared to denounce God and yet people looked up when they muttered a prayer or down when they feared unmentionable evil.

Jacob rattled the ice cubes in his glass indicating he wanted another drink and Micah obliged pouring from the left over bottles neatly stacked on the side.

"When does your brother come?" Asked Micah. Jacob lifted his wrist and glanced at the space where most people wore watches.

"Three hours." Micah's eyes drifted across the room. Nothing had been done to the morass of bottles ash and rubbish. Jacob sighed heavily, looking beyond Micah as he poured.

"I need to tell you some stuff." Said Jacob.

"Is it about you and Imogen. Because I don't want to know and I don't care anymore."
Jacob shook his head sighed again. The stereo hummed electrostatic as the tape spool ran its course. They sat silent listening to it.

"Well?" Asked Micah.

"Yeah. Well, I think I better show you."

"If this is an 'I show you mine, you show me yours' trip then you can fuck right off."

"Huh" Jacob half laughed, half coughed as he stood, steadying himself by dropping the blanket to reach for the wall.

The stereo started up again as auto-reverse spooled the tape over to the other side. The distant throb echoed up the foot of the narrow stairwell where they stood. The first two flights were flooded in daylight but the last flight was pitch black due to the lack of windows. Beyond the landing, beyond the reach of day light streaming through the hallway window, was the inky black pool of shadow leading up the stairs. He blinked hard just picking out a glimmer of an outline of the twelve steps and the door above him.

Step one.
Jacob took a deep breath, allowing himself to be wrapped in darkness. Thick dust scuffed the bottom of his feet like sand at the beach. He wondered if his brother would re-carpet. His hand stretched out with his fingers searching the details of the wall.
Step two.
Another step and he could sense the void above under the eaves where his parents always hung an enormous mirror. Of course he had removed it with all the other mirrors.
Step three.
 His head seemed to pulsate. Thoughts swirled with movement and he blinked, wrestling his conscience. He knew what he had to do.
Step Four

He faltered at the next step. What if Micah hated him? What if after all this time they had found each other's friendship and he blew it? He could count friends on one hand.

He forced himself to take another step then another and another, each feeling heavier than the one before. His gut tightened as he became aware of a presence very close behind at his shoulder. Micah was so close he could only move forward, he was committed now.

"Are we supposed to stop?"
He felt the heat of Micah's breath on his near nakedness. It was always like this.

"I normally say something like, 'We must embrace the dark, confront our fears' something mysterious." Another cough-laugh.

The eighth step creaked as Jacob's bare foot splayed, followed one pace later by Micah's, like an echo. At least it had dried out up here after the long hot summer. He imagined his parents would put central heating in. They would be able to afford it now. Then it struck him. They were not moving back in. This was no longer the family home. That's why his brother had been measuring. They were going to sell it. He had trashed it, sold most of the furniture and generally treated the place as a squat but it was home. He had never lived anywhere else. Parents forgive, that's their job. Sure he knew it would take some time, but he was counting on maternal guilt for going to Singapore. Let that worm bury deep and after a while they would be apologising to him for leaving him in a position where he had wrecked the house.

"Why have we stopped?" Asked Micah.

"Sorry" Jacob reached, turned the brass door knob and fumbled inside for the light switch.

So this was Jacob's temple, the inner sanctum at the top of the house. This was the place that so few were granted entry. Imogen had never been up here he was sure. Exclusivity conjured up a sense of reverence, of mystical allure. Only the chosen saw this place and now Micah was one of them. Micah felt strange standing with so many pairs of sepia stained eyes staring at him blankly from the walls. Jacob stayed silent letting the impact of his scrapbooking take effect. Every inch of space was covered with old photographs. The windows celling, floor, even the light switch was covered by an old picture of a gruff gentleman in a bowler hat with a cane standing formally and awkwardly beside a cheese plant. Jacob depressed the gentleman's bulbous nose and the single naked bulb flickered on. One hundred thousand pairs of eyes stared intently into the camera lens, staring out from the past, watching. Expressions of pride and joy caught on their faces for eternity. The photos were like time portals that worked one way. Books could permeate the future with ideas and philosophies hundreds, if not thousands of years into the future. Photos were just faces staring, caught in a second with nothing to impart, no ideas, no ideals or philosophies. In the middle of the room was a collection of small glass-topped trays, evidently pulled from a display cabinet of some sort. They were arranged in a circle, an altar-like focal point to the room. As Micah's eyes adjusted to the gloom thrown by the twenty-watt light bulb, he could see macabre twisted limbs and thoraxes of dried insects. The specimens were not native to England with spiders the size of Sony Walkmans and beetles with extrusions more elaborate than any stag beetle. Not one insect was smaller than a ten pence piece.

The sepia imbued surroundings watched on, hollow eyes reflecting Micah's imagined horrors. One woman stood with her hand resting lightly on a child, a glazed expression focused at a distant point. Was it disaffection? Had there been death? There was a man in morning suit next to a Great Dane, sorrow gnawing deeply in his eyes. Did he suffer a taste for cruelty? It was all unknown.

"Where did you get them?" He asked needing to break the spell.

"Car boot sale, some guy had a whole suitcase." Judging from the variety the original owner must have been an avid photographer maybe even a professional?

"Fair enough. So why the tour of the inner sanctum now?" Micah was in a boisterous mood.

"To show you something." Jacob went to the corner of the room and stood with his back against the wall.

"You know when I bring people up here they are normally naked. Well nearly naked." He looked embarrassed and added "take a seat."
Micah looked around at the sparse room, the bulb illuminating the lack of any furnishings.

"On the floor." Jacob waved a hand. Micah did as instructed, thankful that he had been allow to be clothed as his carpenter jeans offered some padding against the cold hard boards pressing through the thin veneer of photographic paper. Jacob then took two paces from the wall and as his foot depressed on the second step there was a distinct creak. Jacob rocked on his heal, pinpointing the sound like a sonar ping. He dropped to his knees probing now with his hands looking intently at the photos until he located what he was looking for. Micah tried to act nonchalant but kept staring. What was he doing poking and prodding the floor?

"Here it is" Jacob prized a floorboard loose, the photos lifting up, overlapping to form an exact tessellation to hide the line of the floorboard. Then Jacob reached down into the void underneath the floorboard and pulled out a small black tape recorder holding up like a hard won prize. Micah shrugged again. Jacob depressed the chunky black play button. The box hissed like an angry snake, the volume turned up as high as possible playing recorded silence.

"Great!" Micah shrugged again, irritation beginning to show on his furrowed brow. But this was Jacob building to something and seemed incapable of doing so without a dramatic reveal.

"Oh wait, let me just…" He punched at the buttons fast-forward or rewind animated and almost breathless. Again he pressed play, the same serpentine jeer.

"No. Wait, it will come." Interjected Jacob before his friend could brush it off.

"There. There. Can you hear it?" Micah strained and somewhere in the static the pitch changed, became deeper. Slowly, as they listened, it became deeper and formed into a rhythmic rasping sound.

"Breathing." Said Micah as the audio finally overpowered the background silence becoming a bona-fide sound.

"So this is proof of the after world?" Asked Micah trying to take in what he was hearing.

"What? No I recorded this. Forty-five minutes of silence and then breathing. Of course I have to turn it up full volume so people can here it under the floorboards. It normally starts about five minutes after the mushroom tea kicks in."

Micah sat there trapped in the time capsule of blank expressions suspended like a holocaust memorial, staring from every direction, burrowing into Micah's subconscious. There was the feeling of stories that should have been told, cut short, and forgotten. A feeling that this story, his story, was being cut short or at least being forced into another chapter, a chapter without this friendship as the realisation dawned.

"You lied." Micah mouthed the words almost a whisper, scared to voice his thoughts in case by their very vocalisation they would become real.

"I lie." Corrected Jacob a tentative jeer across his face, his cockiness wavering.

"But last time?" Protested Micah trying to hold on to belief. The last séance had seemed so real, the knocking the temperature change it all seemed too complicated to be a scam. Jacob leant forward, hunching his shoulders in a similar way as he had over the table in Micah's caravan. The knock came once clearly. Then it began to beat out a regular tattoo. With the lack of top Jacob wore, Micah could see his shoulder moving in time jerking forward and backwards.

"Hyper flexible. I can pop the joint in and out when I want. Obviously I wear baggier clothes for a show and sit down."

"Fuck Jacob. Why?" Micah could feel the perspiration wet under his palms as it left a residue on the photos.

"Why not?' He shrugged, exhaling and relaxing his shoulders.

"That's not an answer. I think you owe me an answer." Micah sat up leaving a clear handprint in sweat.

"Mystery, fear, a way to control people, keep them out of my way so I can sell cannabis without too many people poking their noses in."

"But what about the temperature, how did you do that?" Jacob tensed again drawing himself up looking at the ceiling as if he was about to end a relationship.

"Yeah, well that wasn't me. That was odd, I'll give you that."

"Is that why we went to see Ray?" Micah asked.

"It was worth a bit of investigation, after all it scared the shit out of us at the time."

"And what now?"

"Psychosomatic, susceptible minds? Tired, a few drinks. It's not the mushroom tea I usually use but similar effect. Essentially I believed my own hype."

"But the candle? You can't think a candle out, that's ridiculous" Micah began to rock gently.

"Wow a candle is blown out in a draughty old caravan it must be supernatural."

"But it flared up." Said Micah jabbing his finger.

"A gas pocket or oxygen-rich air in a caravan that is shut and carbon-monoxide heavy. I don't know? But come on Micah. I mean, we pump ourselves full of drugs regularly and then we see something weird and you jump to the conclusion that it must be ghosts or what not. Seriously? Fuck off" Jacob was almost laughing now. Swearing more as he struggled to find words to articulate what he thought.

So Jacob confessed like a lapsed Catholic, how he'd used hallucinogenic drugs and then used suggestion with a little trickery. Séances were always him asking open-ended questions. Always allowing the participant to invest as much belief as they wanted. Jacob garbled his sentences referencing techniques and practitioners from the past but all Micah heard was "I exploited you. Used your dad's death to convince people I had occult powers to keep my stash safe."

"Really?" Stuttered Micah, he couldn't manage more. He rocked more erratically.

"Really?" He could feel his face flushing with blood. Jacob retreated back to the corner, the tape recorder hanging limply from his hand, still breathing heavily.

"I'm sorry." Jacob's face looked panicked uncontrolled, his eyes glancing at the door, his exit.

"Fuck. Really?" His voice blustered aggression seeping into the intonation.
"Shall we call it one all? I mean you fuck me off with not trusting me over Imogen." Jacob smiled, hands wide as if proffering a hug.
Micah stared at Jacob then rubbed his hand down his face over his eyes. One thousand thoughts crammed into his head vying for attention. A cacophony of confused, raging, conflicting thoughts. The image of a cigarette flashed in his mind.
He did not crave nicotine. He noticed a pentagram drawn on the door, a five pointed star; Pentateuch - five books, pentatonic verse - five intonations and wondered, was pent up five conflicting emotions? The image of a knife flashed through his mind. He suddenly wanted to be alone, away from the eyes with their blank impassionate stares.

Jacob flinched slightly as Micah got up suddenly to leave. Then was left standing in the corner. He shouted something as Micah ran downstairs, the words bouncing off a hurricane of thoughts. Downstairs he rifled through kitchen draws and cupboards his mind searching for something to grasp on to, something to harm himself with, to stop the world spinning. He discovered Jacob's spirits, an assortment of half empty bottles. *More constructive than cutting himself,* he thought and snatched at the nearest, throwing the stringent liquid down his throat. He then gathered his thoughts. He rested his hands on the kitchen top. Outside, the sun beat down on the browning grass.

"I'm sorry Micah, I thought it would offer you solace. I wasn't trying to be an arsehole."
Micah just stared blankly out of the window.

"Help yourself." Commented Jacob pushing a comedic tone into his voice.
Micah just grunted and took another long, long swig.

"The temperature Jacob?"

"Yeah that." The fridge door opened and Jacob pulled out a beer. More remnants of the party

"I'm pretty sure it was Able-Smythe." Said Micah. The name hung in the air Jacob neither acknowledging nor denying his friend's suspicion. Micah tried to read his face but Jacob looking blank, focused on the rollup cigarette he was now trying to construct with shaking hands.

"Look, I'm sorry, that's all. I shouldn't have tricked you when I did, you know with the shoulder and the leading you on, and the other stuff."

"Let's just call it one all then, as you say."

"Cool" Jacob moved forward intending a reconciliatory hug. Micah recoiled.

"I'm still angry. Just roll me one and leave it at that for now.

As Jacob rolled the door knocked. He glanced down at his wrist and a watch he wasn't wearing.

"What's the time?" Micah shrugged in reply. Then a realisation began to dawn on his face.

"That's not your parents or your brother. Seriously you've done nothing." Micah was feeling uncomfortable, desperately wanting to be anywhere but there.

"No. They don't fly in for another three of four days at least. Can you get the door while I throw some clothes on?" Jacob disappeared upstairs before his friend could protest. Whoever it was thundered on the door again as Micah crossed the lounge.

"Coming." He shouted. But the visitor, impatient or deaf, hammered again.

"Hello." He said curtly, as he swung the door wide catching the dreaded individual off guard, fist poised to knock a fourth time. He recognised the man more from his clothes than his face, dressed as he was, for some kind of guerrilla warfare in khaki combats and boots, replete with shiny dog tag jangling round his neck. It was the friend of Imogen's brother, the dealer.

He couldn't remember the guy's name, he wasn't sure he ever knew it. So led with. "Alright mate? Micah, friend of Jacob's, we met at the student union bar a while back."

The guy grabbed Micah's outstretched hand and twisted his own round it in a series of elaborate moves constituting a hand shake that ended in him clicking his fingers and Micah looking slightly bewildered.

"Is he in? We need to get on."

"Err yeah he is upstairs getting dressed. Come in." Micah turned to call but Jacob was making his way down the stairs dragging a duffle bag and wearing a rucksack.

"Caleb you are early." Said Jacob, passing the guy his bags. He disappeared, leaving the two old friends standing on the threshold looking at each other. Jacob was rummaging in his pocket and came out with his lighter, compulsively flicking it as he shuffled his weight from one foot to the other.

"Ready when you are." Called Jacob's new friend from the back of the rusted van. He leant out from the side panel revealing a rudimental kitchen and bed crammed in to the space. Jacob waved his compliance but did not move.

"I can't be here when they get back." He smiled looking for reassurance. Micah just looked at him, at the van and said nothing.

"I'm going to head for the festivals, hit the hippy trail, maybe go abroad. Caleb says there is a good life to be had travelling down through Spain to Morocco over the Winter." He flicked the lighter repeatedly.

"Hurry up. I don't want to get caught it traffic." Shouted Caleb.

"I'm pretty sure he's got no tax or M.O.T so he wants to get out on the country roads as quickly as possible."

"Right." Was all Micah could muster.

"Sorry." Jacob closed the Zippo and thrust it into Micah's hand. "Look after it until I get back yeah."

"You love that lighter."

"I know and I don't want to leave it behind but I know you'll look after it and it'll be here when I get back. Yeah?"

"Yeah" Micah slipped it into his pocket and watched as Jacob jumped into the back of the van sliding the door shut with a disconcerting crunch. They drove off in a spluttering cloud of blue grey smoke. As they were turning the corner, Jacob stuck his head out the window.

"Help yourself to anything you want and shut the door when you're done." Then the van turned, indicator flickering double time as the bulb struggled on its last legs and they were gone. Micah looked back inside the dim lit half empty house squalid and musty. He had seen better squats. He wanted nothing from the place. He wanted nothing from his friend beyond the one thing he couldn't have but he had known Jacob long enough now to know he was never going to get that. Loyalty. He closed the door, checked it was locked and walked home. The breeze was fresh and, for the first time in months, he wished he was wearing a jumper. Clouds banked on the horizon as a storm front rolled up from the sea following the line of hills to the north. The air smelt of rain. Soon there would be a deluge and all the streets would be washed fresh. Autumn would begin in earnest. Micah liked Autumn.

Epilogue

John Able-Smythe stepped from a doorway further up the road. A cocktail stick flicked from side to side in his mouth as he looked down the road in the van's direction of travel, then back at Micah walking towards town. He pursed his lips with tiny cracks radiating out like an impact crater and pulled the cocktail stick free, flicking it to the curb. Then he stepped in the direction of Micah, a sure bet. He knew that Jacob was the obvious choice, full of vices set on a path of destruction fuelled by self-doubt and a self-loathing born of a necessity to replace a negligent love. But someone that obvious, that stereotypical, even with their stoic non-belief, which Able-Smythe knew was always a bonus, would attract unwanted attention, the kind that would get him in trouble. Micah on the other hand, doubted enough to not believe but believed enough to not warrant some immediate divine intervention. It had been a long time but Able-Smyth remembered the modus operandi. His enemy was a universal constant. He had to admire that, and as such the spiritual triage was predictable, buying Able-Smythe time. He spat on the grey, chewing gum studded pavement, footsteps keeping perfect time with Micah's. Step masked by step rendering him audibly invisible. Ahead Micah stopped and lit a cigarette cupping his hands to coax the flame from the lighter.

"These people are so predictable." Muttered Able-Smythe contemptuously. Micah disappeared out of sight round the corner. No matter thought Able-Smythe he knew where the kid was going. He would head across the park through the trees then pick a path through the back streets to the Park Tavern where he would start drinking. It was the nearest establishment in that direction and with all that had happened he was bound to need a drink. One drink would lead to two then to three, four and so on. The alcohol would make those barriers supple and the liminal spaces would open allowing Able-Smythe to play. He chuckled to himself as he walked, his hand swinging as if an invisible cane imbued him with some kind of status.

    He wound his own route through the back streets, he arrived, imagining it was some minutes after Micah. He slipped into the pub, into a corner escorted by shadows that seemed to hug the walls and grow from the crevices near him until he was virtually invisible unless you sat next to him. He crossed his left leg over his right. His left leg and his left hand were trained dominant for humour sake. He looked around but could not see Micah. He checked the bar then the stalls, then waited in case Micah had gone to toilet when he had first arrived but after an uncomfortably long time Micah was still nowhere to be seen.

    He had been sure those seeds of destruction had been planted that the centre couldn't hold. He had gone to quite a bit of trouble even with how busy he was elsewhere.

    "Hello there, you look sad. Are you sad?" Said the girl, underage and drunk in the afternoon.

"Never mind, there are always others" He mumbled.

"What was that?"

"I said, I regret the choices that people make. Do you regret the choices you make?"

She laughed high pitched, half forced, unsure. "You're strange."

He smiled, his thin grey lips pulling back over his white teeth; a predatory smile.

"Yet I shouldn't be a stranger."

The girl tugged on her denim skirt a little too short for sitting down.

"Buy me a drink?" She said fluttering her eyes. After all this charming young man was paying her attention what harm could there be?